An Unbeaten Man

An Unbeaten Man

Brendan Rielly

Hope you enjoy.

Down East Books

Camden, Maine

Published by Down East Books
An imprint of The Rowman & Littlefield Publishing Group, Inc.
4501 Forbes Boulevard, Suite 200, Lanham, Maryland 20706
www.rowman.com

Unit A, Whitacre Mews, 26-34 Stannary Street, London SE11 4AB, United
Kingdom

Distributed by NATIONAL BOOK NETWORK

British Library Cataloguing in Publication Information Available

Library of Congress Cataloging-in-Publication Data

Rielly, Brendan.
  An unbeaten man / Brendan Rielly.
      pages cm
  ISBN 978-1-60893-587-1 (cloth : alk. paper) — ISBN 978-1-60893-589-5
(electronic) 1. Microbiologists—Fiction. 2. Oil spills—Fiction. 3. Bowdoin
College—Fiction. 4. Brunswick (Me.)—Fiction. 5. Middle East—Fiction. 6.
Russia—Fiction. 7. Political fiction. I. Title.
  PS3618.I39255.U53 2015
  813'.6—dc23

                                        2015024214

♾ ™ The paper used in this publication meets the minimum requirements of
American National Standard for Information Sciences—Permanence of Paper for
Printed Library Materials, ANSI/NISO Z39.48-1992.

Printed in the United States of America

To my best friend and wife, Erica. Thank you.

"The world breaks everyone and afterward many are strong in the broken places."

ERNEST HEMINGWAY—*A Farewell to Arms*

"One beaten man is worth two unbeaten men."

VLADIMIR PUTIN

Acknowledgments

I owe thanks to so many people for helping make this book a reality. This book is vastly improved thanks to their efforts. Any mistakes are all mine.

Thank you to Michael Steere, Meaghan White, and the folks at Down East and Rowman & Littlefield. I apologize for the blizzard of questions I had about the publishing process. Thank you to Professors Anne McBride (Bowdoin College), Rachel Larsen (University of Southern Maine), Peter Woodruff (University of Southern Maine), and Friedrich Widdel (Max Planck Institute for Marine Microbiology) for their technical assistance. Thank you also to Professor McBride for showing me the ins and outs of the Hatch Science Library and Druckenmiller Hall at Bowdoin and the labs where Michael McKeon would have worked. Professor McBride has sworn to protect the location of the ESA's secret and secure location under Hatch and Druckenmiller. So don't ask her.

Thank you to Bill Baker and Amr Ismail for their help in staging locations in the Middle East. Thank you to my Russian expert, Jennifer Black. Thank you to my military jet expert, Art Cody.

Thank you to all my early readers who foolishly believed me when I told them to put aside family and friendship and be honest in their editing and then put up with me when I refused to talk to them afterwards: Ed and Jeanne Rielly, Brigid DelVecchio, Pete and Denise Wilson, Ted Wallace, Maria Dorn and Jeff Dorn. Thank you to Gayle Lynds for sharing her wisdom about writing thrillers and for her help with the title. Thank you to Steve Konkoly for his advice on writing thrillers.

Thank you to my parents, Ed and Jeanne Rielly, for instilling in me a love of learning and writing. Thank you to my kids, Morgan, Shannon, and Maura, and to my best friend and wife, Erica, for giving me the time and space to write (usually in the middle of the night in an undisclosed location) and for giving me the loving, supportive and frequently hilarious family that Michael McKeon is still searching for.

One

~~~

Riyadh

*A*llahu *Akbar, forgive me for my sins. Guide and protect my son . . .*

The *snap-hiss* of a blowtorch silenced Fouad al-Dossary's prayers. A boot slammed against the back of his skull, crushing his nose against the concrete floor and splitting his lip. The Saudi groaned and spat blood; he tried to struggle as one of the attackers yanked off his boots and socks, but someone obscenely heavy dropped on his back, expelling all the air from his lungs. Finally, one of his assailants spoke.

"We know you know about The Global Group."

The Saudi twisted his face away from the warehouse's floor, repulsed by the stench of rotting vegetables and rat droppings. Through a cracked window, he spotted the Kingdom Center, the tallest skyscraper in all of Arabia. On this night, the inverted catenary arch atop the Center, a necklace for the City of Riyadh, glowed a regal purple. As he prepared his soul and body for the agony to come, al-Dossary was proud that the work of his life, spent in shadows and fetid warehouses and moldering docks around the world, had made possible the success of his beloved Kingdom.

The attacker continued speaking in English, whetted by a rough Moscow accent: "We know you know that the leaders of our countries are talking with the American President about a peace plan

1

for the Middle East. And we know that you know that we plan to destroy those talks."

The blowtorch's flame danced in front of al-Dossary's blurring vision. The Saudi's nose twitched at the acrid flame, his face flushed from the heat.

"Now you will tell us who you told."

Al-Dossary closed his eyes and waited for what he knew would come, shivering in the sudden coldness as the blowtorch left his face. Without warning, one of the assailants knelt on his ankles, snapping them like dried twigs.

His scream, through clenched teeth, echoed across the empty warehouse as the blowtorch's flame licked up and down the sole of his right foot.

"Tell me," the Russian said as al-Dossary lay heaving on the cement.

After several moments of waiting, the man blistered al-Dossary's other foot, sending another round of shrieks piercing through the night air. The Saudi was ashamed of his screams, but the pain was too intense, too fast, to control.

"Tell me!"

Al-Dossary bit his own tongue savagely, leaving the tip hanging by a patch of skin.

Then the Russian's breath was on his cheek—sour vodka and stewed cabbage from the man's stomach—as he whispered: "It doesn't matter. We already know about Fyodorov in London. He's next."

As the muzzle flash blazed before al-Dossary's eyes, in the instant before his skull caved in, he grinned a bloody grin.

They didn't know about Longfellow. Even if they got Dmitry, Longfellow could still save their three countries.

———⟊———

London

As Dmitry Fyodorov hurried down Curzon Street toward Berkeley Square, his tailored suit flapping in the brisk evening breeze, he loosened the knot on his blue silk tie. He was sweating despite the damp, raw air. Al-Dossary had missed three check-ins since first sounding the alarm. That could mean only one thing. His old friend and sometime collaborator was dead, killed for the information he had shared.

Fyodorov coughed amid the fogbank of exhaust fumes, trapped by the heavy air, and threaded his way through the sightseers wandering aimlessly along the sidewalk. He couldn't contact his superiors in the *Federalnaya Sluzhba Bezopasnosti Rossiyskoy Federaciyi,* or FSB, because al-Dossary's intercepts indicated that a high-level FSB official was involved. He was isolated, and whoever had gotten to al-Dossary would undoubtedly come for him.

The Russian gave wide berth to a jogger hopping in place and checking her pulse, then cast a wary eye at a man ambling in the opposite direction wearing a New York Yankees cap. A group of glitter-eyed women spilled from a martini bar onto the sidewalk, teetering on their stilettos and screeching with laughter through smudged lips. He wrapped the familiar, cold blanket of paranoia around him, hoping it would save his life one more time.

But there was one person he could trust.

He had formed his collaboration with Longfellow and Fouad for situations just like this, when events moved too fast for the calcified bureaucrats in Washington, Moscow and Riyadh, and the agents on the ground needed to share information quickly and quietly. In dark Viennese alleys, crowded Moroccan markets, and bustling Chinese cities, in searing Libyan deserts, dense Venezuelan jungles, and frozen Swiss peaks, they had saved each other's operations and lives.

There was another reason Fyodorov had to reach Longfellow. He knew something that al-Dossary didn't. The professor mentioned in the intercepts was Longfellow's asset.

L-

F Dead. Your asset in danger. The Global Group after me. Run.

-D.

As Fyodorov finished typing on his smartphone, the man in the Yankees cap brushed past him, having reversed course. Fyodorov eyed the man's back intently, furious at himself for letting someone get close enough to touch him.

He had just reached the Mount Street Gardens when his chest constricted. He placed a hand on the bronze drinking fountain to steady himself before his lungs convulsed with a violent, knife-like twist. He doubled over, gasping for air, then fell at the feet of a woman pushing a baby stroller. He opened his mouth in a silent scream as the baby peered curiously down at him until yanked away by his shrieking mother. A seizure, then another, coursed through him like electrical currents, frying his nerve endings. He could smell himself burning.

Then he collapsed, a dry husk in the evening breeze. A man in a suit peered down at him, blocking the cold, gray sky, shouting something into his cell phone. But Fyodorov's ears had stopped working. As his body stiffened on the stone path, he watched the gray sky swallow the man with the phone, then come for him.

It was up to Longfellow now.

—⌘—

Brunswick, Maine

In the days after the disappearances, the traumatized students and faculty at Bowdoin College gathered together in dorm rooms and living rooms, over hamburgers in the student union, gelato downtown, or beers at Ebenezer's Brew Pub, and struggled to make sense of the sudden loss of four members of their small, tight-knit community. The press conference announcing the professors' discovery of a new microbe had been quickly canceled. Newspaper and television reporters from around the world, accustomed to covering scientific breakthroughs, found themselves caught in a crime scene.

Hatch Science Library and Druckenmiller Hall had assumed the funereal tone of a death watch. Classes were cancelled. Campus security and Brunswick police interviewed and re-interviewed everyone they could find, searching for a clue to explain the unexplainable. Hushed conversations gave way to somber shakes of the head as the campus held its breath. A vigil service was held in the College Chapel, its lights dimmed, its long pews of students and faculty shrouded in shadows.

Father Levasseur stood before them.

"Four members of our family are missing," he began, his clipped French Canadian tones punching the air. "I have known Julia Donatelli since her arrival one year ago. She is not only a brilliant professor, but has worked very closely with our Catholic campus ministry here at Bowdoin. Professor McKeon, I only met recently, here, in this chapel, to pray. And, of course, we must think of Professor McKeon's wife and daughter and pray for their safe return also."

He paused, recalling his first and last exchange with the professor.

What is it that you seek, Michael? A measure of peace?

The snort was his answer.

I don't even know what that means.

You're here for something.

The priest was accustomed to waiting for people to pay out their secrets and sins, and the professor made him wait. Levasseur watched Michael's fingers drum against the railing in an uneven staccato. But they weren't drumming, they were typing. Before the priest could decipher their message, Michael spoke.

I lost my family when I was just a kid. For a long time, I had no one. I didn't want anyone. Then I met Milla and Katya.

Milla is your wife?

Yes.

And Katya is her daughter?

Yes. I adopted her.

And so why are you here?

I'm losing Milla, Father. If I lose her, I lose Katya.

Perhaps we should pray?

The snort again.

My mother always said that the devil likes to listen when you pray.

So why are you here?

A pause.

I'd like to try again.

Father Levasseur glanced at the floor where they had knelt just days before and closed his eyes.

"Let us pray."

Two

———∾∾∾———

Boston

"Michael?"

He was sinking in something black as hell and thick as death. It pulled at his limbs, deadened his ears, blinded his eyes, and filled his lungs.

Photographs fluttered before him like wounded birds. His mother's body under the bush in the park, like a piece of trash snatched from the wind. His sister, tied to her bed, the pale blue of the pillowcase over the window matching her skin. He saw himself, genuflecting next to Katya's bed, checking for breaths, because people died when he wasn't watching.

"Michael?"

Violence begets violence. Father Levasseur's words.

His mother. His sister. The man tied up. The hammer. The gun.

Violence begets violence.

His friend. Threatening. A footstep outside his home. A blaze of pain in his neck. Liquid death.

Violence begets violence.

He tried to catch the photographs; his lips struggling to say their names.

The devil likes to listen when you pray.

"Michael!"

The black waters receded reluctantly, leaving Michael McKeon groggy and disoriented on their shore. He opened his eyes, then instantly regretted it when the overhead lights burned his retinas. As a wave of nausea rolled over him, he clenched his teeth and fought to keep the bile down.

"Wake up, Michael."

The voice was familiar, but he couldn't place it. Male, baritone, but with a sharp edge. He knew the voice, but couldn't get his brain to work.

Slowly, his breathing deepened and his stomach settled. He kept his eyes closed for another moment and tried to take stock of where he was. From the soft padding under him and the squeaks of springs as he shifted, he could tell he was lying on a cot. Beyond that, he had no idea where he was or what had happened.

His throat dry and tight, Michael swallowed and took a chance, opening his eyes cautiously. Light flooded in, bearable this time. He was in an airport hangar with metal-sheathed walls and a concrete floor. A strange-looking, needle-nosed white plane with red striping occupied the majority of the hangar, its engines humming. Through the cockpit windows, Michael glimpsed the pilot and copilot checking their instruments.

A broad, pockmarked face eclipsed the plane.

"How you doing, buddy?"

His old friend.

Michael's head pounded viciously.

"David? Where am I?"

"Good to see you back in the land of the living," David Kenner said, his voice rising over the hum of the plane's engine.

Michael stared blankly.

"You're still groggy. That's the ketamine," David said. "It's a heavy anesthetic. Unfortunately, we needed to knock you out for the trip."

Michael shook his head slowly, trying to clear the cobwebs. David motioned at someone unseen then returned his black eyes to Michael.

"I tried to get you to listen to me," he said. "When you first emailed me about the microbe you'd discovered, I tried to get you to join us."

"Thought you were kidding," Michael replied thickly, trying to work some saliva into his tongue.

"You didn't think I was kidding when I showed up in your living room."

"Thought you were crazy," Michael replied. It had taken some effort, but his hands had finally found the back of his head, which banged like a funeral drum. "Some nonsense about a group of super patriots . . ."

"The Global Group."

". . . fighting the Russians and Saudis. It's nuts."

"We could have been partners, like back in grad school," David sighed. "We were a lot alike back then. Two damaged kids with huge chips on our shoulders." He hunched closer, his voice falling to a whisper. "They said you would never join us. They wanted to grab you weeks ago. I told them that you and I went way back, that we understood each other, that if I talked to you, you'd listen." David slumped in his chair. "And this is how you repay me?" He shook his head, and looked to his right. "Now, they'll *make* you do what we need."

Michael's head was banging so loudly that he was having a difficult time understanding David. Talking took a great effort. He needed to lay his head down, go to sleep, anything to relieve the pain. But David was staring at him intently, waiting for a response.

"Make me do what?"

"We're going to use your microbe to destroy Saudi Arabia's and Russia's oil."

Michael leaned back on the cot and squeezed his eyes shut as the aftereffects of the ketamine hammered the inside of his skull.

"You're out of your mind," he said quietly. "That's not how it works. It consumes oil that's difficult and expensive to pump and produces natural gas that's cheap to capture and use. That's the breakthrough."

"That's not all your microbe does, and you know it." David smiled and slapped Michael's knee. "Time to go."

It was only then that Michael realized they weren't alone. Three men were stationed around him in a semi-circle. The first two wore navy blue sweatshirts and jeans. Both looked ex-military, with thick, muscular chests and arms, chiseled faces, and short, cropped hair. The third was tall and thin and seemed vaguely familiar. Hooded eyes peered from under a New York Yankees cap. The two ex-military types both held pistols, trained at Michael's chest.

Michael slowly raised his hands.

"What's going on, David?"

"You'll find out. Let's go."

"Go where?"

David snapped his fingers and motioned for Michael to stand.

"Are you kidnapping me?" Michael asked.

"That's the plan. Get moving."

"You can't kidnap me," Michael said as a stab of anger erupted in his chest. "We've known each other since graduate school. I trusted you."

"I wouldn't have had to do this, if you'd just listened to me," David said.

Then he turned and walked toward the other men. Closing his eyes against the vertigo breaking over him, Michael struggled to stand on unsteady legs.

"David!" He stumbled drunkenly, but managed, arms and legs wide, to regain his balance. "Don't walk away from me. I'm talking to you. Turn around!"

"Get on the plane, Michael, or they'll shoot you," David called over his shoulder.

Michael blinked rapidly. None of this made sense. His fingers began typing his thoughts, as they always did when he was upset. He shook them loose then froze as the guards inched closer in response. Time to try a different approach, he thought.

"Milla and Katya will worry about me," Michael called after David. "At least let me call them so they know I'm okay."

David paused and turned back to Michael.

"You should worry about *them*."

Michael's heart clutched. The adrenalin suddenly surging through him blasted away the last vestiges of the anesthetic. He stepped forward and the two military-looking guards raised their guns in warning.

"What did you say?" Michael asked in a low voice.

David spread his arms wide.

"I tried, Michael. I tried, but you wouldn't listen, so we needed an insurance policy that guaranteed your cooperation."

David flicked his eyes and the other three men tightened the circle around Michael.

"We have Milla and Katya."

David's words didn't register with Michael at first. He spoke them again.

"We have them."

"What did you say?"

"After grabbing you, we snatched them. They're already gone. Cooperate and they live. Don't, and they die."

Michael launched himself with a roar at David, but before he could reach him, a fist crashed into his kidney, knocking him to the concrete floor. Gasping for air, Michael tucked his knees into his chest and pressed his fists against his burning kidneys.

"It'd be a very bad idea for you to try something like that again," David said as the four men circled Michael warily. "Bad for you and very bad for Milla and Katya."

The thin man shifted slightly and tapped his watch. David noticed and nodded.

"It's time to go."

Michael's kidney throbbed as one of the guards pulled him roughly to his feet. He shoved the guard away, but before he could go after David, the other guard cracked his pistol against the back of Michael's skull. White hot pain exploded behind his eyes, dropping him to one knee. The back of his head was warm and sticky. He pulled his fingers away and found them covered in blood.

The first guard used his knee to send Michael sprawling on the concrete floor. Then both guards dragged him upright and jammed their pistols hard into his neck and ribs before hustling him onto the plane.

"Thanks, Pete," David said, as the shorter, scar-faced guard shoved Michael into a leather chair.

"Adrian, check on our cargo out back, please," David said, gesturing toward the closed door. The other, taller guard brushed roughly past Michael and disappeared into the rear of the plane. "Pete, we're about ready to go. Open the hangar doors."

Michael rubbed his aching kidney and stared furiously at David.

"If you hurt them . . ."

"They're fine, for now," David said. "If you work with us, they'll stay that way. If you're not a good boy, we'll kill them. I don't want to, but we don't have a choice. It'll be slow and painful and we'll make you watch. Do we understand each other?"

Michael ground his teeth, his eyes latching onto David's neck. One swift chop with the hard edge of his hand and David would never breathe again. But he couldn't, not if they had Milla and Katya.

"Yes."

"Good, now, let me tell you what's going to happen."

Three

"As I started to explain at your house last month, a group of us came together a few years ago, concerned about how America's dependence on foreign oil was undercutting national security." David leaned closer and dropped his voice. "We knew that America was bleeding to death, but we also realized that we couldn't depend on our government or our market to stanch the flow. We had to take matters into our own hands. We knew the only way we could change the rules of the game was to knock out Russian and Saudi oil production. Then our country would have no other choice but to use its own resources. We would finally be safe and secure in our own borders."

David paused, waiting for a response from Michael, who pointedly ignored him, glancing instead around the luxurious plane. Cream-colored, leather chairs lined the cabin, interspersed with cherry work tables. Small plasma flat screen monitors adorned the walls.

"Our association, The Global Group, investigated hundreds of possible ways to stop their oil production and even funded attacks on their facilities, but we couldn't find the answer we needed."

Michael's skin crawled as David looked him up and down.

"Until you. If we could introduce your microbes into the Saudi and Russian oil fields, it would destroy their oil from underneath their feet. Before you, we were trying to destroy their facilities or their pipelines, but those can be rebuilt. With your discovery, we can destroy their oil! They would never recover."

David banged his fist on the table.

"This is counter-terrorism at its most literal," he insisted breathlessly. "We tell Russia: you closed your oil pipelines to Europe. You used your oil riches to play hardball with us in Iraq, Iran, Syria, and Sudan. We'll destroy your oil fields. We tell the Saudis: you bankrolled the people who flew planes into the Twin Towers and the Pentagon. We'll destroy your oil fields."

Finally Michael responded. "You're insane."

"It's not insane, and don't pretend to be so naïve. You've heard the reports about how high oil revenues lead to international aggression and domestic oppression. It's no surprise that Russia rattles its saber when oil trades at $100 a barrel instead of $25. You know how high oil prices undercut freedom and democracy around the world and weaken our security here at home."

David's eyes bore relentlessly into Michael's with all the fervor of a true believer.

"We're at war, Michael, and we're losing. It might make you feel better if we continued piddling around with the microscopic advances in alternative energy we've accomplished so far, but if we do, we guarantee ultimate failure. By the time the rest of America wakes up, it'll be too late. The Russians and Saudis will own us. We have to act now!"

David's face was mere inches away, his labored breath hot on Michael's cheeks. His dark eyes had turned glassy, as if they were looking through Michael instead of at him.

"I still don't understand what this nightmare scenario of yours has to do with me or my family."

"You created microbes that consume oil," David began.

"I've discovered a way to convert oil into methane. I was looking for a way to unlock the energy potential of the hundreds of billions of barrels of oil that are too costly or too environmentally dangerous to pump out, like the Athabasca Oil Sands where you work. That's why I told you about my discovery. Canada has 179 billion barrels of proven oil reserves, second only to Saudi Arabia, but almost all of those reserves are oil sands deposits that are incredibly expensive to tap and create an environmental mess. By converting the oil into methane, leaving the bitumen in the ground, and pumping the methane to the surface, we can convert a billion barrels of heavy oil into a trillion cubic feet of methane. We wouldn't have to depend on Saudi Arabia or Russia any longer."

"The Director has other ideas," the thin man said from his seat across the aisle.

"Who the hell's the Director?"

"He's in charge of The Global Group," David replied.

"Does the Director have a real name?" Michael asked.

"Not that you need to know," the thin man said.

Michael heard the grind of the hangar doors opening.

"This is Krzysztof Kasprzyk," David said, nodding to the thin man in the Yankees cap. "Call him Kris. He's a Polish scientist who hates the Russians as much as I do. You got a taste of what he and the guards can do. Believe me, they can do a lot more."

"Don't threaten me, David," Michael bit back. "You know I don't respond well to threats."

Michael glanced at the Polish scientist, recognizing him.

"We met when I field-tested my microbes in the oil lagoon in Poland. I'm guessing that wasn't an accident."

"That's right," Kasprzyk replied. "The Global Group will give you everything you need. This team will support you. We have the means to get you in place. Your job is to destroy the oil. If you do your job, your wife and daughter will be returned to you, unharmed, and we'll provide a story to explain all of your absences." Kasprzyk glared at him. "If you don't do your job, you will have killed your wife and daughter. The Director isn't someone to be played with."

Michael flinched as the cabin door slammed shut. While the engine whined and the plane shuddered towards the opening, he tried to reason with the two men, explaining that the microbes were engineered to turn oil into natural gases like methane, hydrogen and carbon dioxide which could then be captured and used, but weren't designed to simply destroy the oil.

"That's true, but then you created the ability to consume all the gases, leaving nothing behind," Kasprzyk said.

"That was just an academic experiment."

"That academic experiment is what made your microbes perfect for our purposes. We don't want to leave the Saudis or the Russians with anything they can use."

"Other than that field test in Poland, this has never been tested outside the lab. I can't guarantee it will work, especially on oil reserves the size of Russia's and Saudi Arabia's."

Kasprzyk's eyes glittered.

"It'll work. You will make sure of it."

"To make certain you have everything you need, we even brought along your assistant," David said.

"My assistant?"

David gestured toward the back of the cabin with a flamboyant wave of his arm. As if on cue, the door opened and Adrian, the taller guard, stepped through. Michael's eyes widened as Adrian pulled someone after him. A woman with her hands handcuffed behind her back struggled and kicked at the guard. Duct tape covered her mouth and tangled black hair obscured her face. The guard grabbed the top of the woman's head and snapped it back. Caramel-flecked eyes stared out at Michael from a white, panicked face.

"Oh no," Michael breathed.

Julia Donatelli.

Four

Over the Atlantic Ocean

As the plane soared into the night sky over Boston Harbor, Michael shifted in the leather seat and craned his neck to cast a wary glance around the Aerion SBJ. He could just spot the top of Julia's head over one of the seats in the back, where she was being closely guarded by Pete and Adrian. Kasprzyk reclined in the front of the plane, his hands cradled in his lap and his eyes closed, but Michael could tell from the tautness in the man's body that he was still very much awake and alert.

Michael gazed at the man for a moment longer. There was something about Kasprzyk that tugged at the back of his consciousness. He was like no research scientist Michael had ever met. There was a hardness, a sense of certain danger, about the man that Michael had seen in some of the drug dealers who hung around his mother's apartment. It meant they had killed and would think nothing of killing again. Whoever Kasprzyk was, Michael was certain that he was no research scientist.

"Where are we going?" Michael demanded, noting the crystal tumbler that had appeared in David's meaty paw. From the amber color, he guessed David had found a bottle of scotch.

David took a long sip and cast a furtive glance at the Polish scientist before replying.

"To the staging area for our incursion into Saudi Arabia."

"Where's our staging area?"

"You'll find out when we get there," Kasprzyk mumbled from his seat.

David took another deep sip and then gestured around the plane.

"Nice plane, huh?"

"Yours?"

David barked a short, explosive laugh.

"I wish. It belongs to one of the members of The Global Group. It's the latest in private aviation technology. It's supersonic with a top speed of Mach 1.6. It can cut typical flight time in half and it can fly in and out of the United States because it doesn't emit the sonic boom that the Concorde did."

"You sound like a promotional brochure."

"It's a very sweet ride. This is one of the first on the market."

Michael tried again to learn their destination.

"We're clearly headed east, over the Atlantic. Where are we going?"

"You'll find out when we get there." As the plane bounced through several air pockets, David told Michael how he had built a lab in an abandoned factory, modeled after Michael's lab at Bowdoin, but five times the size.

"I'll need glass bottles for the microbial culture, 100 milliliter bottles to start and then a graduated series of larger ones, half-liter, five liter, twenty-five-liter bottles, and lots of them," Michael said.

"Already arranged."

"I'll need oxygen-free containers and tubing systems for the solutions."

"All set."

"And how am I supposed to transport the microbial solution once it's cultured? I can't just walk up to the Saudi oil fields with a test tube and dump it in. We're talking significant volumes here, probably large enough to fill several car fuel tanks."

"You don't need to worry about that."

"I do need to worry about that," Michael snapped. "If I'm somehow able to pull this off in the lab, I don't want you guys screwing up the transportation and insertion." His eyes blazed. "My family's life depends on it."

David drained the glass, wiping his mouth with the back of his sleeve.

"What we need from you right now are the ingredients you'll need to grow the microbes."

"If I give them to you, what's to stop you from killing me and my family and developing the fertilizer yourselves?"

David smiled coldly.

"We might do that if we had more time, but we don't. You've already done the hard work and can get the culture growing immediately." He buried a stubby finger in Michael's chest. "That's your only value."

Through gritted teeth, Michael gave up his secret.

"It's a mixture of nitrates and phosphates. Give me a piece of paper. I'll write it down for you."

David pulled a pad of paper and a pen from his pocket and tossed them into Michael's lap, then nodded as Michael asked whether he would be mixing the culture for both stages, Saudi Arabia and Russia.

"What are the targets?" Michael asked.

"You don't need to know that now."

"Yes I do," Michael exclaimed in exasperation. "I need to know the size of the oil reservoirs so I can calculate how much inoculum we'll need."

"There's a new, largely untapped reservoir of an estimated seven billion barrels. If we knock that out, we cripple Russia. Saudi Arabia is both harder and easier than Russia. It's harder because the target is much bigger, approximately 267 billion barrels."

Michael dropped his pen and stared open-mouthed at David.

"You're talking about contaminating the entire Saudi oil reserve? There's no way I can grow enough microbes. Even if I could, you couldn't transport it. Saudi Arabia has dozens of major oil fields. Fifteen thousand wells. It's impossible."

"Not if you find the choke point and squeeze," David replied cryptically. "We have. That's what makes it easier."

"But the microbes will need a steady supply of nitrogen to continue growing in the reservoir," Michael continued. "How will you supply that?"

"I've got that covered. Finish your calculations and give them to me so I can call ahead for supplies." He winked at Michael. "I want to make sure everything's ready for you. I wouldn't want to slow you up."

As David turned to leave, he motioned for one of the guards to bring Julia forward. "Get some rest. We've got a long flight." He smiled lasciviously at Julia. "If you're not comfortable snuggling up next to him, I'm always available."

Julia Donatelli cast him a cold glance.

"No thanks. I'm fine here."

While David shuffled back to the front of the plane, chortling to himself, Michael turned to Julia. He hadn't had a chance to talk to her since her surprise appearance. Her olive-skinned complexion had turned chalky, and the duct tape had left a rectangular patch of red irritated skin around her mouth. As she brushed hair from her face, her hand shook slightly. She looked like hell, but Michael was sure he didn't look any better.

"I'm sorry you got dragged into this mess," Michael said, his voice low so the others couldn't hear.

"What's going on? I was walking across campus to the field house to work out when a white van pulled up and two men tossed me in the back. They bound and gagged me and didn't say anything. Who are these people? What do they want?"

Michael leaned closer so they could talk without being overheard. Quietly, he recounted David's plans to destroy the Saudi and Russian oil.

"Hal never should have made me include you on this work," Michael concluded. "I never understood why he insisted on it. Required it."

Michael shot a contrite glance at Julia.

"I'm sorry. I didn't mean that the way it sounded. You're brilliant, but I work better alone."

She waved away his apology. "He's our department chair and he thought that my background might help. And he can be pretty demanding." Julia leaned close and whispered: "These people, are they crazy? Do they really think they can destroy all Saudi and Russian oil? That would throw the world into chaos. We can't do that!"

Michael looked around the cabin before answering. Kasprzyk was still pretending to sleep. He took a deep breath and swallowed hard.

"They have Milla and Katya," he whispered as his voice caught in his throat. "They'll kill them if I don't do what they say."

Julia's chalky complexion turned even whiter.

"Oh, Michael, I'm so sorry."

"The important thing is that they're still alive. I'll do whatever it takes to keep them that way."

A shadow passed across Julia's face as she leaned close.

"How do you know that they're still alive? How do you know that this group has them?"

Julia pursed her lips at his blank look.

"Think about it. Maybe they don't have Milla and Katya, or, even if they do, how do you know that your family is still alive? You should demand to speak with them. Insist that you won't do anything unless you hear from them."

Michael seized on the small stirring of hope Julia had given him. Perhaps this was all a horrible bluff. Maybe David didn't really have Milla and Katya.

Julia made a face and sighed. "But right now, I desperately have to go to the bathroom."

She stood up and waved a hand at David.

"I have to go to the bathroom. Your boys there wouldn't let me go earlier. If I don't go now, we're all going to regret it."

David smiled, taking another sip from the glass he'd refilled, and stepped toward them.

"Adrian will be outside your door. If you take too long, he might become impatient. You wouldn't want that."

Julia scowled at David and stepped into the aisle. Stumbling slightly, she knocked the crystal tumbler from his hand, shattering it against the cherry table across the aisle. In an instant, Kasprzyk was out of his chair, wary and alert. David swore loudly as Julia fell to the floor near the glass shards. The two guards lumbered forward with thudding footsteps as the expensive scotch soaked into the carpeting in an elongated s-shape. David reached down and yanked Julia roughly to her feet.

"Clumsy bitch, that scotch is worth more than you are!"

"I'm sorry!" Julia exclaimed as she pulled her hair back from her face. "I tripped. I've been tied up for hours and my legs are weak."

David shoved her toward the two guards.

"Take her to the bathroom, Adrian," he growled. "If she takes longer than two minutes, kick the door in."

A puzzled expression played across Michael's face as Julia marched down the aisle and disappeared into the bathroom. He thought he had seen a flash of something near her pocket as she'd stood up. It was only an instant then it was gone. He glanced down at the shards of the crystal tumbler. David had stormed toward a small closet and retrieved a trash bin. An idea formed in Michael's brain. Mentally, he reassembled the glass. A large piece was missing. The flash he had seen must have been Julia slipping the shard into her pocket. Had she planned to fall and knock the glass out of David's hand, or had she taken advantage of the situation? Either way, Julia now had a weapon.

"David."

His old friend dropped the last of the glass splinters into the trash bin and turned impatiently to Michael.

"What? Do you need to go to the bathroom too?"

"No. I need to talk to Milla and Katya. Now."

Michael heard Kasprzyk's seat creak as he stood up. He kept his eyes trained on David. He needed to gauge the man's response. He saw no shifting of the feet, no flicker of the eyes, no indication the man had been caught in a lie.

"No."

"Then kiss your plans goodbye because I'm not doing anything until I know that they're both alive."

"No."

This time, it was Kasprzyk who had responded. Michael ignored him.

"You tell your Director that I won't lift a finger until I hear from both of them. Go ahead, call him."

Michael held David's gaze. He decided to add a final punch.

"You know I don't make idle threats, David. When I say something, I back it up. Make sure the Director knows that."

Another thought occurred to Michael.

"Tell your Director I want three phone calls. One now. One on our way to the first insertion and one on the way to the second insertion. If Milla and Katya aren't on each of those phone calls, you get nothing."

Michael sat back in his chair.

"You've got one minute for the first call, starting now."

"You don't demand anything!" Kasprzyk growled. Michael braced himself as the man stepped toward him, but David stopped Kasprzyk with a hand to the chest. Michael caught the calculating glint in David's eyes.

"I don't want him to have any doubt that we really have his wife and daughter, or what will happen to them if he doesn't cooperate. You should make the call."

A long moment passed filled only with Kasprzyk's wheezy breathing. Then, finally, he relented. A cruel smile snaked across his lips.

"That's why you're here. I'll make the call."

Kasprzyk spun on his heel and stepped toward the cockpit, pausing at the door to punch some numbers into his cell phone. Michael strained to hear, but the hiss of the plane's air conditioning and the vibration from the wind drowned out the man's hushed conversation. A soft touch on his shoulder nearly sent Michael out of his seat. He hadn't heard Julia return from the bathroom.

"What's happening?" she asked quietly.

"They're getting Milla and Katya on the phone," he whispered tensely, never taking his eyes off Kasprzyk.

At that moment, the Polish scientist pivoted and marched down the aisle, beaming in triumph. Michael hesitated before snatching the phone. It was warm and slightly sweaty in his ice cold hands. He fought to keep his expression neutral as he pressed the phone to his ear.

He could hear someone breathing. Long, shaky nasal breaths, like a runner trying to slow her pulse.

"Milla?"

He heard the breath catch with a panicked *snick*. In that instant, even before he heard her voice, he knew Milla was alive. The euphoria quickly turned into despair as he realized that David hadn't been bluffing. He really had Milla and Katya.

"Michael?"

"It's me. Are you okay? Where's Katya?"

Her words tumbled through the phone like a rockslide.

"They came to the house. They grabbed Katya. I couldn't do anything. I tried to stop them. They said they would hurt Katya then they forced us into a van."

"Is Katya okay?"

"She's here with me. We're okay, for now."

"Where are you?"

"I don't know."

Milla's husky voice dropped to a low whisper.

"I'm sorry about what I said last night."

"Don't worry about it," Michael replied, swallowing hard.

"It was horrible and I shouldn't have said it." She paused. "They want you to do something. Please, Michael, do whatever they want."

Her voice cracked upward like a broken hinge. Panicked.

"They said they would kill Katya! Please, Michael, please! Do what they want!"

He heard the sounds of a struggle. Someone was trying to take the phone from Milla.

"Milla!"

"Michael!"

Her voice was muffled, as if from a great distance. He heard a click. Then nothing.

"Milla!"

She was gone.

Slowly, he lowered the phone. His ear throbbed where he had mashed the phone against it. He stared at the blank display, wanting to climb through it to rescue Milla and Katya. A hand appeared on the edge of his vision, demanding the phone's return. He threw the phone into the dark recesses enveloping him. Julia placed a hand on his twitching fingers, but he shook it off.

As his surroundings slowly leaked back into Michael's consciousness, he realized that Julia was staring at him.

"We need to talk," she whispered.

Michael turned away, but she leaned close so her lips brushed his ear.

"We need to find a way to get a message out, so people can start looking for Milla and Katya. And for us."

Michael shook his head.

"Too dangerous."

"We need to contact someone who can help us."

"I won't risk it. I'm sorry you're caught up in this, Julia, but I won't give them a reason to kill my family."

"You know they may not let any of us go."

"I know that," he snapped, then raised a hand in apology. "I'm sorry, but I'm not stupid. They can't release us; we know who they are." Michael took a breath before continuing. "I know they're going to kill us."

He was surprised how easily the words had come out. He repeated them quietly, without looking at Julia, his fingers typing each letter on his lap.

"We only have one chance; give the Director what he wants and pray for a moment when we can make a move."

"What kind of move?" she asked.

He glanced around, but no one was listening.

"You saw what happened with the phone. The path to the Director is through Kasprzyk. David and the guards are expendable. If I can get rid of them, I'll make Kasprzyk lead me to the Director."

"How?"

Michael shook his head grimly as his thoughts careened back to the last time someone he loved had been taken from him.

"Everyone talks eventually, given the right encouragement."

Five

Aboard Air Force One
Charles De Gaulle Airport
Paris

As *Air Force One* lifted off the tarmac, Deputy NSA Director Melissa Stark dug her knuckles into her eyes until the pressure squeaked out of the sockets. She'd gotten two hours of sleep in the past twenty-four, preparing for the President's breakfast meeting with the French and his evening summit with the Russians and Saudis. She'd hoped for a little rest on their mid-morning flight to Moscow, but the phone call she had just received changed all that. Red-haired and green-eyed with a slight lisp, Stark had been a Secret Service agent, then a field agent for the NSA before being appointed Deputy Director. As her boss, NSA Director Stanley Billings, stormed down the aisle toward her, Stark wished that she were back in the field.

"Director, we have a situation."

"Not now, Melissa. After listening to that preening French bastard lecture us about international organizations, I have to brief the President on the latest attack by ISIS."

The lightning quick charge through northern Iraq by the Islamic State in Iraq and Levant, or ISIS, and the equally rapid retreat by the American-trained Iraqi military was the latest crisis of the moment.

"Sir . . ."

But Billings had disappeared into the presidential suite.

Frustrated, Stark dialed her cell.

"Jigger, what have you learned?"

The NSA computer analyst's excited voice poured out of her phone.

"The field agent who told you about the professor's disappearance ghosted this guy's laptop and sent it to me. I've just started digging, but McKeon was doing amazing stuff. Microbes that eat oil? They could've cleaned up the BP spill in the Gulf like nothing. They can also turn oil that you can't get to into natural gas that's easily tapped."

Melissa sighed. She could picture the frizzy-haired tech pacing around his lab in his jeans and Green Lantern t-shirt.

"I know all this, Jigger. That's why we've been monitoring his work."

"So then he just disappears?"

"He was supposed to meet the college president last night, but never showed. When our field agent couldn't find him, he checked out his house. McKeon and his family were gone."

"Maybe they just went somewhere."

"No. McKeon was announcing his discovery of this microbe on Friday. It was the most important day of his career. The *New York Times*, the *Washington Post,* some international papers, a slew of government officials, national security folks, oil companies, the American Petroleum Institute, they were all going to be there. Energy security, peace in our time, that sort of thing. He wouldn't just disappear. His wife's purse was in the kitchen and their clothes and suitcases weren't missing."

"So who nabbed him?"

"That's what I want you to tell me."

Melissa waved at a passing secret service agent she had trained before leaving the service.

"I need to talk to you," he mouthed.

She nodded, tapped her watch to signal *later*, then slipped into an empty conference room and kicked the door shut, waiting for Jigger to continue. A television on the wall showed silent video of the new caliphate in Iraq. As Melissa waited, she heard the *click clack* of Jigger's fingers pounding out keystrokes.

"Well, I found something weird."

"What?"

"Some of his lab notes show that he tweaked his experiments to capture and destroy the natural gases created by the destruction of the oil."

Stark sighed again.

"I already know this, Jigger. One of the reasons I'm talking to you is because I'm afraid that someone wants to weaponize McKeon's discovery and use it to destroy oil fields."

"Can it do that?"

Melissa's silence was a sufficient answer for the analyst, as his fingers returned in a flurry to the keyboard.

"Got it. Got it. I'd already started a search for any email about his work and I have the results now. There's not much. He kept things pretty quiet. The college president, his department chair . . . wait. Here's something."

"What?"

Just then, Stark jumped at a knock on the door behind her. She turned and spotted her aide, who was pointing urgently at her watch. *Damn! She was late for a meeting with the Deputy Chief of Staff.*

"What did you find, Jigger?"

"Approximately one year ago, Michael emailed a man named David Kenner at the Department of Energy's Savannah River National Laboratory about his research. Kenner runs DOE's explorations in the Athabasca Oil Sands."

"Get me everything on Kenner. Find out what his connection is to McKeon and call me back in fifteen minutes."

Stark yanked open the door and took a briefing memo from her assistant. As she hurried down the hall, she couldn't take her mind off McKeon. *Where the hell was he?*

Fifteen minutes later, Melissa Stark stepped out of her meeting with the Deputy Chief of Staff, a pompous weasel of a man who always set her teeth on edge, particularly now. It seemed that they had spent their first two years in office lurching from one crisis to another, but the current unrest sweeping the Middle East and Northern Africa was unprecedented. Protesters had toppled Mubarak in Egypt before the military outlawed the Muslim Brotherhood again. Syrian protesters were running for their lives. The ISIS jihadis, too violent even for al-Qaeda, now controlled most of Iraq. Iran was on the rise everywhere. The entire region was one match strike from exploding. In response, the United States, Russia and Saudi Arabia had begun top-secret negotiations to create a new framework, like the Marshall Plan in post–World War II Europe, to lift the millions of protesters out of grinding poverty and away from the grip of the Iranian mullahs and the new ISIS jihadis. The President was flying to Moscow to try to close the deal.

Melissa stretched her knotted neck muscles side to side. That moron of a Deputy Chief of Staff had proclaimed that *failure was not an option* in these talks. *Idiot.* Failure was always an option, often a bitter reality. Melissa gave the success of a Middle East Marshall Plan a one in a hundred chance, but it was still their best and only chance to avoid catastrophe.

She stared at her phone, willing it to ring.

And if some group is trying to use an American discovery to destroy Saudi and Russian oil, then that'll blow the talks all to hell, and with it, any chance to stop the Middle East from burning up.

She needed information to share with Billings, if he'd ever listen to her.

Her phone rang and she immediately answered.

"What did you find, Jigger?"

"David Kenner and McKeon were in grad school at Notre Dame at the same time. I've sent you a picture of Kenner."

Melissa opened the attachment while the computer analyst kept talking. She gazed thoughtfully at the man staring unpleasantly into the camera: thick-necked and broad-faced, with a bent nose and a buzz cut.

"Kenner studied engineering while McKeon was getting his Ph.Ds in Biochemistry and Biomolecular Engineering. Nothing much about their time together except both were arrested for fighting a group of undergrads in a bar in downtown South Bend. They were released and no charges were brought."

Melissa handed off the files from her meeting with the Deputy Chief of Staff to her aide and kept walking to the galley. She was starving.

"What else?" she asked.

"After graduating, Kenner joined the DOE's Savannah River National Laboratory, but he's spent most of his time in the Athabasca oil sands in Alberta, Canada. He's been working on the cutting edge of the oil sands extraction technology, but it's a mess."

"What do you mean?"

"To extract the oil, they blast steam into the reservoirs to loosen the bitumen so it flows into wells, then they pump it to the surface. It's incredibly complex and expensive. And inefficient. With all the piping and the sludge they leave behind, they don't make any friends in the environmental world, either. I found several online videos of protesters at the Athabasca Oil Sands."

"So McKeon emails Kenner that his microbes could solve Kenner's problems."

"Right."

"What does Kenner do?" Melissa asked as she grabbed a banana and peeled it.

"Well, that's the interesting part. He never passed on the information to anyone at the oil fields or at the lab."

"No one?"

"Nope."

"Why wouldn't you tell your bosses about a breakthrough that could revolutionize your work and make you a ton of money?"

"Good question."

"Tell me you have a good answer, Jigger," Melissa said, popping a piece of banana into her mouth.

"Not yet. On your authority, I sent some agents over to his apartment and lab. They'll send me anything they find. I did find something, though."

"What?" Melissa mumbled through a mouthful of banana.

"I checked flight records and found that he flew to Portland, Maine, the day before McKeon disappeared. He flew on a round trip ticket, but wasn't on the return flight."

"Find him, Jigger. And let me know as soon as you have anything from his apartment or lab."

"You bet. Hey, uh, Longfellow and McKeon are very close, right?"

"Right."

Melissa was ashamed of the sour note that had crept into her voice. *That was ten years ago. It's over. Leave it alone.* She unconsciously rubbed the scar on her shoulder.

"Does Longfellow know McKeon's disappeared?" Jigger asked.

Melissa stopped rubbing and sighed.

"Not yet. The Director sent him on a mission to London and I want to have something concrete before I call him. Otherwise he's likely to abandon his mission and race back to search for McKeon and the others."

Melissa sighed again as she spied her aide approaching with another stack of files. *Even on its worst day, field work is still better than this.*

"I've got to go. Call me as soon as you have anything."

"You bet."

Six

As the conference room aboard Air Force One emptied, Melissa Stark leaned back in her chair, kicked off her pumps, and rubbed her shoulder. With McKeon's disappearance, she'd been thinking about Moscow, ten years before, when Longfellow had left her alone for her first solo mission.

Moscow's Novodevichy Cemetery had closed hours ago, but she had entered with a key left for her under a bench outside the gate. She tasted the soot that fell like damaged snow and glanced around her surroundings apprehensively. Black shadows licked at the rows of monuments. Up the hill, the moonlight glistened off the white walls and gold-trimmed green domes of the Cathedral of Our Lady of Smolensk, one of the two main cathedrals in the Novodevichy, or New Maiden, Convent. Its sister, the Gate Church of the Intercession, somberly watched over the monuments below, its deep red muted in the twilight.

As she crept silently through the cemetery, looking for her contact, a flash of light blazed to her left, followed immediately by a soft handclap, then the bone and ligaments in her shoulder exploded in a burst of agony. As she fell, the only sound she heard was running footsteps.

Melissa jerked awake as her phone chirped.

"What do you have, Jigger?"

"Good stuff."

Melissa leaned forward at the excitement in the analyst's voice. "Talk to me," she said.

"Our agents found a laptop in Kenner's apartment. They ghosted and mirrored it for me, but it was scrubbed clean."

"You mean he deleted everything?" Melissa asked. "That doesn't sound like someone taking a simple trip to visit a friend."

"Right. I ran some very sophisticated software that can recover just about everything. People think they can delete stuff, but digital is forever. I found McKeon's email to Kenner."

"Did he send the email to anyone?"

"Yep," Jigger replied. "He forwarded it to two different email accounts."

"We need to trace those."

"I'm working on it. I'm betting that he bounced the email through a number of servers designed to hide the identity of the recipient. If he did it well, it's very difficult, if not impossible, to identify the recipient, but I'll do my best."

"We need to know who he told about Michael's work," Melissa said as she waved away her aide who had appeared at the conference room door with another stack of files.

"I found something else," Jigger replied hurriedly. "This dude's a serious conspiracy nut."

"What do you mean?"

"I'm sending you a link."

Melissa opened the link on her phone and a blog appeared under the banner of a waving American flag.

"This is a fringe blog about threats to American security because of our dependence on foreign oil," Jigger explained. "Kenner was a regular poster. He was all worked up over Russia and Saudi Arabia. He keeps writing how they are bleeding America and that we need to go for their jugular. He says that they will destroy America unless we take drastic action."

"Does he say what action we should take?" Melissa asked as she scrolled through several screens of retrieved posts.

"No, he's not specific."

"When was his last post?"

"Two days ago."

"The day he flew to Boston to see Michael," Melissa said.

"The day before everyone disappeared," Jigger replied. "And take a look at Kenner's last post."

Melissa scrolled to the last page, then gave a low whistle.

"*Pay attention, patriots. A new revolution starts soon. Freedom from the oil tyrants is days away.*"

"Damn it. Kenner's the guy. Kenner must have learned that McKeon's microbe could destroy the oil and decided to deploy it in some plot, most likely against Saudi Arabia or Russia. All right, Jigger, Kenner's your number one priority. Everything else can wait. I'll brief the Director as soon as he's free. Find Kenner."

"I'll start with the airports."

"Contact Homeland Security. Give them Kenner's picture and have them run a facial recognition scan on all their airport security. Start with Portland and Bangor, Maine, then Manchester, New Hampshire. If they're flying to Saudi Arabia or Russia, they'll connect in Boston. If they don't find anything, check New York, Newark and Philadelphia."

"I'll run an algorithm for probable flight patterns."

"We have to find this guy fast, Jigger. If he attacks Russia or Saudi Arabia, the summit will fail and we'll lose Northern Africa and the Middle East to the Iranians forever."

"On it." Jigger paused before continuing. "Uh, boss, there's something else you might want to see."

"What?"

"I pulled McKeon's deep background file. I'm sending it to you now. Check out his childhood. It's, uh. . . ."

Melissa could hear the hesitation in the man's voice.

"What, Jigger?"

"It's some of the worst stuff I've ever read. If half of the stuff is true, this Kenner guy doesn't know who he's dealing with."

As Melissa ended the call and opened McKeon's file, she shook her head at her aide, who was approaching with yet another stack of files.

"Not now, Dani, I'm going to plant myself outside the Director's meeting and wait for him to finish with the President. There's an emergency I have to tell him about."

As she headed toward the President's quarters, Melissa began reading the file. Halfway down the aisle, she stopped as her hand flew to her mouth.

"Oh my God," she breathed, turning pale.

She steadied herself against the wall, sickened by what she had read, and closed the file, wishing she'd never read it. She told herself that she had an asset to recover and an international disaster to stop. This couldn't become personal. But as she clutched the file to her chest, she knew it already was personal, for Longfellow and for her. Now she understood why Longfellow had abandoned her ten years ago in Moscow. She had to call him, but she knew nothing good would come of it.

Seven

—⦿⦿⦿—

London

"It's a trap!"

The NSA agent code-named Longfellow ducked behind a crate as the three men he had come to meet opened fire. As their submachine gunfire chewed into the crate, Longfellow nodded to the retired FSB agent he'd dragged with him.

"Sorry, Grisha."

"Where are the centrifuges?" Grisha Medvedev demanded as another fusillade sent them sprawling to the cement floor.

"I don't know. My bosses sent me here to meet a Pakistani American scientist who was supposedly selling nuclear-grade centrifuges to Iran, but there's nothing here."

Medvedev yanked his Makarov out of its holster and shot blindly around the crate.

"Why do you hold onto that artifact?" Longfellow chided his old friend, as he pulled out his trusty Sig Sauer P220.

"Old habits die hard," Medvedev grinned. "Speaking of which, you should have listened to me. I told you that I hadn't heard of your scientist."

Longfellow banged off several rounds then ducked under a shower of splinters as their assailants continued the onslaught. He grimly surveyed their surroundings.

"Bit of a tight spot. The only exit is in back of them. Can you sneak around to your right?"

Medvedev rolled to the edge of the crate then quickly scrambled back as another hail of gunfire erupted.

"No good. They've fanned out. We're stuck. I told you coming here was a bad idea."

"That's why I'm glad we were never partners," Longfellow replied, letting another couple shots loose before ducking back. "You always have to be right."

"In our profession, being right usually means being alive."

Longfellow jumped as a new round of gunfire erupted.

"Those are different weapons. Who the hell else is shooting at us?"

After several moments, the gunfire finished echoing off the concrete block walls and a voice shouted in Russian.

"Yasno! Grisha?"

Hearing the "all clear" signal, Longfellow shot a quizzical look at Medvedev, who shrugged and smiled.

"I told you coming here was a bad idea, so I arranged some back-up." He stood up and waved cheerily. Longfellow followed suit, a little more warily. At the sight of the two men, their four rescuers lowered submachine guns. Their three assailants were dead on the floor, their blood turning the cement dust pink.

"It's good to be right . . ." Longfellow began.

"And alive," Medvedev finished.

The two men quickly searched the dead assailants, but found nothing to identify them.

"If this was part of a deal gone bad, I'd expect to find some identification," Longfellow said. "There's only one type of person scrubbed so clean that they can't be identified."

"A professional," Medvedev said.

"So why were three professionals sent to kill me?" Longfellow asked.

"More importantly, who sent them?" Medvedev responded.

As the wail of sirens filled the warehouse, Medvedev clasped Longfellow's hand in his.

"Time to go. If you need anything, you know how to find me."

"Thanks, Grisha. I owe you."

"I think we're even." The Russian grew serious as he picked a gray hair from Longfellow's shoulder. "There is one favor you can do me."

"What?"

"Retire. We're both getting too old for this."

Eight

—ᘛᘚᘛ—

Southwark Street, London

As Longfellow threaded his way through the throng of morning shoppers in the Borough Market in London's South Bank, he luxuriated in the Market's warm chaos. The comforting scents of coriander and cinnamon mingled with the cacophony of colors from the vegetable and fruit stands, distracting the spy from the ominous gray skies and his troubling questions about the ambush at the warehouse. He knew he should report in, but his gut told him to wait. Something was going on and until he knew what, it was better to stay quiet and below the radar. He bought a bag of dried apricots and honey cashews at a stall and began scrolling through the various email accounts he maintained. Midway through the Market, he froze, an unchewed apricot on his tongue, as he read Fyodorov's email.

> L-
> *F Dead. Your asset in danger. The Global Group after me. Run.*
> -D.

Fouad was dead?

Longfellow spit the apricot on the floor, ignoring the disgusted stare of a frumpy matron in a housecoat and Wellingtons, and read the email again. Only Dmitry, Fouad and he had access to the email account. The email had to be genuine. With a growing sense of apprehension, he dialed their phone numbers.

No answer. Damn!

He threw the apricots and cashews into a trash can and hurried through the market, dodging merchants and shoppers. He had to check in. If anything had happened to Fouad or Dmitry, Melissa would know. Or she would find out. She owed them that. He scanned the faces of the nearby shoppers as he dialed, looking for any sign of a threat.

"Longfellow?" Melissa's voice spilled into his ear. "I, uh, was about to call you."

"I just received an email from Dmitry that he sent two days ago," Longfellow interrupted in clipped tones. "Fouad's dead."

"What?" The surprise and pain were evident in her voice. "How?"

"That's what I need you to find out."

"Let me patch Jigger in."

A heartbeat later, the analyst was on the line.

"Hi, Longfellow. You need me to look for someone named Fouad al-Dossary?"

"And Dmitry Fyodorov."

"On it."

"Do you think something happened to Dmitry, too?" Melissa asked.

"In his email, he said something called The Global Group was after him."

"Nothing on al-Dossary," Jigger replied shortly, "but Dmitry Fyodorov died two days ago. He collapsed on Curzon Street in London. Suspected heart attack."

Longfellow grimaced in pain.

"Was he a friend?" Jigger asked.

"Yes," Longfellow and Melissa replied simultaneously.

"Jigger, look into The Global Group and call me as soon as you have anything," Melissa said.

"You got it, boss," Jigger replied, hanging up.

"I'm sorry," Melissa said softly. "They were both good agents."

"Good men," Longfellow replied, shaking his head sadly.

"We'll find out who did this to them," Melissa promised. Then she remembered McKeon.

"There's something I need to tell you," she began.

"Dmitry's email also said my asset was in danger," Longfellow interrupted again. "There was only one asset of mine that he knew about. Where's Michael?"

Melissa swallowed.

Longfellow's voice tightened. "Where is he, Melissa?"

"We were watching him, but we didn't have any warning."

"What happened?"

"He was supposed to meet the college president at his lab yesterday, but never showed. He was at his last class of the day, which ended at 4:30 p.m. Some time between then and 9 p.m., he disappeared."

Longfellow swayed amid the eddy of shoppers swirling around him.

"About six months ago, Michael emailed a man named David Kenner about his discovery," Melissa said. "They went to Notre Dame together. Did Michael ever mention him?"

"Michael doesn't have many friends, but I don't recall that name."

"Michael emailed Kenner because he thought the microbe could help Kenner's work in the Athabasca Oil Sands, but Kenner never passed it along to his superiors. Instead he emailed it to two accounts we're tracing right now. A couple days before Michael disappeared, Kenner posted a blog entry that America's freedom from Saudi and Russian oil tyranny was coming soon."

"Shit."

"Right. Then he wiped his laptop clean and flew to Portland. We're looking for them both now."

"That means that Kenner knows that Michael's microbe can consume everything it comes into contact with."

"Yes, we're assuming he intends to use the microbe to attack Saudi Arabia and Russia." Melissa took a deep breath. "But that's not all. Michael's wife and daughter are missing too."

Longfellow spun and kicked a nearby trash can with a loud clang, sending a flock of pigeons fluttering into the air.

"They're holding them hostage to force him to cooperate," he spat.

"Homeland Security is running facial recognition scans on airport security videos for all of them," Melissa said.

"Where was Julia when they took Michael?" Longfellow asked.

"She's missing too."

"Son of a bitch! Don't any of your agents know what it means to watch an asset, Melissa?"

"Don't yell at me. We had people watching him. This was a professional grab."

Longfellow stalked in a circle by the entrance to the market. Finally he slowed.

"I should have been there," he groaned. "Why the hell did the Director send me on this dead end mission?"

"I don't know. He doesn't include me in his operational decisions."

Several beats of Longfellow's pulse passed before Melissa continued.

"I read his deep background report," she said quietly, "the one you prepared." She paused again. "Is everything in there true?"

"Everything."

"Good God. How do you think he's handling this?"

Longfellow squinted into the gray, lifeless sky and turned up his collar as pedestrians scurried to escape the cold rain that had begun to fall. He faced southeast toward the dangers burning across the Middle East and Northern Africa. Somewhere out there was a man whose discovery could save or destroy his country's national security, but at what cost to his family? Longfellow's mind drifted back to the angry young man he had met at the Mission Possible Teen Center in Westbrook, Maine, who had been ordered there after breaking a chair over another student's head.

You like fighting?

He was picking on another kid. But, yeah, I like fighting.

You should spend more time studying than fighting. Your test scores are astronomical. Have you ever thought about college?

Not for me. I'm too busy. . . .

Too busy doing what?

But Longfellow soon learned what kept Michael busy, stealing food and money, fighting off the predators who had realized he was alone in his mother's apartment, and hiding his secret from the police and school officials.

I know about you.

What do you know?

Everything. So here's the deal. You want to fight? Three times a week, you come here and fight with me over math and science.

If I don't?

If you miss one lesson, I'll call the police and tell them you're living alone. And stop stealing. After each lesson, I'll take you to the grocery store and you pick out what you need.

Michael came. He never missed a lesson, slicing through everything Longfellow taught him with deadly precision, but he never talked about his family. Not once. The scars were too hard and thick. For twenty years, Longfellow had watched Michael channel that ferocity into his studies and then his work, but had never once gotten Michael to talk about his past. Longfellow never revealed that he already had unearthed all the horrors that Michael thought were buried. But, in all those years, Longfellow had never seen anyone get past the scarring, until Katya and Milla. Then he had seen Michael bleed for the first time.

Longfellow wiped the moisture from his face, which he told himself was rain, and returned to his conversation with Melissa.

"He's in hell," he finally replied. "And he'll do anything to save Milla and Katya. Anything."

Melissa knew she had to choose her next words carefully.

"Longfellow? Rescuing Michael and his family and Julia is obviously our priority, but his discovery can't be used to attack Russia and Saudi Arabia, especially not now when our president is one hour from landing in Moscow to meet with the Russian president and the Saudi king in our last best chance to save our asses in the Middle East."

"I know."

"That means that if our choice is between rescuing those four or stopping the attack, we must stop the attack. National security is more important than friendship or loyalty."

"It won't come to that."

"If it does . . ."

"It won't."

"If it does, do you understand your obligations?"

"I don't know who the hell taught you to abandon friends in need, but it wasn't me," Longfellow snapped as he hurried down Storey Street to the London Bridge Underground station.

"Tell me you understand."

"I understand," Longfellow spat.

Aboard Air Force One, Melissa's shoulders sagged. She felt relieved and sick all at once.

"Good. We'll keep you updated. What's your next move?"

"Dmitry's apartment, in case he hid anything there."

"Be careful. Whoever killed him is probably watching the apartment. With Fouad and Dmitry dead, they may be coming after you."

Longfellow terminated the call with a look of disgust.

"I understand," he muttered to himself as he reached the metro stop. "I understand that I'm not taking orders from anyone anymore." An instant later, the darkness of the London Underground had swallowed him whole.

Nine

Aboard Air Force One

When the door to the conference room finally opened, unleashing a babble of voices, Melissa stepped toward Director Billings. Tall and thin, with intense blue eyes and close-cropped gray hair, Billings always looked like he was gritting his teeth, perhaps because he had spent a lifetime giving bad news.

"Director, I need a few moments to update you on the crisis I mentioned earlier," Melissa said.

Billings checked his watch and motioned for her to follow him. He finally stopped at the base of the stairs leading up to the communications deck.

"Another group of Iraqi soldiers we trained just dropped their weapons and ran into the desert," Billings said. "ISIS is spitting distance from Baghdad. What is *your* emergency, Melissa?"

With a deep breath, Melissa began. As she recounted the developments, Billings' eyes locked onto hers, unblinking in their intensity. Melissa had grown accustomed to Billings' dislike of long-winded briefings. Minutes later, when she had finished, Billings tapped his chin twice before speaking.

"Where's Longfellow now?"

"In London."

"Call him home. I don't want Longfellow on this. He's too close."

"Sir, Longfellow's going to want to be involved."

Billings blinked once, slowly.

"I'm not interested in what Longfellow wants. I'm interested in stopping this before it escalates further."

"Who do you want on this?"

"I'll mobilize some assets already in the area."

"Should we notify the Saudis or Russians?"

"Leave that to me."

"Yes sir."

Billings stepped away, then stopped and looked back over his shoulder.

"Get Longfellow off this. Now."

"Yes sir."

Ten

Berkeley Square, London

As Longfellow hurried down Curzon Street on the eastern border of the Mayfair District, he kept a wary eye out for surveillance, but nothing triggered any alarms. He stepped into a doorway across the street from Dmitry's apartment, out of the cold rain that had already soaked his jacket and corduroys, and carefully surveyed his surroundings. Dmitry had always lived life large. His choice of apartment reflected that. The site had originally been the Third Church of Christ, Scientist. The owners had retained the original church façade while renovating it into some of the most exclusive apartments in London. Longfellow knew that the entrance led into a beautifully landscaped private courtyard.

Longfellow had to assume that someone was watching Fyodorov's apartment. If so, the courtyard was a deathtrap. He'd be spotted instantly. Instead, he made his way around to a private underground parking lot off Clarges Mews then used Fyodorov's code for the elevator.

As the door opened on the third floor, Longfellow slipped the Sig Sauer from its holster and stepped quickly into the hallway. Finding it empty, he hurried to Dmitry's door, where several issues of the *Times* had accumulated. Longfellow checked the door then removed a set of lockpicks from his pocket, glancing up and down the hallway as he jiggled the pick. After a few seconds' work, he was inside.

Longfellow locked the door behind him and looked around the apartment, a bemused half-smile flitting across his face at Dmitry's bourgeois taste. A sunken living room with oak flooring and luxurious crimson-colored couches screamed opulence, if not refinement. Floor to ceiling windows gazed towards Berkeley Square. Off to the left was a modern kitchen with chrome appliances and speckled Italian marble. Despite his taste for the finer things, Fyodorov had always been a Russian pretending to be British.

Longfellow's trained eye told him that the apartment had been searched. The carpet runner leading from the door to the hall bore the marks of many different shoes. As he sniffed the air, his nostrils flared at the hint of cigarette smoke. Dmitry didn't smoke. Longfellow doubted that the searchers had smoked in the apartment, but they had spent enough time for the smell to migrate from their clothing into the air.

The grandfather clock in the living room ticked. Outside, a few pigeons cooed and flapped away as a delivery truck rumbled past. Otherwise, the apartment was quiet. Gun ready, Longfellow crept down the hall towards the bedroom; as good a place as any to start. In one fluid movement, he banged the door open and slid through. A quick check of the closet and underneath the bed revealed no one. The bathroom was similarly empty. Finally, he entered Dmitry's office.

Longfellow stared in dismay at the desk, barren except for a wooden container holding several pens. Someone had taken everything. The desk, filing cabinets, closet—all were empty. He checked his watch again. He didn't have time to be quiet or careful. With a silent apology to his dead friend, Longfellow ripped the desk apart, looking for hidden compartments. Then the closet. He yanked out the drawers from the filing cabinet and turned it over. With a rising sense of frustration, he unscrewed door knobs, looking for anything hidden inside the doors, but still found nothing.

Just then, he heard someone's foot scuff across the carpet in the living room. He was not alone.

He stepped quietly into the hall and blinked as a burst of static sounded from the living room, followed by a Russian voice: *We're arriving out front now. We'll meet you at the third floor elevator. Make sure he doesn't leave.* The advance guard, perhaps wanting to be a hero, had left his post and entered ahead of his team. Longfellow had no delusions about holding off a well-armed squad. He had to escape before the team arrived.

Betting that the message had momentarily distracted the guard, Longfellow launched himself into the living room, firing in the direction of the noise. A tall, stocky gunman with long blond hair recoiled as two shots struck him in the chest, but the black Kevlar vest he wore saved his life. Wincing, the guard aimed at Longfellow, who had landed on his shoulder and was skidding across the kitchen tile. Longfellow squeezed off one last burst as the gunman fired.

The spy's left shoulder exploded in agony. He jammed his foot against the kitchen island to stop his slide and raked the pistol across the living room, but the gunman had disappeared. He leapt to his feet, his shoulder throbbing. Warm blood soaked his shirt. The guard had fallen onto one of Dmitry's couches, blood pumping from a bullet hole in his neck. Longfellow's last shot had severed the man's jugular vein. His pallor had already turned ashen.

Longfellow spotted the man's gun, picked it up, and stepped close. He only had seconds before the rest of the man's team would arrive. He had to leave, but first, he needed to learn what he could about his attackers. He pointed both guns at the man.

Kto vam? Who are you?

The guard smiled. A red bubble escaped his lips.

Ne-kto. No one.

Then his eyes shut and his face sagged. A last wet wheeze escaped the man's lips. The man's direct-connect walkie talkie barked again. *Where are you?* Longfellow turned and raced for the bedroom, tearing open the window and stepping onto the windowsill. Just out of arms' reach, a drainpipe ran down the side of the building to the street two floors below. He lunged and wrapped his hands around it, groaning as the bullet wound in his shoulder tore open. The pipe squealed and pulled away from the building, but the bolts held. Longfellow's feet slipped twice on the rain-slicked brick exterior before he was able to wedge his toes and walk himself down the side of the building.

Angry cries from inside the apartment told him that the crew had found their dead comrade. It would be only seconds before they spotted the open window. He looked down. There was approximately fifteen feet to go. If he fell onto the street below, he'd break his legs, but he had no choice, relaxing his grip on the pipe and letting himself slide down towards the street. Halfway down, a loose bracket sliced through his left palm. Longfellow cried out and pulled his hand away, his foot banging against the wall, sending him spiraling towards the pavement. He flailed helplessly for a moment before crashing onto the pavement.

Longfellow gasped for breath as he tried to roll onto his side, his left shoulder and hand screaming in agony. A hail of bullets chewed up the pavement around him as he reached a nearby trash dumpster. Black spots danced before his eyes from the impact with the pavement. His left arm dangled lifeless, but he knew he had to move or die.

Forcing himself to his feet, he used the dumpster as cover to pump several rounds at the window, shattering glass and forcing the gunman back inside. Longfellow seized the opportunity to race across the street, reaching the shelter of an enclosed doorway just as another round of bullets splattered the sidewalk.

He knew he was in a dangerous position. The gunman upstairs would try to pin him down long enough for the rest of his team to trap him. He emptied the gun he had taken from the dead man at the window then tossed it in the dumpster and darted around the corner into a back alley.

A chuck of concrete molding exploded by his head, slicing his cheek and forehead. Longfellow dropped to one knee as he slammed another clip into his Sig Sauer. The gunmen had stationed a man in the alley in case Longfellow broke through the first line of containment. With a single spit, Longfellow shot the guard in the face then jumped into the man's Saab.

With a grinding of gears, he backed up just as two more gunmen raced out of Dmitry's apartment building, unleashing another futile volley as he squealed out of the alley. Longfellow heard the sirens as he shifted one-handed onto Berkeley Street, but he quickly disappeared into the morning traffic on Piccadilly.

Heading west toward Piccadilly Circus, Longfellow realized that his phone was gone. He groaned and inspected his injuries. His shoulder and hand throbbed, but his bullet wound was the most troubling. He couldn't go to a hospital. He blinked the sweat from his eyes and pressed his hand against the wound, trying vainly to stop the blood flow. There was one man who could get him patched up, provide him with a new gun and cell phone, and get him out of England. He shivered and flipped on the heat full blast, but he didn't have much time. He was already growing cold.

Eleven

—⊶⊷—

Aboard Air Force One

As *Air Force One* descended toward Vnukovo Airport, southwest of Moscow, Melissa stared at her phone in frustration. With the two-hour time difference between London and Moscow, it was mid-afternoon. She had left four messages for Longfellow, but hadn't reached him to relay Billings' order. Just then, her phone rang. She eagerly peered at the screen, hoping it was Longfellow, but it was Jigger instead.

"What do you have, Jigger?"

"Nothing on The Global Group, but I did make some progress on one of the emails Kenner forwarded."

"What did you find?"

"Like I told you, Kenner forwarded McKeon's email to two email addresses. One of the recipients is using a series of extremely sophisticated servers, fake addresses and anonymous email accounts to hide his identity. I'm running into dead end after dead end, but the other recipient isn't so clever. I traced that forwarded email to an account registered in Houston, Texas, but no name."

"I need a name, Jigger."

"I know. On a hunch, I hacked into the search records for the online service providers for Houston, looking for anyone searching for information on Michael McKeon within a week of the date Kenner forwarded the email."

"What did you find?"

"Duncan Berry, an energy broker. He searched for information on Michael McKeon the day after the email was sent. And he used the internet service he registered for in his own name."

"Get an address and send a team."

"On it, boss. Also, I cracked the code for a secure blog site that this guy posted to. He wrote 'freedom from the Russian and Saudi petro-dictators is coming soon.' He also referred to 'TGG,' which must be The Global Group."

"Good. What about Homeland Security?"

"Nothing, but that wouldn't hit the private planes, so I checked flight plans for private planes out of Boston over the past week and found one that was interesting the day after McKeon disappeared."

"Where did it go?"

"Moscow. Sheremetyevo Airport."

Melissa punched the air in satisfaction.

"Find me everything you can on that flight."

"Do you want me to contact airport officials?"

"Not yet. I don't want to have to explain to them why we're looking. Do it from your end."

"You bet. Should I send this to Longfellow?"

Melissa glanced toward the presidential suite. Billings' orders had been clear, but she also knew that Longfellow would never follow them. She wasn't sure if she even wanted him to. Longfellow, on the books or off, was their best bet to find Michael and stop The Global Group. To do that, he needed information. She made her choice.

"Send it."

Twelve

London

Longfellow grimaced and slowly rotated his bandaged left shoulder. His eyes watered as the pain knifed through him.

"I'd take it easy on that shoulder," Medvedev cautioned as he packed away the gauze and bandages. "You're lucky that the bullet just grazed you. Surgery isn't a skill I want to develop."

Medvedev smiled and gingerly flexed the fingers he had slashed on the drainpipe during his escape from Dmitry's apartment.

"I wouldn't put anything past you, Grisha. You've always been able to get me anything I need. Thanks for the dry clothes, too." The work pants, wool sweater and lightweight anorak clearly had not been intended for the rotund Grisha because they fit Hal's trim frame perfectly.

"I'm sorry you couldn't come to my townhouse," Medvedev said, looking around the cluttered apartment. Unopened boxes of cell phones and i-Pads leaned against stacks of laptops. A giant safe in the corner held passports and currencies from various countries. The Russian pursed his lips as he swirled a glass of cognac in his long, thin fingers. "My wife will be home soon from her Pilates class and she doesn't like me to conduct *business* in our home."

"Understood. Laura was the same way, God rest her soul." Longfellow pointed at Medvedev's ample stomach straining against the cashmere sweater. "Marriage seems to suit you, though, Grisha. Who would've thought?"

The Russian patted his stomach ruefully. "I was a whippet when I worked for the FSB; rail-thin, hollow-eyed, twitchy from the methamphetamines I needed to get from mission to mission, to do the things I had to do." He shifted uncomfortably. "I'm still not used to all this extra weight."

"If I was looking for the famous Russian assassin code-named the Sword, I wouldn't even recognize you," Longfellow said.

"*Mech*," Medvedev whispered, staring vacantly past Longfellow's shoulder, as he uttered the Russian word for *sword*. "I haven't heard that name in a long time." He cast a guilty glance at Longfellow. "You know, there was one mission I always meant to tell you about."

Longfellow waved him away.

"We all bring our own baggage. Some things are best left unsaid."

Medvedev nodded gratefully. "Anyway, I suppose chocolate is a better addiction than my old ones, even if I can't see my toes!" A deep, rumble of a laugh burbled out of his chest. Longfellow joined in until wincing in pain.

"I'm sorry," Medvedev said, placing a hand on the American's shoulder. "Forgive me for getting caught in the past. Walking backward is a very Russian thing to do. We must face the future, like you Americans always do." He hoisted himself upright and began pacing around the small apartment. "This organization called The Global Group has managed to kill Fouad and Dmitry, tried to kill you, and has captured McKeon. The NSA thinks they plan to use McKeon's microbe to destroy Russian and Saudi oil. Again, forgive me, but this sounds like something out of one of those thrillers you Americans love."

"It's very real, Grisha," Longfellow replied grimly. "I assure you."

"But can this microbe really destroy such vast quantities of oil?"

Longfellow finished adjusting the bandages on his hands and looked the Russian in the eye.

"It's never been done before, but the lab results say yes. Most importantly, The Global Group believes it can and intends to deploy it."

"Where do you think they will strike first, Saudi Arabia or Russia?"

"I don't know. And even if we knew the country, each country has so many possible targets, it's nearly impossible to predict where they will strike."

"I haven't heard of The Global Group," Medvedev said as he pulled out his cell phone, "but I still have some sources."

"You always do," Longfellow replied with a grin. "Who are you calling?"

"A friend. He owes me. You can listen in."

He dialed quickly. As it rang, Longfellow swallowed a handful of aspirin. When the voice answered, Grisha got directly to the point.

"Sergei, it's Grisha. I need some information."

"It's always good to hear from you, Grisha," the man replied, his frigid tone clear even to Longfellow.

"Dmitry is dead."

"I know. I was very saddened to hear the news," Sergei replied laconically.

"Do you remember Kazakhstan, Sergei, when you were the Deputy Energy Secretary?" Medvedev cut in. "Do you remember that prostitute, that *young girl*, and what her pimp was going to do to you?"

"I repaid my debt to you and Dmitry long ago," Sergei spat.

"You repaid nothing. Now, you are a member of the Federation Council. A big shot. Perhaps one day you will be the new Putin? Tell me, Sergei, what do you think the story of you and that little girl will do to your career?"

Sergei's labored breathing filled Medvedev's apartment. Longfellow shifted uncomfortably as he waited. His shoulder was killing him. Finally, the other Russian responded.

"What do you want?"

"I want to know who The Global Group is."

When the Russian politician replied, fear and resignation rang in his voice.

"I don't know."

"Not good enough!" Medvedev thundered.

"All I've heard is that the Americans are involved."

Longfellow and Medvedev exchanged a glance.

"What do you mean 'the Americans'?" Medvedev demanded.

"The NSA, the CIA, look, Grisha, I don't know. Even if I did, I can't help you with this. Do what you will." The Russian's voice had fallen to a whisper.

"Sergei—"

"No. There is nothing I can do. Grisha, trust no one. No one is who they seem. You're on your own. Tell whoever's listening in that he's on his own, too."

Medvedev and Longfellow stared at the cell phone for several seconds after Sergei had hung up.

"He doesn't frighten easily," Medvedev said, as he scratched furiously at the bridge of his nose. "Whenever my nose itches, it means danger."

"I know."

"What is this about the Americans being involved?" Medvedev asked.

"There is at least one American involved, but, as far as I know, no one from the NSA or CIA."

"Can you be sure?" Medvedev asked.

"No," Longfellow replied, letting a hint of exasperation creep into his voice. "Can we be sure that he wasn't making that up?"

"No," Medvedev said, "but let's not quarrel. There are a few other contacts I can try, but I have to do it alone. You're welcome to wait here."

Longfellow cast a doubtful eye at the stained couch along the wall.

"No thanks. I need to walk and think. Call me on the new cell when you have something. I'll also check in with my boss. See if they learned anything."

Grisha smiled knowingly.

"You don't want to talk here because you think I've bugged the apartment."

Longfellow returned the smile as he waved the cell phone in the air.

"I'm pretty sure you've bugged this phone, too, Grisha, but I'm not concerned about that right now."

Thirty minutes later, Medvedev dropped Longfellow off along Mayfair's southern end on Piccadilly, in front of the Ritz Hotel, and promised to call within the hour. Longfellow gave the trunk an affectionate swipe as the Russian pulled away, quickly disappearing into the traffic flowing down the wide and straight street. The American spy turned to gaze at the Ritz. He'd always admired it for its attempt to evoke Paris' *Rue de Rivoli*, and had even brought Laura once, the year before she died. The rain had lifted, leaving behind a damp gloom that fit Longfellow's mood perfectly. He sighed and decided to stroll toward the aristocratic Hatchard's Book Shop, to give himself time to work through the developments of the past few hours.

He had only taken a few steps when the barrel of a gun pressed into the small of his back.

"Please get in the Mercedes at the curb," said a Russian-accented voice.

"I'd rather walk," Longfellow replied.

"I'd rather not shoot you," the voice replied, "but I will if you don't get in now."

Angry at himself for dropping his guard, Longfellow stepped toward the silver Mercedes limousine at the curb just as its rear passenger door opened. The man at his back had made a fatal mistake. *If you're close enough to touch someone with your gun, you're close enough to lose it*. Longfellow tensed, ready to spin and disarm the man, but the unseen gunman stepped back to a safe range.

"My men are better trained than that, Longfellow," said a deep voice from inside the car. "Please join me. I have information about your friend, Michael McKeon."

With a last look up and down Piccadilly, Longfellow reluctantly slid into the back seat. Facing him was a broad-shouldered man dressed in an impeccable Savile Row suit with silk shirt open at the neck. Longfellow judged him to be in his late forties despite the black hair prematurely graying at the temples. The man had a swarthy complexion stippled with the shadow of a beard recently shorn. Slightly oval-shaped eyes hinted at an eastern heritage. The gunman, a short stocky fellow with tufts of curly black hair spilling over his tight-fitting dress-shirt, slid in after Longfellow, gun at the ready.

"All right," Longfellow replied as the limousine slid into traffic. "You know me, but I'm afraid I haven't had the pleasure."

The man smiled, but didn't extend a hand.

"Forgive me. My name is Colonel Vadim Akhmetalin."

"Colonel?"

"With the FSB."

"To what do I owe this honor?"

Akhmetalin smiled again, displaying a full set of luminescent white teeth. Between Akhmetalin's smile and the other man's gun, Longfellow preferred the gun.

"I believe you and I may have come into similar information."

"What's that?"

Longfellow was stalling for time, waiting for a quick stop, bump in the road, for the gunman to glance out a window, any opportunity to turn the tables.

"You and I have both learned about The Global Group's plot to attack my country and Saudi Arabia."

Longfellow wasn't about to reveal anything to this man.

"I don't know what you're talking about."

"Fair enough," Akhmetalin said, with a slight nod of his head. "Professor McKeon has created a microbe that consumes oil. His intent was to use it to convert oil that was difficult and expensive to extract into natural gases that could easily and cheaply be captured, helping your country reduce its dependence on foreign oil."

When Longfellow remained silent, the colonel continued.

"But Professor McKeon also discovered that the decomposition of the oil could be altered slightly, so everything was destroyed, leaving nothing of value. This turned his microbe into a very potent weapon that could be deployed against any country with significant oil reserves, such as my own country."

Longfellow's eyes darted between the colonel and the gunman. He already knew all this.

"Two days ago, The Global Group kidnapped the professor along with his wife and daughter and his assistant. They are holding his wife and daughter hostage until he uses his microbe to successfully attack my country and Saudi Arabia."

Akhmetalin raised a hand as Longfellow opened his mouth.

"Don't ask me how I learned this. It was in much the same manner as your friends, Fyodorov and the Saudi, al-Dossary."

Longfellow's teeth clenched shut at the mention of his dead friends.

"You said you had information about Michael," Longfellow muttered.

Akhmetalin smiled again.

"Yes, I know where The Global Group is holding his wife and daughter."

Thirteen

—⟡—

Mayfair District, London

"You know where Milla and Katya are?" Longfellow asked in disbelief.

"I'm glad to see that my information about how close you are to the professor and his family is correct," the colonel replied. "Yes, I know where they are."

"Where the hell are they?"

Akhmetalin raised a finger.

"That information comes with a price."

Longfellow liked this guy less by the second.

"What price?"

"I want you to stop Professor McKeon from attacking my country."

Longfellow sat back, puzzled.

"What do you mean?"

Akhmetalin spread his hands wide.

"I think, in this instance, our interests are aligned. You want to find him, and your country does not want to be accused of having a role in attacking my country and Saudi Arabia at the very moment it is trying to reach agreement on a new *Marshall Plan*, I believe the term is, for the Middle East and North Africa. And I don't want my country to lose its oil."

"So why do you need me? Send your agency after him. Go rescue Milla and Katya, then The Global Group won't have any leverage over Michael."

The smile disappeared from Akhmetalin's face as he leaned closer, but still out of Longfellow's reach.

"I am concerned that elements of the FSB may be involved in The Global Group," he said quietly. "I don't know who to trust."

"But, still, why me? I'm a little below your pay grade. You should be reaching out to my bosses."

The smile returned.

"You're far too modest," Akhmetalin said, wagging a finger at Longfellow before turning serious again. "I also have information that someone in the American intelligence system, perhaps in your own agency, is also involved. Again, I don't know whom to trust."

When Longfellow remained silent, a sour look on his face, the FSB Colonel continued.

"Why trust you? Because of your personal relationship with the professor. You will find him and stop him because that's the only way to save him."

"Fine. Tell me where they are."

"I'll fly you there," Akhmetalin said, gesturing to the men in the front. "My plane is waiting."

"No. I've had bad experiences when the FSB promises to take me somewhere. You'll forgive me if I don't trust you. Give me the address and I'll rescue them, then I'll find Michael and save your oil."

"I insist."

"I don't give a damn."

An electric silence crackled between the two men until the smile reappeared.

"Very well."

The colonel gestured again and the limousine returned to the curb in front of the Ritz Carlton, having looped entirely around the

Mayfair District. The gunman opened the door and, as Hal slid out, Akhmetalin gave him the address.

"Don't forget what I said about trust," Akhmetalin called after him. "I've just learned that your own agency has issued an order for your arrest for sharing secrets with Fyodorov and al-Dossary. Curious timing, wouldn't you say?"

As Longfellow's eyes widened, Akhmetalin landed a final punch. "I'm counting on you to stop him. If you double cross me, your previous experiences with my agency will seem like a walk in the park."

As the limousine slipped away, Longfellow yanked out his cell phone and started to dial Melissa's number then stopped. He didn't have time to deal with whatever was going on in the NSA. Stomach churning, he dialed Medvedev's number. Only one thing mattered now: getting to Moscow as fast as possible.

Fourteen

―∾∾―

Ritz-Carlton, Moscow

Melissa padded across the Portuguese marble floor in her suite's bathroom, fingered the plush terry robe, and thought longingly of a long, hot shower, but there wasn't time. Once the American and Russian presidents were finished with their reception in Vnukovo's VIP Hall, her president would be ready for a round of briefings on the situation in the Middle East and Northern Africa, which was deteriorating faster than expected. Instead, she tossed the last of her grilled chicken and penne pasta dinner into the trash and poured herself a small glass of wine. There'd be no heavy drinking until the summit was finished. Then she collapsed onto the leather sofa in her tastefully decorated living room and barely had time to admire the dark cherry and burl wood décor before her phone rang.

"Boss?"

Melissa sat up straight at the urgency in Jigger's voice.

"What's wrong?"

"I really shouldn't be calling you about this, but you've always been very cool to me. I like working with you," Jigger said.

"What's wrong?" Melissa repeated.

The analyst blew out a long breath before continuing.

"First, that Texas energy broker who received McKeon's email? He's dead. The team found him in his indoor lap pool."

"Accident?"

"Doesn't look like it. The back of his skull's caved in."

"Damn."

"But that's not the bad news."

"Spit it out, Jigger."

The analyst blew out a noisy breath.

"All right. Here's the deal. I finally identified the second recipient of the email Kenner forwarded."

"That's great!"

"It's not so great."

"What do you mean?"

"That email ping-ponged through servers around the world, but it ended up . . ."

Melissa couldn't stand Jigger's hesitance any longer. She didn't have time for this.

"Where, Jigger? Who received that email?"

"You."

Melissa laughed.

"Very funny."

"I'm not kidding, boss. I traced the email to a g-mail account in your name. It arrived one week ago."

"That's crazy. I don't have a g-mail account."

"I don't know what to tell you, boss, but I wasn't the only one snooping around."

A cold tendril of fear wriggled inside Melissa. The glass of wine and briefing books lay forgotten on the coffee table.

"What do you mean?"

"I set off all kinds of alarms. Some suit called me before my fingers even left the keyboard. I'm on my way to his office right now."

Melissa stood up and began pacing.

"I'm calling you on a cell phone I keep under my sister's name. I didn't want to use my company phone or the personal one they know I have." Several seconds of ragged breathing came over the line, before Jigger continued. "And there's more."

"More?"

"Before I was frozen out, I found another message in your g-mail account."

"What was it?"

"Confirmation of a deposit in some offshore bank account. Five million dollars. Boss, you're rich."

"That's not funny," Melissa replied, kneading her suddenly throbbing shoulder.

"No, it's not. And that's not the worst." When Jigger's voice returned, it was muffled as if he had cupped his hand over his mouth. "They've issued an order for your immediate arrest."

"What?"

Shocked, Melissa sat down on the couch, then immediately stood back up and resumed pacing. Icy prickles danced up and down her body as she noticed she was shivering.

"This is crazy," Melissa said. "I never created that g-mail account. I don't know what that five million dollars is. Someone's setting me up."

"Looks that way, boss. Uh-oh, some suit's coming my way. I gotta go."

"Wait, keep this phone with you," Melissa said.

"Okay, but I don't think they're going to like us talking."

"Just do it until I get this straightened out," Melissa said. "Please."

"You got it. One more thing."

Melissa had almost reached her door when she stopped.

"What?"

"They also issued an arrest order for Longfellow for sharing state secrets with members of foreign intelligence services."

Melissa shut her eyes. *Madness.* The NSA had known of Longfellow's cooperation with Fyodorov and al-Dossary for years. *Why move now?*

"Thanks, Jigger. I owe you one."

"Look forward to collecting, boss. Boy does this suit look pissed."

Melissa terminated the call and stood in front of her door, trying to collect her thoughts. She needed to get to Billings and explain that she knew nothing about any of this. They could trace who opened the g-mail account, follow the funds back to their source, do *something*. Her aching shoulder pulsed along with her racing heart and she balled her hands to stop them from shaking. She'd faced danger, nearly been killed more than once, but she'd never had her integrity attacked. *An arrest order? I've got to find Billings now.*

After memorizing the phone number Jigger had used, she yanked open her door then froze in mid-step, finding Director Billings glaring at her, blocking the doorway. Behind him stood two secret service agents, weapons drawn.

"You're not going anywhere, Melissa," Billings said.

Fifteen

—∽∾∽—

Melissa backed away in shock as the two secret service agents followed Billings into her suite.

"Stan, there's been a mistake," she stammered. "I just learned that someone opened a g-mail account in my name and deposited five million dollars in some account I've never heard of. Someone's setting me up. We need to track down who . . ."

"Stop it," Billings interrupted, as he held up a hand. "Stop talking."

Melissa gritted her teeth, waiting, as Billings composed himself. His normally gray pallor had flushed scarlet and his eyes snapped dangerously. Billings ran a hand over his forehead, smoothed down his tie, buttoned his suit jacket, then, finally squared his shoulders and looked her in the eye; all the while she wanted to scream.

"I don't know what to say, Melissa."

"We need to track . . ." but she stopped as he raised his hand again.

"We have tracked them. The g-mail account was opened through your computer at work, using your secure log-in. The account in the Caymans was opened the same way. We have your log-in times for that day, which put you at your desk at the times the two accounts were opened. We even have key-stroke monitoring, as you know."

"Why would I do this, Stan? It makes no sense."

The Director sidled closer but Melissa held her ground.

"Who knows? Jealousy? Longfellow used to be your mentor until he turned his sights to McKeon. Or maybe you just got greedy. Either way, I don't give a damn and I don't have time to deal with you right now."

Billings snapped his fingers and the two secret service agents closed in. For one crazy moment, Melissa thought about trying to escape, but she'd be dead before she cleared the couch.

"At least lift the arrest order for Longfellow," she tried. "He's our best chance to rescue Michael and the others."

"Rescuing Michael is no longer my priority," Billings retorted. "Stopping him is."

Melissa hadn't thought she could sink any lower, but she was wrong. As the agents placed her in handcuffs, she gaped at Billings.

"You can't," she whispered.

"You've left me no choice," Billings snapped. "If McKeon's microbe is deployed, the Middle East and Northern Africa will burn and the world will blame us. McKeon, his family, Donatelli—their lives mean nothing in that calculus. Take her away."

The next hour passed in a semi-conscious blur for Melissa as she was frog-marched from her suite into the elevator and down to a windowless room in the basement in which the two agents locked her. From the smell of gasoline and sounds of traffic, she was vaguely aware that she must be in the hotel's underground parking lot. As the shock receded, she gradually took stock of her surroundings. They had taken her phone. She was alone in a room not much bigger than a utility closet, bare except for a single chair. She slumped, completely defeated.

By the time the doorknob turned, a blazing fury had replaced the numbing shock. She again thought of trying to escape. Her feet were free, but her hands were still handcuffed, and the agents at the door would be armed and ready.

It's hopeless.

The identity of the agent entering the room surprised her. It was Barry Nelson, the agent who had wanted to talk to her aboard Air Force One, her protégé before she left for the NSA. Melissa's face burned with embarrassment.

"So, there was something you wanted to tell me?" Melissa tried gamely.

Nelson shifted uncomfortably.

"Spit it out, Nelson," Melissa said.

The agent smiled a half-smile.

"It doesn't really matter now, but I wanted to tell you that I just got promoted."

"Congratulations," Melissa said, a little too acidly. She blew out a breath. "I mean it, congratulations Barry. You deserve it."

"I owe it all to you."

Tears brimmed in Melissa's eyes as her anger and embarrassment overwhelmed her.

"That's not true."

"It is. You taught me everything I know. And you fought for me when they wanted to kick me out because of my sister."

"Just because your sister lit a few fires to protest the Iraq War didn't mean you wouldn't be a good agent."

Nelson shuffled from foot to foot in the ensuing silence.

"I didn't do what they're accusing me of," Melissa said. "I'm being set up. It's important to me that you believe that, even if they don't."

Nelson nodded sadly before motioning toward the door.

"I'm sorry, Melissa, but I have to move you now."

Nelson backed away from the door as Melissa stepped out of the room. She *was* in the hotel's underground parking lot.

"Barry," Melissa said as she peered around in the dim light. "Where are the other two agents?"

At that moment she heard a click and her arms were free.

"What are you doing?" Melissa asked, wide-eyed, rubbing her wrists.

"There's a loose piece of concrete curbing by your foot," Nelson said, looking around the garage. "Hit me with it before the other agents come."

"I can't do that," Melissa said. "I won't."

"Quickly! It's the only way you can prove your innocence. I told the other agents they were needed upstairs. They've probably already realized that's wrong. You don't have any time."

Melissa reluctantly picked up the concrete chunk. It was heavy with a serrated edge where it had broken free. She rotated the blunt end outward to avoid slicing the agent's face open.

"Make it look real," Nelson urged as he closed his eyes and steeled himself for the blow.

"I'm sorry, Barry," Melissa said as she swung. She tried to hold back, but the concrete still smacked into the agent's temple with a sickening, wet thud. Melissa instinctively dropped the block and caught Nelson as he collapsed.

"I'm sorry," she whispered again as she lowered him onto the asphalt. She checked his pulse, relieved that he was still breathing, but the right side of his face was already turning a dark purple and a thin stream of blood trickled down his cheek. Just as she turned toward the exit, a shout rang out.

"Hey! Stop!"

Two agents had just stepped off the elevator. Melissa turned and raced up the ramp toward the exit as they opened fire.

Sixteen

———⚬⚬⚬———

As bullets chewed the asphalt at her feet, pinging off nearby cars, Melissa burst onto *Ylitsa Tverskaya*. To her left, a series of black SUV's was approaching. *The president's motorcade!* The whine of a bullet passing her ear sent her racing past the motorcade. Reaching *Ylitsa Moxobaya*, she quickly oriented herself then sprinted down the street, against the go-home traffic, toward *Alexandrovsky Sad*, or Alexander Garden.

Ducking and weaving around the oncoming cars amid screeching brakes and blaring horns, she had almost reached the other side when a tan Nissan jackknifed toward her, tires squealing. Melissa gasped and dove for the curb, landing roughly on her shoulder as the Nissan's driver, now blocking two lanes, screamed angrily at her. Picking herself up, she spotted the two agents in the street. One, almost at the Nissan, stopped to aim. Bullets pinged off the cast iron gates as she raced past a group of college students diving for cover.

She had to find a place to hide. The Tomb of the Unknown Soldier was to her left, but, if the black-booted guards didn't stop her, the secret service agents would quickly corner her inside. She sprinted east toward the Kremlin's walls, hoping to disappear among the hot dog stands and throngs of tourists.

They won't shoot near civilians.

Just then, a volley of gunfire dug up the manicured tulip beds to her right. Melissa gasped for breath as she slammed through a crowd of camera-toting tourists. Arms and legs pumping, she had almost reached the Kremlin when four Moscow police officers appeared, drawn by the sound of gunfire.

"Help me! Those men!" Melissa panted to the officers in Russian. "*Mafiya! Narkartikov deelera!*"

The secret service agents had just raced into view around a grove of lindens. Melissa dove in back of a peanut cart as the lead agent raised his gun.

"*Brosseye oryzhyc!*" *Drop your weapon,* one of the officers yelled just as the agent opened fire. Muscovites and tourists scattered, screaming, as the bullets dug into the squat, ugly Kutafya Tower in back of Melissa.

The volley stopped as abruptly as it had stated. Peeking over the peanut cart, Melissa spotted the four Moscow police officers, weapons drawn, advancing on the two red-faced agents. Before the agents could identify themselves, Melissa slipped through the throng of crouching onlookers, ducked in back of a dense patch of evergreen shrubs, then raced for the *Alexandrovsky Sad* metro station.

She reached the tunnel leading to the subterranean station just as another police officer stepped into the sunlight, walkie talkie pressed to his ear.

". . . American woman, well-dressed, running south in the park," the static-filled receiver barked, ". . . American Secret Service looking for her."

Melissa immediately stuck her head and torso into a nearby garbage can and wailed: "*Moya kolso! Moya kolso!*" *My ring! My ring!*

After the officer passed, she stood up, wiping the ketchup and god-knows-what else on her pants with a look of disgust before hurrying down the tunnel. She had the beginning of a plan and knew where to go, if only it was still there. When she reached the station, instead of waiting for the metro, she took the escalators down to the ornate central hall of the *Arbatskaya* station. There she stopped at a souvenir stall under one of the station's rounded arches and purchased a sweatshirt and baseball hat, into which she stuffed her riotous hair. With that minimal change of appearance, she strolled down another tunnel, as calmly as possible, to a set of stairs taking her to the *Biblioteka Imeni Lenina* station. From another stall, she bought a garish pair of yellow sweatpants with "Moskva" across the rear and pulled them on in a nearby bathroom, stuffing her pants into the trash. With one last look around the station, she crossed the platform and stepped onto the train. The familiar warning of *dveri zakrivayite* sounded. An instant later, the doors closed, and she was off.

Two stops north, she exited the train. The Lubyanka metro station was not as elaborate as many of the other stations, with its modernist feel, squared-off entrance and plaster ceiling. None of this interested Melissa as she circled the station three times, checking for surveillance, before finally stepping into a small alcove. Crumpled newspapers and dirty wrappers had collected against the rusted door recessed into the wall. After another furtive look over her shoulder, Melissa keyed a combination into the touchpad next to the door and yanked on the handle, mouthing a silent prayer of relief as the door screeched open on rusty hinges.

"Thank God the combination still worked," she murmured to herself.

Cautiously, she slipped through the door into the darkness within, pulling the door shut behind her. From memory, she reached out to the right and found the light switch. The dim light revealed a dusty room, no larger than a storage closet, which is what she had always suspected this place was when Dmitry and Fuoad had brought her here, near-death, before spiriting her to safety. This was one of Dmitry's bolt-holes, and he had given her the access code in case she ever needed it again.

You saved me again, Melissa thought as she padded around the room, inspecting the seedy mattress on rusty hinges in the center of the room. She shivered, hoping that wasn't the same mattress she'd bled on as Longfellow's two friends had made their hasty calculations to save her life. She passed another door that she vaguely recalled led to a series of tunnels through which Dmitry and Fouad had carried her, and opened the cupboard along the far wall, running a finger along dusty packages of crackers and sardines. Outside, another train came and went with a roar muted by the thick stone walls.

She was safe for the moment, but she needed to think. As she traced a lazy "*m*" in the dust on top of the tin of sardines, her hand started to shake as the hopelessness of her situation crashed over her. Accused of treason, isolated from anyone who might help her, with no phone and no contacts, she was on her own. She shook herself violently and squared her shoulders. No, she thought, there was one person left, if it wasn't already too late.

I've got to warn Longfellow then we can find McKeon together and clear both our names.

The slightest waft of air brushed against the back of her neck, sending a prickle of fear up and down her spine. Out of the corner of her eye, she noticed that the door to the tunnels was now open. She smelled sweat. Male sweat.

Then something heavy crashed into the back of her head, and she collapsed to the floor, unconscious.

Seventeen

NSA Director Billings threw the file on the desk and stared balefully at the Secret Service special agent standing in front of him.

"How the hell does someone like Melissa Stark, unarmed and in custody, overpower a trained Secret Service agent and escape two more agents on foot? Tell me, Frank, how the hell does that happen? Jesus Christ, you guys are supposed to protect the fucking President and you can't even hold onto Stark. Should I be worried about the President's safety?"

The special agent bristled, but remained silent.

"What the hell are you going to do about it, Frank?"

"Since I'm not aware that the Deputy Director poses any threat to the President, I would respectfully suggest, sir, that she is your problem, not mine, especially since you find my men to be so incompetent."

"And I'd respectfully suggest that you go fuck yourself."

Billings continued to fume as the agent turned and marched stiffly out of the suite.

"Un-fucking-believable," Billings spat as he turned his attention to the television on the wall. Syrian soldiers were bombing another village again, turning rubble into rubble. The chirp of his cell phone brought him back.

"Viktor, thanks for getting back to me so quickly. Listen, I have a situation. My Deputy Director, Melissa Stark, has gone rogue. We had her in custody, but she escaped. I want this quiet so I don't want to use any of my official operatives or notify the Russians. That's why I have you. Find her and bring her back immediately."

"What are my parameters?" said a rough voice.

Billings closed his eyes for a moment.

"I'm not authorizing lethal action, not yet. Anything short of that, but find her, and find her now."

—◆◆◆—

Even before her eyes opened, or the muted roar of the passing metro trains returned, the blazing headache told Melissa that she was still alive. She gingerly lifted a hand to her skull, expecting to find it cleaved in two, but instead found a bag of ice. She hesitated. The smell of male sweat was gone, but someone was in the room with her. She could hear him breathing.

Slowly, she opened her eyes. A soft moan escaped her lips as the room spun wildly.

"Easy," said a man's voice as she clutched her stomach, trying not to vomit. "You took a nasty blow to the head. Just stay still."

The voice sounded familiar, but, in her fogged state, she couldn't place it. She opened her eyes again and, this time, the room didn't move. Gradually, her senses returned enough to piece together the face of the man staring intently at her. Gray, slightly shaggy hair covered the tips of the ears. Wrinkled, leathered skin had just started to sag off a strong jaw. With a gasp, she struggled to sit up.

"Longfellow! How did you find me?"

The spy smiled worriedly.

"I didn't. I was surprised to find you here."

"Did you hit me?" she asked, pressing the ice pack more firmly against her still-throbbing skull.

Longfellow shook his head.

"No, that wasn't me. I arrived afterwards. When you break into a den of spies, you have to be careful."

"Then who hit me?"

Longfellow turned toward the open door to the tunnels. "Him."

A man stepped through the doorway just as Melissa laboriously turned her head. A giant stomach draped off what had once, clearly, been a thin man. Piercing blue eyes peered from under black eyebrows as thick and bushy as the hair covering the rest of his face.

"I'm sorry for hitting you. I didn't recognize you in that horrendous outfit."

It was the eyes that Melissa first recognized. Suddenly, she was back in Moscow's Novodevichy Cemetery, just as her contact opened fire at her.

"The Sword!" she cried, scrambling upright, headache forgotten as the bandages fell to the floor. She grabbed for Longfellow. "He tried to kill me. He's an assassin. Shoot him!"

Melissa cast about, frantically, for a weapon as the assassin stepped forward. She had no gun. There was no loose pipe, no piece of stone, nothing! Why wasn't Longfellow reacting?

"Melissa," Longfellow said, trying to stop her retreat around the room. "He used to be *Mech*, but he's no longer an assassin for the FSB. He quit ten years ago."

"He tried to kill me!"

"If I had tried to kill you, you'd be dead," the assassin responded.

Melissa finally stopped pacing and leaned against the cupboard, breathing heavily. She pressed a shaking hand against her forehead. The savage headache had returned.

"Please sit down and we'll explain everything," Longfellow said.

Melissa contemplated standing, but the room had begun to spin again, so she let Longfellow guide her back to the cot, where she perched warily next to him while the assassin settled uncomfortably into the chair facing them.

"Melissa," Longfellow began, "meet Grisha Medvedev, a friend of mine and someone who is going to help us rescue Michael and his family and Julia."

Eighteen

"This monster is your friend?"

Longfellow laid a comforting hand on her arm.

"Let me explain. Ten years ago, Medvedev was the FSB's top assassin, code-named *Mech*, or the Sword, as you know, from the old symbol for the KGB: the sword and the shield."

"I never liked the name, myself," Medvedev replied. "Too grandiose. Assassins need to work in the shadows."

"This'll go a lot quicker without the interruptions," Longfellow chided Medvedev, who ducked his head apologetically. "Grisha had had enough and wanted out."

"My wife hated what I did," Medvedev interrupted again. "I never told her, of course, but she knew. She always said she could smell other people's blood on me. When I returned home from my last assignment, she had burned all my clothes. . . ." He paused and took a deep breath, the piercing blue eyes turned inward. "I found her in our bedroom. She had used one of my guns. She left a note, saying that I needed to throw myself in the fire and burn for my sins."

The large man stared at his hands, fragile and long-fingered, like a pianist's. Melissa remained next to Longfellow, eyes fixed on the assassin, as Longfellow picked up the story. Outside, another train rumbled past.

"No one quits the FSB," Longfellow said, then pointed a finger at Melissa. "That's when you entered the picture. I had left you in Moscow . . ."

"To run to Michael," Melissa said.

Longfellow acknowledged the rebuke with a shrug before continuing. "I was confident you could handle a solo mission, but I asked Dmitry and Fouad to watch your back."

"You did?" Melissa asked in surprise.

Longfellow shot her a quizzical look.

"Do you mean you never wondered why they were there to save you?" When Melissa didn't respond, he continued. "While I was gone, Grisha received the order from his superiors to kill you." Melissa glared at the assassin, who continued examining his hands. "He tried to warn me."

"I knew you were his protégé," Medvedev said, raising his hands in defense. "After my wife, I just couldn't."

"But if he didn't, someone else would," Longfellow said. "When he couldn't reach me, he contacted Dmitry and Fouad. Together, they decided that Grisha would shoot you then they would get you safely out of Russia. Grisha would disappear before you resurfaced."

"Hold on," Melissa said to Longfellow. "They agreed that he would shoot me?"

"Shoot, not kill," Medvedev replied, as if that explained everything. Melissa stared aghast.

"So Grisha disappeared for several years, changed his appearance, even got married," Longfellow said.

"To an American in London," the Russian added with a grin. "Very smart and beautiful. She does the Pilates. You'd like her."

Melissa rolled her eyes. "So, he works with you?" she asked Longfellow.

"From time to time. He saved my butt the other day in London when that mission you all sent me on turned into an ambush."

"What ambush?"

Medvedev tapped his watch.

"We have to move. My friend parked our car a few minutes ago. I don't want to leave it unattended."

"Go where?" Melissa asked as Longfellow pulled her upright.

"To rescue Milla and Katya. We received a tip that they might be here in Moscow. Grisha has arranged some supplies."

Melissa stopped in the middle of the room.

"I don't trust him," she said, pointing at Medvedev.

"I do," Longfellow replied. "He's earned it."

When she didn't move, Longfellow sighed.

"We don't have time. They may move Milla and Katya at any moment. Look, when we get to the car, I'll give you a gun. If Grisha does anything suspicious, shoot him."

Longfellow grinned.

Medvedev gestured toward the tunnels.

"I believe you've been this way before."

"Don't think I won't do it," Melissa snapped as she stepped past the Russian.

"Remember: shoot, not kill," he retorted.

Nineteen

Billings settled into a scallop-backed chair across the table from Melissa Stark's assistant in the glass-domed O2 lounge atop the Ritz Carlton and did his best to look sympathetic. Outside, the lights of Moscow winked brightly.

"I know you're upset, Dani, but Melissa's in trouble and I need your help."

The stricken woman fidgeted on her seat, tugging at her sleeve and smoothing her skirt over and over.

"People are saying that she's some kind of traitor," the assistant replied, barely above a whisper. "I just don't believe it. She would never do anything like that."

Billings stifled his irritation. He hated tearful, whispery voices and maudlin sentiment almost as much as he hated anyone whom he perceived as a threat to his country.

"I'm hoping that this is all a mistake, but I have to tell you that it doesn't look good. I need to find her before this situation gets any worse. Can you think of any place she might have gone? A friend? A favorite hotel? Anything?"

Billings closed his eyes and counted to ten as Dani dabbed at her eyes with a napkin.

"No sir."

Billings reached for his glass of Bordeaux, terminating the interview, but the assistant was not quite finished.

"I did see something before we left Washington, though, sir."

The glass paused at Billings' lips before he returned it to the table.

"What did you see?" he asked, his voice tight with impatience.

"About a week ago, I saw a man sitting at Melissa's desk. I asked him what he was doing and he just brushed past me without saying anything. He was pretty rude."

"Did you recognize him?"

"No. I've never seen him before."

"Could you identify him if you had to?"

"Probably. I have a good memory for faces."

Billings waited another beat before responding.

"Anything else?"

Stark's assistant shrunk at the clipped tone and scurried away. Billings took a slow sip of his wine and watched her disappear, then made a call.

"Have our substation listen for any mention of Melissa Stark or Michael McKeon in any communications they intercept. And I want a tap on Stark's assistant's phone and computer. If Stark tries to contact her, I want to know."

Twenty

---∽∾∿---

Moscow's Industrial District

"This is a really bad idea," Medvedev warned for the seventh time since the three operatives had left *Lubyanka* station through the warren of tunnels leading to a store room full of dusty icons in the *Zaikonospassky Monastery* in the *Kitay-Gorod* district.

"It's not like we can call in any help from the NSA or anyone else," Longfellow replied as the three huddled behind a rotting wood fence. During the drive across Moscow in the olive Volvo that Medvedev's friend had left for them, Melissa had brought Longfellow up to date on the arrest orders for both of them and her recent escape from the secret service.

Melissa squinted at the shuttered glass factory barely visible through the sooty, night air and checked the illuminated face on her watch. It was nearly ten o'clock, just a few hours since Billings had shown up at her door with the Secret Service. She closed her eyes as a wave of nausea rolled over. *Madness.*

She blinked against the swirling grit as a light breeze sent crumpled newspapers scurrying past her feet, then focused on the spot between Medvedev's shoulder blades and briefly considered using the Makarov now nestled in the small of her back. But there would be plenty of time to shoot him later.

She cast a warm glance at Longfellow. She felt a little less isolated and desperate having her old partner by her side. She was also thankful for the black fleece, jeans and hiking boots she had purchased with Medvedev's rubles at a sporting goods store on the way. She couldn't very well sneak up on anyone in the day-glow sweats she had purchased in the metro station.

"I don't trust Akhmetalin," Medvedev hissed.

Melissa started at the name.

"What's he have to do with this?" she asked.

"He's the one who told me that The Global Group is keeping Milla and Katya in that factory," Longfellow replied.

"The FSB colonel? You can't trust him. I was investigating him ten years ago for running rogue operations. He's as slippery and manipulative as they come."

"He was right about the arrest order against me."

"That doesn't mean anything," Melissa said. "This could be a trap."

"Especially if he had known you would come," Medvedev told Melissa.

"What do you mean?" she asked.

"He used to be my boss," Medvedev replied. "You must've found some good intel on him ten years ago, because he's the one who ordered you killed."

"I don't trust him either," Longfellow said as Melissa opened her mouth in shock, "but what other options do we have? The only way to stop The Global Group and save the Middle East Marshall Plan is to rescue Michael and his family and Julia. If there are Global Group operatives in there, they may be able to lead us to Michael and Julia. You said that Jigger had traced that plane to Moscow. At the very least, if we rescue Milla and Katya, then The Global Group loses its leverage over Michael." He turned and looked Melissa in the eyes. "It's also the only way you and I can clear our names and avoid being shot by some NSA or Secret Service agent."

Longfellow was right, and the others silently began pulling their gear from the bags Medvedev's friend had left in the Volvo's trunk. Sub-vocal microphones, shock grenades, Kevlar vests, nightvision goggles, extra ammunition, and a particularly lethal-looking knife for Medvedev.

"You know, if Akhmetalin knows you're here, you're dead, too," Melissa told Medvedev, who grinned.

"Good thing he hasn't been able to find me," Medvedev said as he distributed the ammunition in various pockets. "Still, I'll be much happier when I'm back in London."

"Let's go," Longfellow ordered.

Like wraiths, the three spies slipped through the shadows along the fence toward the factory, a two-story, crumbling concrete relic from the Soviet Union. Greasy windows, many broken, stared blankly into the night. Medvedev pointed to a nest of pigeons in one broken window.

"Doesn't look like anyone's home," he subvocalized through the microphone attached to his throat.

Longfellow nodded.

"I'll check the landing bay in the rear. You two take the front."

Melissa opened her mouth to protest but Longfellow had already melted into the dark. She slipped the Makarov from her belt and grimly chambered a round before following the Russian across the garbage-strewn sidewalk with a dark sense of foreboding.

As they crept toward the decaying factory, Melissa kept a fearful eye on the dark windows, too encrusted with filth and grime to see through, and waited for a shot to ring out. The thought occurred to her that someone like Akhmetalin undoubtedly had a long list of people he wanted dead, but she was certain that she and Medvedev were both on that list.

So why are we going exactly where he told us to go?

A small parking lot stretched between them and the factory, once big enough to hold ten cars, but now rutted with frost heaves and potholes. The two agents picked their way carefully over the undulating terrain. Melissa's pulse quickened as a siren sounded in the distance, but the night was otherwise strangely silent.

As they reached the front door, Medvedev's voice whispered over her earpiece.

"Old door, but new lock. Entrance is clear of dirt and debris. Someone's been in and out recently. Longfellow, where are you?"

After several moments of silence, Medvedev tried again.

"Longfellow?"

Nothing.

"Longfellow, report in," Melissa demanded.

Medvedev shook his head and pulled a pair of bolt cutters from his backpack. Melissa grabbed his arm.

"What are you doing? We should find Longfellow."

"There may be a reason he's not responding," Medvedev said.

"Right, like he's hurt or captured."

"Or he needs to maintain silence," the Russian responded. "Either way, our job is to go in the front. We find what we find and respond."

As Medvedev snipped the lock, Melissa surveyed their surroundings once again. *If The Global Group is holding Milla and Katya here, where are the guards? Wouldn't they post someone outside?* The fact that she couldn't spot anyone only increased her anxiety. They also had no idea how many guards might be inside, where Milla and Katya might be in the building, or what the guards might do when attacked. Melissa shook her head. She never would have approved an operation like this with no prior reconnaissance and based on such incomplete intel. *And why the hell isn't Longfellow responding?*

At that moment, headlights appeared, coming toward then on the otherwise deserted street.

"Quick!" Melissa said, giving Medvedev a light shove. "Inside now!"

The two agents snapped on their goggles and slipped inside, pulling the door shut behind them. The factory's interior, suffused in an eerie green light from the nightvision goggles, yawned menacingly before them.

Melissa held her breath as she pivoted around the Russian, peering into the shadows that lapped up the walls and across the concrete floor. The building was small by Russian standards. Melissa estimated the first floor at approximately two thousand square feet; a forty by fifty rectangle, with a conveyor belt in the middle, leading to a mammoth glass furnace. On the right wall, a set of metal stairs led to the second floor. Inside the thick walls, she couldn't hear if the car outside had continued on, or stopped.

She nearly jumped when Medvedev touched her arm and pointed at the floor. A series of footprints had disturbed the dust in, more or less, a straight line toward the steps. Melissa nodded and, together, they stepped away from the door toward the stairs.

If Melissa hadn't been listening so intently for the car outside, she might have missed the soft *click* that sounded just after they stepped. She peered around, looking for the cause of the noise, and what she spotted made her heart stop. On either side, two small lights, two to three inches off the floor, glowed red.

"Medvedev!" she shouted, forgetting the subvocal microphones in her panic. "Run!"

The Russian yanked the earpiece from his ear and spun angrily toward Melissa, then stopped, wide-eyed, as he spotted the motion detectors.

A blinding white light filled the factory. She felt, rather than heard, the blast as a wall of air slammed into her, blowing her off her feet and sending her cartwheeling toward the door. A terrible shriek ripped through her, then the world fell on top of her, and she knew nothing more.

———⟡⟡⟡———

An hour later, Billings's phone rang as he finished telling the President that a U.S. drone strike had missed a top-level al-Quaeda operative in Yemen, destroying several homes and killing an undetermined number of civilians.

"Excuse me, sir," Billings said, as he ducked into the hall.

"An abandoned glass factory on the city's northern side just exploded," said Billings' operative, Viktor.

"And?"

"And an eyewitness reported seeing a man drag two bodies from the rubble: a man and a woman. Both appeared to be dead."

"And?" Billings demanded, even more forcefully.

"The eyewitness snapped a picture, which I've just emailed to you."

With a flash of irritation, Billings checked his phone. The photo was grainy and dark, obviously snapped by some cell phone of inferior quality. A flash of light illuminated the left half of the picture. A man was hunched over an unconscious woman, whose pale face was turned toward the camera. Billings sucked in his breath.

It was Stark.

He also recognized the man. What the hell was Longfellow doing in Moscow?

"Check all the hospitals and the morgues. Work the police. Find out what they know, but don't tell them anything. And find that man who's with her!"

Billings terminated the call and stared at the blank wall, calculating his next move.

Twenty-one

—◦◦◦◦—

Dubrovitsy, Russia

She had to be dead.

She had no fingers, no toes, no body, no pain, no sadness or anger or fear. She was conscious, but detached, floating even.

It was the only explanation. She had to be dead.

Then, the sluice gates opened, and the pain and horror of the explosion flooded through her, like sewage after a storm.

With a sharp cry, she opened her eyes to find Longfellow, for the second time in less than twenty-four hours, staring at her in concern. He moved his mouth to speak, but the *wuh-wuh* of his underwater words was lost on her. She struggled to sit up, but he pressed her back.

Then she passed out again.

—◦◦◦◦—

FSB Headquarters, Lubyanka Square, Moscow

The operative known as "Viktor" to NSA Director Billings rapped on the door to the office of FSB First Deputy Aleksandr Yakovlev.

"*Prihodeetee,*" the First Deputy responded. *Come in.*

"Good morning, Mr. First Deputy," the agent said. "I wish to report that I've been contacted again by NSA Director Billings."

"Very good," Yakovlev replied, stroking the red goatee that made the paunchy man look like a fat Lenin. "And he does not know that you are an FSB agent?"

"He still thinks I'm one of his off-the-book assets."

"What does he want?"

"His deputy director has gone rogue and missing. He asked me to find her."

"What did she do?"

"I don't know, but in looking for the deputy director, I have come across something that will be of great interest to you."

With that, the agent reached behind him and slammed the door shut.

—⦵⦵⦵—

Dubrovitsy

What seemed an eternity later, Melissa Stark awoke again, this time to a muted buzzing in her ears and a coppery taste in her mouth.

"How are you feeling?" Longfellow asked from the chair by her side.

"Like I've just been blown up," she murmured. "Where am I?"

Longfellow helped her sit up, propped a couple pillows against her back and handed her a glass of cold water, which she gratefully pressed against both temples before sipping cautiously. After most of the coppery tang had been washed from her mouth, she tried again.

"Where am I?"

"Dubrovitsy. It's a small town about fifteen miles outside Moscow. We're in a home owned by Grisha's friend, the one who provided us the car and weapons."

"What happened?"

"I'm not sure. The factory's rear door was welded shut. My microphone and earpiece weren't working so I didn't know what was happening with you and Grisha. I had just reached the front when an enormous explosion blew out all the windows. There was a giant hole where the front door had been. Most of the second floor had collapsed, but I found you and Grisha under part of the furnace. You were lucky. That furnace kept you from being crushed."

"Where's Medvedev?"

Longfellow grimaced.

"He wasn't so lucky."

Melissa gasped.

"He's dead?"

As much as she had fantasized about shooting him, she felt an inexplicable sadness at his death.

"No, he's not dead, but he's in rough shape. I found him on top of you. It looked like he had been trying to cover you when that part of the furnace landed on you both. He's in one piece, barely. Grisha's friend's daughter is a trauma nurse in Moscow. She's looking after him in the next room. He's been mostly unconscious since I pulled him out last night."

Melissa closed her eyes.

"We tripped a motion detector. The factory was a trap."

Longfellow nodded.

"We've been monitoring police radios. The entire first floor was lined with explosives, but only those in the middle detonated. Lucky."

"So Akhmetalin was trying to kill you, and we're no closer to stopping The Global Group," she said wearily.

Melissa could sense Longfellow's hesitation as he rocked in his chair.

"What else?" she asked.

"The police reported finding the incinerated remains of two bodies in the factory," he said quietly.

A cold dread seized her.

"Not . . ."

"No identification was possible, but the skeletons were of a woman and a young girl," Longfellow replied.

A tear slipped down Melissa's cheek. She'd never met Milla and Katya, but the idea of Michael losing another family knifed through her.

"Were they dead before the explosion?" she asked, a slight tremble in her voice.

"The police can't tell," Longfellow said, "but I don't think it's them. It wouldn't make sense to kill them until Michael has done what they want him to do."

"Maybe he's finished preparing the microbes," Melissa said.

Longfellow shook his head.

"Doubtful. Even if everything went perfectly, he'd still need forty-eight hours for a complete culture and growth cycle on the scale they'd need to launch a significant attack either here or in Saudi Arabia. And they'd want to keep Michael around in case anything went wrong and they needed him to make more. They'd have to keep Milla and Katya alive until they knew their attack had worked, and if it was working, we'd have heard about it."

"They could just tell Michael that Milla and Katya were still alive," Melissa said.

Longfellow shook his head again, a slight smile tugging at the corners of his mouth.

"You don't know Michael like I do. He's the most stubborn bastard I've ever met. He wouldn't do a damn thing without proof they were still alive. No," Longfellow said, bringing the argument to a conclusion, "we have to assume they're still alive."

"Okay," Melissa said, still unsure, "but that doesn't help us find them."

"I've been thinking about that," Longfellow said. "I have a new burn phone. Do you still remember the number for the cell phone Jigger used to warn you?"

Melissa nodded.

"But it's risky to call. What if the NSA is monitoring it?"

Longfellow laughed for the first time in days.

"Jigger's pretty paranoid. If anyone can hide a phone from the NSA, he can, besides, we need information and he's our best chance to get it."

Longfellow dialed as she rattled off the number, pleased that being knocked unconscious twice hadn't rattled her memory.

"Macy's Pizzeria," a man's voice responded.

"I'd like a large pepperoni and sausage and any information you can give me about The Global Group, Jigger," Longfellow chuckled.

"Longfellow! How'd you get this number?"

"Melissa's with me."

"You're kidding. She got away?"

"She's pretty resourceful."

"No shit. Did she tell you there's an arrest order out for you, too?"

"I've been chased by worse. Listen, Jigger, we're trying to locate Michael and his family and Julia and we need some help."

"Those bastards locked me out and sent me home on leave. I can't access any of my computers from work."

It was Longfellow's turn to swear.

"But, my sister has an even better system," Jigger continued. "Real kick-ass. Better than the NSA's. Well, almost."

"If the NSA locked you out, they might be monitoring your sister's system, too," Longfellow said.

"No way. First, she's not really my sister. No one knows about her, but that's a story for another day. Second, this system's as secure as it gets. What do you need?"

"You tracked a plane from Boston to Moscow," Longfellow said.

"That's right."

"We need any video that might have captured who was on that plane and where they might have gone. Also, find out anything you can about an abandoned glass factory in Moscow." Longfellow gave him the address. "Then start digging into FSB Colonel Vadim Akhmetalin. Finally, can you send me a layout and description of the Saudi and Russian oil storage and distribution systems? They can't hit everywhere. I need to identify possible targets."

Jigger whistled.

"Tall order. When do you need it?"

"Five minutes ago."

"You got it," Jigger replied, laughing, as he hung up.

"So, do we go after Michael and Julia or Milla and Katya, as-suming that they're still alive?" Melissa asked, finishing the glass of water. "If we rescue Michael and Julia without having secured Milla and Katya, The Global Group will kill his family."

Longfellow shot Melissa a curious glance.

"What happened to 'mission first'?" he asked.

"This is about the mission," she insisted, a little too heatedly. "It's not personal."

Before Longfellow could respond, a burly man with thick, curly blond hair appeared in the doorway.

"Melissa, this is Grisha's friend," Longfellow said.

The man gave a curt nod.

"I have bad news," the blond man said. "I've been tipped off that the FSB will be here any moment. There's a BMW out back, gassed up." He handed Longfellow a black backpack. "Money, weapons, ammunition."

Longfellow had helped Melissa struggle to her feet, where she wobbled slightly.

"Passports?" Longfellow asked.

"Irish and Canadian, like you requested."

"What about Grisha?"

"My daughter and her boyfriend are moving him to a van right now. We'll take care of him, but, please, you must leave now."

"Thank you," Melissa said, extending a hand, then finding her-self enveloped in a furious embrace.

"Anything for friends of Grisha," the man said when he had finally released the shocked Stark. After exchanging another embrace with Longfellow, the man hurried them through the house to a back door that looked out on an alley. A black BMW waited outside the door, steam rising from its warm engine.

Melissa, still a little unsteady, zipped her fleece against the cold, clammy morning air and held onto Longfellow's arm down the stairs to the car.

"I hate leaving Grisha," Longfellow said, glancing back at the cottage in frustration.

"We don't have a choice," Melissa said as they got into the car. "We can't stop The Global Group if we're locked up in Lubyanka. Besides, this guy seems to know what he's doing. He'll get Grisha somewhere safe."

Just then, a black SUV screeched to a stop at the end of the alley, red light flashing on its dashboard.

"They're here!" Melissa shouted.

Longfellow slammed the BMW into reverse and peeled back down the alley, tires smoking, as the SUV gave chase. The SUV's grill had almost reached their front bumper when the alley emptied onto the main road into town. Longfellow spun the wheel and flung the car into drive just as submachine gunfire stitched across the BMW's trunk. Melissa dove for the backpack and pulled another Makarov out as the car leaped forward.

"They don't give much of a warning, do they?" she asked, checking the clip to make sure it was fully loaded.

"That *was* their warning," Longfellow replied, shifting gears and flooring the accelerator. In drive, the BMW's engine was powerful enough to maintain the small distance Longfellow had created, but not enough to lose the SUV.

As they roared east toward the small town center, another volley of submachine gunfire shattered the rear window. Wind howled in, whipping Melissa's auburn hair into a blazing fury.

"Look out!" Melissa shouted as two boys dove off their bicycles onto the sidewalk. "Don't hit anyone."

Longfellow gripped the wheel even tighter in response. Melissa glanced back at the SUV, but Longfellow was zigging and zagging so fast that a shot was impossible. Suddenly Longfellow hit the brakes, downshifted and veered to the left, slamming Melissa against her seat. A delivery truck had backed out, blocking the road.

"Oh my God!" Melissa cried as she spotted where Longfellow was heading, directly for the town's salmon-colored municipal building. The BMW banged and bounced across the dirt parking lot as men and women darted out of the way. The SUV remained hard on their heels as Longfellow sawed the steering wheel back and forth, trying to keep control of the bucking BMW.

Melissa, for an instant, thought he was going to drive right up the town hall's front steps, but, at the last second, Longfellow whipped the wheel to the right. Bullets chewed into the steps, spraying concrete shards over the cluster of workers racing into the building. Melissa sighted the Makarov, but couldn't squeeze off a shot at the SUV dancing in and out of the missing rear window.

"We need to find an open stretch of road," she started to say, but the words died in her throat as the BMW bounced off a grass embankment with a bone-jarring shudder. Longfellow snapped the wheel to the left and the BMW clawed across the lawn toward the adjacent Church of the Sign. Both spies ducked as another hail of bullets blew out the driver's side windows.

"Get us out of here!" Melissa shouted as she climbed into the glass-strewn back seat. The drive shaft screamed in protest as Long-fellow locked the BMW in a tight counter-clockwise spin around the cylindrical church, sending worshippers scurrying for safety. Me-lissa, slammed against the rear passenger door by the vicious centrif-ugal force, snapped off one shot through the clods of dirt flung into the air by the BMW's rear tires, exploding the SUV's side mirror, but doing nothing to slow it down.

As the BMW skidded out of its circuit, Longfellow whipped the wheel to center, sending them flying through the gates and across the dirt parking lot with the SUV right behind.

"Get ready to shoot the tires," Longfellow ordered.

Melissa wrapped one seat belt around her torso and braced a foot against the far wall, trying to hold the Makarov steady. With an angry squeal, the BMW's tires grabbed purchase on *Ylitsa Belyae-vskaya* and raced east out of town.

"Ready," Longfellow called. "Now!"

Melissa opened fire as they crossed the bridge out of town, exploding both of the SUV's front tires before she emptied her clip. The SUV, traveling too fast to recover from the blown tires, lurched to the left and crashed through the guard rail into the river below.

Longfellow and Melissa paused for an instant, hearts racing, as the SUV slipped below the surface, before speeding away.

Twenty-two

———✦———

Forty minutes later, Longfellow slowed, reversed the BMW, and backed into a copse of trees until they were fully hidden from the road. Then he turned the engine off and the two agents sat silently, catching their breath while the cooling engine ticked away the seconds.

"Nice shooting," Longfellow said.

"Where do we go now?" Melissa asked.

"Let's check in with Jigger and see what he's found," Longfellow said.

Melissa dialed and placed the phone on speaker.

"Hey guys!" Jigger's voice was uncomfortably loud in the quiet copse. Melissa instinctively glanced around, but they were alone. "I was about to call you."

"What'd you find, Jigger?" Melissa asked.

"I'm sending you detailed maps of the Saudi and Russian oil storage and transmission facilities. If you need something more on that, let me know."

"Thanks."

"I haven't had time yet to find much on Akhmetalin except that he's one scary dude. He was in charge of FSB assassins, you know, the ones who carry poison walking sticks and stuff like that."

"Or just shoot people," Longfellow replied drily.

"Right. He used to be some power broker in the Soviet government, but a couple years ago, reports stopped mentioning his name. It looks like he's on the outs."

"Interesting," Melissa said.

"But that's not all. I was able to hack into airport security video at Sheremetyevo Airport, where the plane from Boston landed, and guess who met the plane?"

"Akhmetalin?" Longfellow asked, surprised.

"Right. The cameras caught him leaving a private hangar with McKeon's wife and daughter and a bunch of muscle."

"Were Michael and Julia with them?" Longfellow asked.

"Nope. I don't think they were on that plane. I ran the video forward and they never got off."

"So we know that Milla and Katya were in Moscow at one point," Melissa said.

"And that Akhmetalin knows where they are," Longfellow added.

"Which means that Akhmetalin is involved in The Global Group," Melissa concluded.

Jigger tried to interrupt. "Guys?"

"Why would an FSB colonel be involved with a group that wants to destroy Russian oil?" Longfellow asked.

"Guys! I checked out that factory you asked about. Hey, did you know that place just blew up?"

"I was in it when it did," Melissa said.

Jigger whistled.

"Damn, boss, I don't want to know how many lives you have left. Anyway, property records in Russia are a nightmare so I can't tell who owns that building. I'm trying to see if Akhmetalin owns any property anywhere, but, like I said, I'm not optimistic. But I did find something."

"What?"

"After the explosion, the police pulled all the video from the area near the factory and dumped it on an unsecure server. One of the cameras at a used car dealer across the street captured the front door to the factory. At that distance, it's grainy during the day and pretty useless at night, which explains why I didn't see you two enter the factory, but the video did show a certain FSB colonel taking McKeon's wife and daughter into the factory."

Melissa felt sick.

"Did it show Milla and Katya leaving?"

"No, but they could've gone out another entrance or at night and the video wouldn't have caught them."

"That's not good news, Jigger."

"Sorry boss. I just report it, good or bad."

During Jigger's and Melissa's back and forth, Longfellow had fallen silent, puzzling over something.

"You're sure Michael and Julia weren't on that flight from Boston to Moscow," Longfellow asked the computer analyst.

"Unless they're still hiding on the plane."

"Then where did they go?"

"I'm glad you asked. When I realized that they weren't on that plane, I started over. I assumed that they'd want to make those microbes not too far from where they were going to use them. Is that right?"

"Yes," Longfellow said.

"I also figured they'd stay on private aircraft to minimize exposure. Using those parameters, I searched for flight plans leaving Boston, connecting through other cities, but ending up in or near Russia or Saudi Arabia."

"What'd you find?" Longfellow asked.

"Nothing."

"Damnit, Jigger, stop screwing around!" Longfellow exploded.

"Then I checked to make sure that all private craft filing flight plans out of Logan actually ended up where they said they were going, and I found something."

The agents waited impatiently for Jigger to continue.

"An Aerion, a brand new, high-tech plane filed a flight plan to Halifax, Nova Scotia, but never arrived."

Longfellow felt a zing of excitement.

"I finally tracked it down," Jigger continued.

"Where?" Longfellow interrupted.

"Sharjah, in the United Arab Emirates."

"This Aerion," Longfellow said. "How fast does it fly?"

"Top speed of Mach 1.6," Jigger said. "It can cut typical flight time in half."

Longfellow pounded the dashboard in frustration.

"With that kind of head start, the culture may already be finished," he said.

"If they flew into Sharjah, they're attacking Saudi Arabia, first, not Russia," Melissa added.

"We're in the wrong place," Hal said grimly. "And we may already be too late."

Twenty-three

~∾∾~

Sharjah, United Arab Emirates
The day before

As he disembarked the plane, the furnace-like heat blasted over Michael, squeezing the breath out of his lungs. Sweat instantly soaked his shirt and pants, coursing down his face and neck in thick rivulets. Having spent most of his life in Maine's cold, northern climate, Michael had never experienced anything like the searing heat now boiling his blood. As he struggled to breathe, Michael thought: *this is why the word "hell" was created.*

"Welcome to Sharjah International Airport," David boomed as he stretched his arms wide, grinning behind dark sunglasses. Julia stood next to Michael, gasping in the heat baking off the tarmac in shimmering waves. Kasprzyk silently took the lead, seemingly unaffected by the heat. The two guards, Pete and Adrian, fell in behind, grumbling loudly.

"We're about ten miles from the Dubai border and a mile or two from some of the other emirates," David continued. "Imperial Airways, the predecessor to British Airways, built this place in 1932 as a stopover en route to India and Australia. The United States used it for air transport command during World War II. The Air Force flew out of here during Desert Shield/Desert Storm in the early 1990s. Now, Sharjah is principally a cargo airport, although it does have passenger flights."

"I've heard of this place," Julia said. "Arms dealers and heroin smugglers love it because almost anyone can fly in and out of here. Anything goes."

"Why do you think we flew here?" David replied as the bus transport arrived, reeking of stale sweat, to take them to the passenger terminal. The high-pitched whine of the transport's struggling air conditioner made conversation nearly impossible. As the small group rode in silence, Michael examined the Canadian passport Kasprzyk had handed him on the plane. He flipped it open and saw his own mugshot staring back at him, but with a new name and identity.

Julia and the two guards breathed a sigh of relief as they entered the cool, air-conditioned terminal. Michael shivered as the sweat trapped between his skin and clothes cooled and condensed. With Kasprzyk in the lead, they followed the colorful signs toward Immigration. As they passed the duty free shops, Michael heard a voice that sounded disturbingly familiar.

"But Mama, I *vant* it!" cried a little girl's voice in a Russian accent.

"Katya!"

The word rocketed from Michael's lips before he could stop it. He spun towards the little girl's voice. His eyes devoured the milling crowds in the terminal, chewing and spitting each one out until he spotted her. When he did, his shoulders slumped. A girl with short brown hair, perhaps two or three years older than Katya, pointed at a Toblerone bar in the duty free shop.

"I *vant* it!" she exclaimed, stamping her foot as her mother shook her head no.

It wasn't Katya.

One of the guards elbowed him in the ribs to move him along, but Michael remained rooted in place. He watched as the mother dragged the pouting girl by the wrist toward the bathroom. A shove this time from one of the guards, rougher. Still Michael couldn't move. Finally, he felt an arm slip through his.

"It's okay, Michael," Julia said quietly. "It's not her."

She tugged gently on his arm.

"We've got to move," she reminded him.

Michael nodded numbly and shuffled alongside her toward Immigration. As he handed his passport to the officer, he craned his neck one last time to look for the little girl with the Russian accent.

He couldn't find her.

She was gone.

Twenty-four

— ∞ —

"Hurry!" Kasprzyk snapped as he hustled them all through the airport's underground subway to the parking lot, where a white Yukon Denali was waiting for them. He had just unlocked the driver's door when a Sharjah police officer in his baby-blue uniform with maroon epaulets and beret rounded the corner.

"Stop!"

Kasprzyk ignored him and unlocked all the doors.

"Get in," he ordered, then, quietly to David: "Grab the bag under the seat."

"We don't want trouble with the Sharjah police," David hissed back.

"I'll talk to him, but we don't stop for anyone," Kasprzyk said. "Be ready."

The officer shouted again, hand on the revolver at his hip, and approached warily. Kasprzyk shot a look at David then both men walked to the Denali's rear. Michael and the others watched as the officer held up a warning hand.

"What's wrong, officer?" David asked.

"That vehicle is impounded," the officer replied.

"What for?" Kasprzyk asked.

"For suspicion of illegal activity."

Kasprzyk laughed, but Michael watched intently as David's hand drifted toward the zipper on the black duffel bag slung over his shoulder that he had retrieved from under the seat. The sharp odor of burnt oil and exhaust hung alongside the muted sounds of traffic in the thick air. Michael checked their surroundings; there was no one else around.

"What do you mean, 'illegal activity'?" Kasprzyk asked. "It's been parked here, waiting for us."

"We have had problems in the past with undesirable activities."

Michael watched as Kasprzyk drifted to his right, drawing the officer's attention away from David. "What kind of 'undesirable activities'?"

"Smuggling. Arms dealing. Airplanes and vehicles with contraband stored inside, left to be retrieved at a later date. Your vehicle was flagged because it was parked too long."

Kasprzyk laughed. "We're not smugglers. We're Canadians, here on a business trip. This is all just a misunderstanding."

Michael glanced at the officer in the semi-darkness of the underground garage. He was young, his face darkened with the beginnings of a beard. The officer's eyes darted nervously between Kasprzyk and David.

"Officer, we're pressed for time. We have to get on our way."

"You must come with me."

Kasprzyk's face reddened.

"We don't have time for this."

As the officer undid the flap on his holster, Michael's eyes darted to David, who had unzipped the bag far enough to insert his hand. Michael gritted his teeth. He had a good idea of what was inside that bag.

"I must insist."

"You're wasting our time," Kasprzyk snapped, stepping further to his right. The officer's eyes darted uncertainly from Kasprzyk, to David, to Michael's group at the Denali, then back.

"Sir, please step back to the vehicle."

"No. This is ridiculous."

"Sir!"

But Kasprzyk ignored him.

The situation was deteriorating rapidly. Michael's mind whirred, trying to find a way to turn the circumstances in his favor, but, any way he looked at it, getting captured by the Sharjah police didn't help Milla and Katya, so he kept quiet and waited for what he knew was coming.

"Sir!"

The officer reached for his gun as Kasprzyk continued to stalk away. Clearly, the inexperienced officer had not drawn his weapon often. By the time he freed it on the second tug, David's hand had snaked out of the duffel bag, holding a Makarov. The pistol barked twice, echoing painfully off the concrete walls and floor. The officer's body jerked as two slugs tore through his torso. The two guards pinned Michael and Julia against the Denali as Kasprzyk and David raced to the fallen guard. In the grim silence that followed, a wet wheeze escaped the dying man's lips, then Kasprzyk spoke.

"Finish him. Then let's get out of here."

Michael watched through narrowed eyes as David hesitated.

"Finish him!" Kasprzyk barked.

David flinched, re-set his grip, hunched his shoulders, and fired once more, taking off most of the young officer's face.

"Let's go," Kasprzyk said as he ran for the driver's door. But David remained rooted to the spot, staring down at what remained of the young guard. Pete opened a side door and shoved Julia in. Before Adrian could do likewise, Michael shrugged off his grip and stepped toward David, who had finally backed away from the dead officer. There was a message he had to give his former friend.

"Look at you," he snapped. "You're pale. Your heart's racing. You look like you're about to throw up." He jabbed a finger into David's chest. "It's easy to threaten people when you're not the one pulling the trigger, but if you touch Milla or Katya, I'm going to do to you much worse than you did to that guard."

Michael gave David a final shove before Adrian grabbed him by the back of the collar and hauled him into the Denali. A moment later, David had slipped into the front passenger seat, and they were off.

———✦———

"See anyone?" Pete asked as the Denali careened southwest down Sheikh Zayed Road on the outskirts of Dubai.

"How the hell can you tell if someone's following us?" Adrian demanded, bracing himself as Kasprzyk swerved across two lanes, jamming their white Yukon Denali into a space that didn't look like it could fit a motorcycle. "These people drive like maniacs. They're all over the road. No one brakes or stays in a lane or uses a blinker for Christ's sake. It's like we're all in some kind of death race. How the hell fast are we going anyway?"

But Kasprzyk ignored him, sawing the Denali's steering wheel back and forth one-handed while he pressed his cell phone to his ear. He had called the Director as they left Sharjah behind to report the officer's death. David had continued to stare silently out the window, not seeing the traffic hurtling toward them. Michael had seen him flinch several times, reliving each shot over and over. After a hushed conversation, Kasprzyk terminated the call and slid his phone into a holder on the console.

"Looks like we're clear."

"Ah, boss," Pete said from the back seat. "You spoke too soon. We've got company."

The Denali's inhabitants craned their necks to spot two Dubai police cruisers racing toward them, lights flashing and sirens blaring.

"Maybe they're after someone else," Adrian said. But that hope was soon dashed when the first vehicle slipped behind them, quickly closing the distance to their bumper while the other flashed alongside.

"Hold on," Kasprzyk muttered.

They couldn't have chosen a better location for a high speed chase than the Sheikh Zayed Road through Dubai. As the wide, multi-laned ribbon of tar snaked through the flamboyant, modernist, high-rise fantasyland, the other drivers, accustomed to high speeds and erratic driving, took no notice of the Denali hurtling onward, paced by the two police vehicles.

"They're still there!" Adrian called as they flashed through downtown Dubai. Michael twisted in his seat, losing the cruisers in the glare from the reflective glazing of the mammoth glass and aluminum Burj Dubai, the tallest building in the world. As Kasprzyk yanked the wheel to the right, sending the Denali careening across three lanes, the two vehicles followed suit.

"They're good," Pete said.

David finally stirred. "We have to get rid of them before they call in backup and barricade the road."

"Should we get off?" Adrian asked.

David shook his head. "No, if we get off, they'll trap us easily. Our best bet is here."

Without warning, Kasprzyk slammed on the brakes. Michael's and Julia's necks whip sawed as the trailing cruiser slammed into them then spun out, peeling off the Denali's rear bumper with a screech of metal. Michael and Julia twisted backwards in time to see a black Toyota Land Cruiser plow through the disabled police car. Before they could react, Kasprzyk floored the accelerator and snapped the wheel to the left, catching the other police car on the right rear, sending it spinning into the concrete bunker with a sickening crash.

The flood of vehicles along the Sheikh Zayed Road consumed the carnage and continued flowing, carrying forward the Denali, dented and battered, but still operational. As Dubai receded in their rear window, Julia slipped a hand into Michael's, shocked at the three deaths.

"Nice driving!" Adrian yelled while the guards pounded the back of the scientists' seat. David twisted around and pointed a finger at Michael.

"Whatever it takes, Michael. Remember that."

Michael returned the stare.

"I remember everything, David. Everything."

Ninety minutes later, they reached Abu Dhabi without further incident. Within minutes, the Denali sped past the capital and headed toward the remote and desolate desert stretching towards the Saudi border.

"We're going to need a new vehicle," David said to Kasprzyk. "We can't take a chance on the Ruwais police finding it."

Kasprzyk nodded. "I'll call the Director."

"What's Ruwais?" Julia asked.

"It's an oil refinery town about 150 miles west of Abu Dhabi on Highway 11 toward the Saudi border. I found a factory that Ruwais Fertilizer Industries isn't using, right on the waterfront. I leased it and outfitted it with all the lab equipment you'll need."

"Is it close to our target in Saudi Arabia?" Michael asked.

"Nice try," Kasprzyk snapped.

"It's not far from the Saudi border," David replied. "That's all you need to know."

As Kasprzyk placed another call to the Director, Michael slumped in his seat and, once again, tried to work through the unprecedented task of creating enough microbes to destroy the Saudi and Russian oil reserves. Simply increasing the lab size did not solve the problem, although Michael knew he would need every square inch of cultivation surface. The most vexing problem was that cultivation took time, something he didn't have. Even the rapid cultivation he had achieved in his lab did not necessarily extrapolate to production on the scale that he was about to attempt.

Despite the seemingly insurmountable obstacles facing him, he couldn't force himself to slog through the methodologies he would need. Each time he tried, images of Milla and Katya dragged him back into a hellish pattern of questions and no answers. Where were they? Had they been hurt? Michael had imagined a thousand times over what might be happening to them. It was a nightmare that he couldn't stop.

Outside the vehicle, the barren desert flashed past, with its scattered clumps of date palms and occasional clusters of goats or camels plodding along near the road, like a scene from *Lawrence of Arabia*. The stark landscape reinforced the desolation and isolation that had seized Michael. As the miles sped past, Michael finally succumbed to the despair and let his eyelids slide shut, his fingers continuing to type Milla's and Katya's names over and over.

——*◊◊◊*——

He didn't even notice that they had reached Ruwais. When the Denali turned off Highway 11 and headed toward the water-front, past the giant GASCO plant and the oil refinery, Julia stirred, woken by the slower pace of the vehicle. She gently nudged him awake.

As the diaphanous waters of the Persian Gulf burst into view, filling the windshield with their almost painful sparkle, David glanced over his shoulder at Michael.

"We're here."

Twenty-five

─◦◦◦◦─

Ruwais, U.A.E.

David entered the abandoned factory like a proud parent, chest puffed out and arms spread wide.

"Look at the lab I've built for you," he crowed. "You'd be hard-pressed to find a better equipped one anywhere!"

As David's voice echoed off the concrete floor and cinder block walls, Michael had to admit that the facility was impressive. The factory consisted of one floor that stretched almost the full length of a football field. Banks of industrial lighting blazed thirty feet overhead, turning the somber, gray stone a sickly green. Michael spotted one set of large, metal receiving doors on the rear wall that rolled up, like garage doors. One open door on the left wall led into what appeared to be an office. There was another door, approximately fifteen feet down the left wall from the first, but it was closed. Long tables with flat, air-tight, transparent cabinets on them ran from one end to the other. Michael had expected an abandoned factory in the desert to be searingly hot, but the air was surprisingly cool, although the pungent smell of ammonia reminded him that the facility had been used to manufacture fertilizer.

"First order of business was to jack up the air conditioning in this place," David said, pointing to a series of industrial blowers scattered around the factory floor. "That also helped remove some of the ammonia stench. There's an office to the right that Kris and

I will use and a break room I've set up with a refrigerator, a micro-wave, a hot plate, and some cots for people to grab a quick rest."

"But there won't be much time for rest," Kasprzyk broke in. "You have too much work to do."

Michael shrugged off the man and followed David toward the first cluster of tables. Thousands of small glass bottles lined the cab-inets on the tables. As he looked across the giant room, he noticed that the glass bottles grew larger as the tables extended away from him. David watched Michael's reaction with keen interest while Julia followed close behind. The two guards roamed in a half arc behind Michael, uninterested in the layout of the lab.

"I've arranged it so you can scale up, starting with the initial cultures in the 120 milliliter bottles in this section," David explained as he led Michael to the nearest tables. "He swept a hand towards the other tables. "As the cultures grow, you can move across the floor to the half-liter bottles, liters, five liters, and ultimately to the twenty-five-liter bottles, which will be delivered soon. Each bottle is fitted with rubber stoppers and aluminum crimped caps after the solution is prepared."

The sheer number of bottles took Michael's breath away.

"David, in my lab I worked with a handful of bottles at a time. There are thousands here! How am I supposed to prepare the anaerobic microcosm in each bottle? Each bottle needs to be stirred slowly to fos-ter the cultivation and equipped with oxygen sensors to ensure there's no oxygen in the containers and the tubing system. As the inoculum grows inside each bottle, it emits gas which will crack the bottles if it's not released. On top of all that, the cultures need to be transferred from the smaller bottles to the larger ones to permit continued growth."

Michael paced restlessly as the impossibility of his situation struck him.

"It can't be done, not on this scale."

David chuckled at Michael's distress.

"You underestimate me, Michael. But then, you always did."

David stepped over to the first table and pressed a button. With a soft click and whirr, a thousand robotic arms rose from the table and hovered over the stoppered ends of the bottles.

"It's all computerized. You give the command and the robotic arms will slip a needle and syringe through the stopper to add the inoculum and the stopper then self-seals of course. This all occurs inside anaerobic chambers."

Michael's mouth hung open in astonishment. This wasn't a lab, it was a production facility.

"How do we stir the cultures and release the gas?"

"Each bottle contains a computerized stir bar that you control from your keyboard. The transfers to the larger bottles are also computer-controlled." David gazed proudly at his creation. "I worked on this with a guy who used to head up research and development for one of the largest pharmaceutical companies in the world. He had no idea what I was going to do with it, of course. This can take what you did in your lab and expand it to any scale we need."

David turned to Michael and stared grimly into his eyes, making sure his message was received.

"With this equipment, there is no excuse for failure, Michael."

A loud metallic bang startled Michael. He spun around to see that Pete had locked the door with a thick chain and padlock.

"You're locked in," Kasprzyk said. "All the doors and windows are chained and locked shut. Don't even think about trying to escape."

"Shut up, Kasprzyk," Michael snapped. "You know I'm not going anywhere until I have my wife and daughter."

David snorted with laughter as Kasprzyk's face reddened. Michael turned to Julia.

"We'd better get to work."

David pointed towards a line of barrels stacked against the wall.

"We've obtained everything you asked for. Samples from an oil reservoir in Saudi Arabia, deionized water, bicarbonate, sulphides, phosphates, and so on."

"What about carbon dioxide, nitrogen and hydrogen?"

"All set. Get started."

"Wait, what about samples from the Russian oil reservoir?"

"Kris obtained those," David said.

"No, I didn't," Kasprzyk replied.

David and Michael exchanged anxious glances as the giant room fell silent.

"What do you mean you didn't?" David demanded.

"I didn't get them," Kasprzyk said, shrugging. "There wasn't time."

"I assembled this entire lab," David snapped, flushing dangerously red. "Obtained all the chemicals, the Saudi sample, everything Michael would need. The one thing you had to get was the Sakhalin sample. You assured me you would get it."

Michael started at David's slip. He now knew where the second target was: the Sakhalin Islands in Russia's Far East.

"My supplier didn't come through. We don't have it," Kasprzyk said, his voice dropping several degrees. "Move on."

"I need samples from the oil reservoirs where the culture is to be inserted," Michael told both men. "I have to work with the microbes that are already in the reservoir because they have adapted to survive in that environment. Underground oil reservoirs are extremely harsh environments. Foreign microbial strains most likely won't survive."

Kasprzyk responded without removing his eyes from David, standing inches away. The two guards had crept closer, drawn by the conflict.

"You'll prepare for the Saudi insertion and that will have to work for Russia, too."

Michael's temper crackled amid the electrical storm brewing between Kasprzyk and Kenner.

"It doesn't work like that. If you want the culture to work, I need samples from the targeted reservoir."

In an instant, Kasprzyk's pistol was pressed against Michael's forehead. Michael didn't flinch.

"Do your job," Kasprzyk said.

"Do yours," Michael replied. He stared down the barrel until, with a cold smile, Kasprzyk holstered the gun and strode across the floor into the office.

"Come on, David," he called over his shoulder. "I'll call the Director to see if he's arranged for our alternate transportation and then we'll find a place for you to hide the Denali. You can make yourself useful."

David glowered after the man for several beats before relenting.

"Dinner's in three hours," he muttered before storming after Kasprzyk.

As the two guards returned to their posts on opposite sides of the lab, Julia appeared at Michael side, breathing a sigh of relief.

"It's probably not a good idea to antagonize someone who has a gun to your forehead," she said.

"It's not the first time," Michael said quietly, turning to the laptop that would control the experiment. "It's only when they pull the trigger that you have a problem."

Julia shook her head as she slipped onto a stool next to his. Despite their dire situation, the scientist in her could not help but be curious about what they were about to attempt.

"Tell me again how this works."

"Over time, if left alone, a small amount of oil will degrade naturally in the underground reservoirs," Michael explained as he powered up the laptop. "Anaerobic microbes, ones that don't need oxygen, digest the hydrocarbons."

"And you need microbes that are indigenous to the reservoir?"

"That's right, but, since we don't have a Russian sample, we'll work with what we've got. If it works in Saudi Arabia, I hope it'll work in Russia too."

A window popped up on the laptop's screen. Michael continued explaining the process to Julia as he entered the amounts of each solution and chemical to be injected into each bottle.

"As with any microbial culture, we start small."

"The 120 milliliter bottles."

"Right. We add one hundred milliliters of our solution, leaving twenty milliliters of head space, which we gas with a mixture of nitrogen and carbon dioxide. We then inject a brackish solution consisting of the oil sample, deionized water, bicarbonate, sulphides, phosphates, nitrates, vitamins and trace minerals."

"And it's the mixture of the phosphates and nitrates that will speed up the cultivation?"

"Yes."

"Brilliant," Julia murmured admiringly.

Michael shrugged off the compliment and kept typing.

"If I recall from your report, it's a two-step process," Julia continued. "In the first step, the microbes will break the hydrocarbons in the oil down into acetic acid, CO_2, and hydrogen. In the second step, the acid and gases are degraded into methane."

"Right, but we won't see that here. Hopefully, that will happen in the reservoir."

Michael blew out his breath.

"But this still won't work without a constant source of nitrogen."

"What do you mean?"

"Living organisms need carbon and nitrogen to grow. The oil is a great source of carbon for the microbes, but anything trying to grow in it would quickly run out of nitrogen. David says they've figured that out. If they haven't, this won't work. The inoculum will grow only a little, then stop once the nitrogen source is used up."

Michael finished entering the data as Julia ran her fingers through her hair, breaking up some of the tangles and knots that had formed during her abduction and flight across the globe."

"I could really use a shower," she said.

"Good luck with that," Michael replied. "I doubt they built showers into their fertilizer factories."

"A hot shower, a lot of food, and a long nap," she continued. She arched her back and twisted side to side, trying to work out some kinks, then made a face at her blouse and pants. "And a change of clothes. These are disgusting. They smell."

Julia turned to Michael.

"How are you holding up?"

He shrugged and stared forcefully at the laptop.

"You do what you have to do."

An uncomfortable silence settled over Michael once more as Julia continued twisting side to side, stretching her back muscles. Michael let his gaze drop to the laptop, but all he could see were ghostlike images of Milla and Katya, distorted, mouths open, screaming silently.

"Michael, we need to talk," Julia began then stopped as she spotted the anguish in Michael's eyes. She hesitated then gave up. A dark look flitted across her face, but Michael, still trapped in his nightmare, saw nothing. With a frustrated sigh, she reached tentatively for Michael's arm.

"You're going to get through this, Michael," Julia told him.

Michael shifted. The nightmarish images disappeared, leaving behind the laptop screen, blinking patiently for him to initiate the cultivation.

Julia's eyes followed his to the screen.

"What are the odds this will work?" she asked quietly.

Before responding, Michael glanced quickly toward the guards to make sure they could not hear.

"Not good."

Julia nodded silently.

"Here goes everything," he murmured as he pressed the enter key and listened to the *snap-whirr* of the robotic arms springing to life.

Twenty-six

David sat down on a stool across the table as Michael and Julia tossed the melon rinds, chicken bones, and crusts of flatbread into the trash, remnants of their first real meal in twenty-four hours. From her perch next to Michael, Julia peered at the gas readings scrolling across the laptop's screen. As a strand of hair slipped past her ear and dangled toward the table, a lecherous grin slid across David's face and he leaned across the table. With a surprising swiftness, Julia grabbed his outstretched hand and pulled it toward her, stretching David across the table. Before he could regain his footing, she snapped his wrist sharply against the edge of the countertop. From the sharp crack, Michael figured she had broken David's wrist.

David reared back, roaring in pain. He cradled his wrist against his chest and gingerly flexed his fingers. Julia was on her feet, staring defiantly across the table at David. The gold flecks in her eyes sparked dangerously.

"Try to touch me again and I'll break it."

As David stormed around the table, Julia dropped into a defensive posture, her muscles tensed like coiled springs. Michael scrambled off his stool and stood between them. The two guards had raised their weapons and were slowly approaching.

"Leave her alone, David," Michael cautioned.

Red-faced and huffing, David glared over Michael's shoulder at Julia. He slowly rotated his right wrist. Gradually, David's jaw muscles slowed their pistons-like pumping.

"Keep her in line. Otherwise, you'll be working alone."

A banging on the door silenced them all. Both guards raised their weapons as Kasprzyk appeared like magic. With a warning look at Michael and Julia, he whispered to the guards: "Police. I saw them making their way down the row of warehouses."

"How'd they find us?" Pete asked.

"Traffic cameras. Security cameras, probably," Kasprzyk replied quietly.

"Where's the Denali?" Adrian asked.

"At the bottom of the harbor," David replied *sotto voce*.

They fell quiet at another round of banging, more insistent this time, followed by voices shouting in Arabic. Michael didn't speak Arabic, but could guess the meaning. *Open up!* Kasprzyk nodded at the two guards, who crept toward the door, guns at the ready. More shouts then the door shook as one of the officers put his shoulder to it. Michael held his breath. They were sitting ducks. Another round of gunplay would bring the Ruwais police swooping down on them. Then their operation would be busted and any chance to save Milla and Katya would be gone.

Michael's field of vision narrowed to the four foot span between the guards and the door. With each bang on the door, the guards' fingers tightened on the triggers. He prayed that the guards' patience would last as long as the doors did. Just then, Pete's nerves snapped and he raised his weapon to fire. But the next knock never came. Kasprzyk raced into the office, where Michael assumed he had a window, and reappeared a few moments later, smiling.

"They're gone."

David smiled in relief and headed for the break room as the two guards slung their submachine guns over their shoulders and retreated to their corners, but Michael was still uneasy as he slid back onto his stool. The police may have left, but would they be back? As Julia sat next to him, he remembered that he had another problem.

"What you did earlier was very stupid," he muttered under his breath.

"I'm not going to let him touch me."

"Still, you didn't have to try to break his wrist."

"If I'd tried to break his wrist, it'd be broken."

Michael shook his head at her false bravado.

"Look," he began, keeping his voice low and level, "we have to keep our heads down, do what they tell us to do, and wait for an opportunity to save Milla and Katya."

"Is that what you were doing when Kasprzyk pulled his gun on you?"

"Don't jeopardize my family."

Julia raised her hands in surrender.

"I would never want to jeopardize your family." She paused. "But, you aren't really going to give them what they want, are you?"

"I'll give them whatever they want if it gets my wife and daughter back."

Julia bent over, placing her head near the laptop as if she were peering closely at it. She continued speaking without looking at Michael.

"I know you want to save them. I do too. But think of what will happen if you give The Global Group the culture. The world economy runs on oil. It will be shattered. People's lives will be destroyed. And Saudi Arabia and Russia will trace this back to you and to the United States. They'll consider it an act of war. Even if they don't, we'll have terrorists dropping from our skies and crawling out of our sewers. You can't do this."

"I don't care about any of that. I'm only interested in finding Milla and Katya."

Julia slowly pivoted on her stool as if she were stretching. Instead, she was locating each of their captors. David and Kasprzyk were still out of sight. The two guards were twenty feet away and beginning to show the first signs of boredom and fatigue, with one inspecting his machine gun and the other looking at the ceiling.

"Michael, is there a way that you can make a large enough batch so they'll think it'll work, but not large enough to actually make it work?"

Michael could not help the angry edge that crept into his voice. "I'm not playing games with my family's lives, Julia."

"I'm not asking you to," she whispered urgently. "I'm asking you to buy us enough time until we can let someone know where we are."

"I'm sorry you're mixed up in this, Julia. I really am. But I'm not interested in being rescued, at least not until I've found Milla and Katya."

Michael needed to move. He walked across the room to the tanks of nutrients, inspecting each tube, more to occupy himself than for any real purpose, before finally returning to his seat, where Julia was waiting to resume their argument.

"The best way to save Milla and Katya is to get word out."

"And what would that do? We don't know where they are or who has them. By the time we find them, they'll be dead."

Michael shot an angry glare at Julia, silencing her response.

"We have to get closer to the Director," he said. "The only way to do that is to go along with them for now and wait for our opportunity."

"Opportunity for what?" Julia hissed.

"An opportunity to kill David and the guards and make Kasprzyk take me to the Director."

"Who's going to do that? You?" Julia flushed and quickly changed her tone. "I'm sorry. I just meant to say that you're not trained for situations like this."

"I'm done talking about this."

Julia turned red and marched stiffly down the long table, peering intently into the glass bottles. Michael watched her go, his restless fingers tapping out the last of their conversation. He hoped she got the message. She was swimming with sharks. This was no time to splash around.

He checked his watch. One more hour and then it would be time for the first transfer.

Approximately one hundred feet away, in the warehouse office, Kasprzyk listened to the clipped tones of the Director.

"Be patient," the Director cautioned. "The time for action will come soon."

A smile as wide and cold as the Siberian steppes spread across Kasprzyk's face. He would wait to kill, but not for long. Then he would kill them both, as the Director had ordered.

Twenty-seven

———⟪∾⟫———

"I'm sorry."

Michael glanced up at Julia in surprise.

"For what?"

"For what I said earlier," she said quietly as she slipped onto the stool next to his. "It was insensitive. You're focused on getting your wife and daughter back and that's where you should be." Julia folded her hands in her lap. "This is hard enough for you without me making it harder. What can I do to help?"

"I'm all set," Michael replied, a little gruffly.

"Please."

Michael hesitated then relented.

"I need to input the stir rates."

"Let me do that."

Julia flashed a smile as he handed her a sheet of notes, but her smile quickly faltered as she pointed toward the break room.

"Your friend wants you."

David fidgeted, shifting impatiently while Michael trudged toward him.

"What do you want?" Michael asked.

"Our supplier is arriving at the dock with the twenty-five-liter bottles. You're going to help me offload them. Just in case you get any ideas about escaping, Adrian will be guarding you and Julia will remain here with Pete and Kasprzyk. Let's go."

The dock was a dilapidated structure of rotting wood covered in green slime, restrained from slipping into the Persian Gulf by its last few rusty bolts. Although the dock was less than a hundred yards from the factory, Michael was soaked with sweat by the time he and David had dragged the flatbed to its edge. Through the melancholy orange glow suffusing the harbor, the dirty *spit-put* of a balky outboard engine reached them. A slight breeze carried the stench of petroleum and rotting seaweed.

"Why are you doing this, David?" Michael asked as they waited for the boat to approach. It was the first chance he'd had to talk to his former friend.

"Because he didn't have the twenty-five-liter bottles before."

"No, I mean, all of this. Why are you involved with this insane plot? Why are you doing this to me and my family?"

David smiled wryly.

"The biggest surprise of all this is that you actually care about someone other than yourself. After your sister, I didn't think that would ever happen. You're not the same guy I knew at grad school."

"Right back at you."

"Hey, you're not the only one who's lost someone," David bit back, giving Michael a rough shove. Michael stumbled then braced himself, clenching his fists as Adrian raised his machine gun in warning. "I lost my sister, too."

"What sister? You don't have a sister."

Michael flinched as David's hand whipped something black from behind his back, but it was just a wallet. His former friend's stubby fingers fumbled with the wallet's contents before thrusting something at Michael. It was a picture of a young woman smiling directly into the camera. High cheekbones elongated her thin, but attractive, face. Long, blond hair was pulled back in a ponytail. Bright green eyes sparkled. The photo was taken outdoors in the fall.

"Her name was Sarah. She was my step-sister. I didn't even know about her until after we graduated. Same father, different mothers." David shrugged. "Dad was never much for sticking around."

He took the picture back and gazed at it, his rough features momentarily softening before he stuffed the picture back into his wallet.

"Summer of 2001, she found me. She was a senior in high school. Wanted to be a reporter. Smart kid. Big smile. Her mother must've been a lot more put-together than mine. She got better genes somewhere."

"I met her twice," David continued after casting a long glance across the harbor, "but then she got on a plane. It was September 11. She got on Mohammed Atta's plane."

David looked out to sea again. The boat had almost arrived. An Arab in a white, linen shirt waved from behind the wheel.

"Protecting our national security was the whole reason I got into my field in the first place," David said softly, his words almost lost in the boat's backfiring, "but after Sarah, there wasn't any more time for half-measures or baby steps. It was time for the jugular."

The small outboard bumped against the dock with a wet slurp.

"Hello, my friend, I have the supplies you requested, but I'm afraid they were more expensive than I had expected."

As David opened his mouth to retort, a triple-tap from Adrian's machine gun shattered the morning quiet, sending a flock of seagulls screaming into the air. The supplier's body shook as the slugs ripped through his chest, then pitched overboard, where a dark crimson cloud quickly bloomed around his body as it floated face down.

"What are you doing?" David demanded of the guard. "I didn't tell you to do that."

"Orders from Kasprzyk. He said to remove the supplier and sink his body." The guard tossed a length of rope to David and pointed at a cement block on the dock. "Use that. And, professor, you unload everything quick."

Twenty minutes later, David burst into the factory, followed by a huffing, sweating Michael pulling the loaded flatbed, then Adrian.

"Kasprzyk!" David bellowed, racing into his office. "I give the orders around here!" He slammed the door, but the men's shouts still echoed through the factory.

Michael plopped down on the edge of the flatbed and wiped the sweat from his forehead. He had seen too much violent, sudden death to be shaken by the killing of the supplier, but the man's murder confirmed one thing. Kasprzyk and the Director intended to kill them all.

Across the floor, at the computer, Julia finished the last entry and closed down the window. With a guilty glance at Michael's back, she balled up his notes and threw them in the trash can, hoping that Michael never found out what she had done.

Twenty-eight

—⦿—

"Why don't you get some rest on one of those cots in the break room?" Julia suggested as Michael's eyelids slid shut once again.

"No, I'm good." He blinked his eyes, red-rimmed with exhaustion. Julia sighed, exasperated.

"You haven't slept. You're chewing yourself up worrying about Milla and Katya." She gestured at the long rows of cabinets. "We've been watching microbes grow for six hours. It's not exactly scintillating. Go get some rest. You need to be sharp when this process gets closer to completion. If there's any problem, I'll shout for you immediately."

Michael reluctantly agreed. He was having a difficult time staying awake amid the constant hum of the air conditioning units and the occasional whirr of the stir bars and robotic arms. Pete and Adrian stiffened as Michael stood up and slowly made his way toward the break room.

"Just catching a little shut-eye, guys."

He stepped into the break room and looked around. A gleaming white refrigerator occupied one corner. He was too numb from exhaustion to be thirsty or hungry. Three green army surplus cots were lined perpendicular to the far wall. He picked the farthest from the door and collapsed onto it, using his arm as a pillow.

Just then, the guard named Pete stepped into the room and stood inside the doorway, eyes trained on Michael.

"Are you going to watch me while I sleep?" Michael groaned.

Pete shrugged.

"Orders are orders," he said flatly. "We're never supposed to leave you or the lady scientist alone."

"And you drew me?"

"My bad luck."

Michael gave up and closed his eyes. As his body sank into a dark sleep, the nightmares he had fended off while awake broke over him like a tidal wave.

After watching Pete follow Michael into the break room, Julia waited several minutes to make certain that Michael was asleep and that Pete wouldn't leave him. This was her chance. She wasn't going to let Michael's misgivings stop her from getting them rescued.

Julia slowly raised her eyes from the laptop's screen until they met the guard's and let a smile flit across her face.

"Would you like me to show you what we're doing?" she asked, a little embarrassed at the coquettish lilt she had forced into her voice.

Adrian stirred uncertainly.

"We're just supposed to watch."

"Oh, come on," Julia replied as she slid off the stool and walked toward the guard. She tucked a strand of hair behind her ear and flashed her brightest smile at him. "Let me show you."

She led him to the nearest line of cabinets, aware that he was checking her out as he followed. She stopped at a microscope she and Michael used to examine microbial samples.

"If you look through here, you can see the microbes we're culturing," she said, motioning toward the microscope.

Adrian shook his head.

"I don't need to look at no microbes."

Julia pouted playfully, pulled her hair back, and bent over the microscope, giving Adrian time to enjoy the curve of her back side and her long legs. The brown slacks and pink sweater she had worn to class the previous day were grimy and worse for the wear, but still hugged her lithe form. She casually glanced up and then waited for him to notice that she had caught him ogling her. When he did, she smiled again. A grin slipped across his face, then disappeared. She laughed and straightened up.

She stepped into him, careful to stay on the other side of his body from his gun, not wanting to alarm him. She sighed.

"I've been at this for hours. I'm really thirsty." She cocked her head toward the break room. "Are there any Cokes in the refrigerator in there?"

"I think so."

Julia touched the guard's bicep, lightly, just a hint, then removed her hand.

"Could you get me one?"

The guard's eyes shot toward the closed office door.

"You'll have to come with me. I'm not supposed to leave you alone."

Julia let her face sag in disappointment.

"I have to stay here and watch the readouts. If I left and anything happened out here. . . ." She left the statement unfinished.

She touched his arm again and left her hand there this time. She could smell the harsh bite of stale beer on his breath mingled with dried sweat. She kept the disgust out of her face and voice as she leaned against him.

"Please?"

Adrian shot another cautious glance toward the closed office door. He was clearly weighing the dilemma. Julia tried to look as harmless as possible. The possibility of pleasing a beautiful woman was too strong for the guard to resist.

"Wait right here," he ordered while he lumbered off toward the break room.

Julia waited until he disappeared through the doorway then sprang into action. She knew that she was taking a terrible risk. She only had a minute before Adrian hurried back with a Coke. She pulled from her pocket the cell phone she had slipped off the guard's belt clip while touching his shoulder. She had to let someone know where they were and what was happening. Then she'd slide the phone across the floor toward where Adrian had stood, as if he had dropped it. No one would know.

She quickly dialed Hal's cell phone number. Before she could finish, a hand knocked the phone from her grip, sending it clattering across the cement floor. Two hands grabbed her arms and shook her violently.

"That was a very stupid thing to try," Kasprzyk hissed directly into her face. The veins in his temples pulsed. Julia struggled in vain as his fingers dug into her biceps. Without warning, he threw her to the floor. Her shoulder crashed painfully against the hard cement. Black dots danced before her eyes as her head smacked against the concrete. She pulled her feet under her, ready to run, but he was too quick. He grabbed her hair and snapped her head back, exposing her neck. Julia gasped and reached to claw at his hand. She froze as she felt the cold barrel of his pistol press against her right temple.

"Now you're going to pay."

Twenty-nine

———

Kasprzyk ground the barrel of his gun into Julia's temple. "Adrian!" he bellowed. "Where the hell are you?

The guard came running and dropped the two cans of Coke as he spied Kasprzyk holding Julia on her knees at gunpoint. As the cans clanked on the floor and rolled away with a tinny clatter, the guard stared dumbstruck at the scene.

"Your phone's on the floor in back of me," Kasprzyk shouted across the room.

The guard checked his empty belt clip and turned red.

"The bitch stole your phone," Kasprzyk spat.

Drawn by the shouting, David stepped out of the office as Adrian approached Kasprzyk and Julia, his expression both sheepish and murderous. In back of him, Julia saw the other guard shove a groggy and disheveled Michael out of the door. She closed her eyes. She couldn't face Michael. She knew she had jeopardized not only their lives, but his family's lives as well.

"What's going on?" David demanded.

"It's a good thing I came out of the office when I did," Kasprzyk replied, giving Julia's head another sharp yank. She gritted her teeth and said nothing. "She stole a cell phone from this idiot guard you hired and then sent him to get her a Coke. As soon as he went into the break room, she started dialing. I stopped her before she could make the call."

The others had reached Julia. She opened her eyes to find Michael staring horrorstruck at her. Adrian had found his cell phone.

David angrily yanked it from his grasp and checked the list of calls placed before tossing it back to the guard.

"It looks like you're right, you stopped her before she placed the call." He looked hesitant. "What do you plan to do?"

Kasprzyk bared his teeth in a feral smile.

"I plan to kill her."

Julia's heart beat uncontrollably. As her hands shook at her sides, she promised herself that she would not beg for her life. There was one thing she had to do, though. Taking a deep, shaky breath, she opened her eyes to apologize to Michael.

Before she could, one quiet word reverberated in the silence.

"No."

Michael had pulled free from Pete's grip and stepped forward. He didn't look at Julia. He glared at Kasprzyk, his shoulders squared, his chin up, his eyes ablaze.

"No what?" Kasprzyk replied.

"No, you won't kill her."

Julia felt the man's fingers tighten around her locks.

"You're not in a position to issue any orders, McKeon," Kasprzyk said coldly and evenly. "After I kill this bitch, you better pray that I don't decide to kill your wife or your little girl, too."

Kasprzyk pulled Julia roughly to her feet. She steadied herself and held a warning hand to Michael.

"Michael, don't," she said. "Don't let him hurt your family."

Michael still didn't look at her. He continued to stare down Kasprzyk as he took a deep breath. His voice throbbed with emotion as he bit off each word.

"You won't hurt anyone. You won't hurt my daughter, my wife, or Julia. If you do, I won't finish the culture, and you can explain to the Director how you caused the entire mission to fail. I wonder how long he'll let you live after that."

"You'll do what we say when we make your little girl cry," Kasprzyk snarled.

"The second you lift a finger against any of them, you may as well kill us all because I will never give you the culture," Michael promised. "What do you think the Director will do to you if that happens? You want to sign your own death warrant? Pull the trigger."

Michael saw Kasprzyk's finger tighten on the trigger. The end was moments away. He knew it. Julia saw that realization in his eyes and closed hers. For a long moment, no one moved or spoke. Then David stepped forward.

"Let her go. We still need her."

He took another step and raised his hands.

"I'm here because I know him," David continued, jerking a thumb at Michael. "You've made that clear. I'm telling you that if you shoot her, he won't do a damn thing. He's that stubborn. You shoot her, you blow this entire operation."

Kasprzyk pressed the barrel against Julia's temple. Just then, his cell phone rang. He released Julia's hair and stepped back to check the caller's identity. The gun remained pointed at her head.

"It's the Director."

"Jesus Christ," David breathed. "Put the gun away and take the call. And don't tell him anything about this."

Kasprzyk hesitated for a long moment while his phone rang twice more, harsh and shrill in the cavernous silence of the factory floor. Then, with a last snarl, he shoved Julia toward the group, holstered his gun, and hurried toward the office.

"Yes, Director," Michael heard him say. "Everything is still going according to plan."

Julia staggered into Michael then picked herself up.

"I'm sorry, Michael," she said as he turned away.

Michael didn't respond. He wasn't sure why he had risked everything to save Julia. He just couldn't stand one more person dying because of him, even if he had only merely delayed the inevitable.

"All right then," David exhaled loudly. "Everyone back to . . ."

An alarm from the laptop silenced him.

"What the hell's that?" demanded Pete, the nearest one to the laptop.

David shouldered past the guard and hunched urgently over the computer. Michael reached it a second later, followed by Julia. An error message flashed on the screen. Michael pressed a few buttons. His stomach dropped as an explanation scrolled across the screen.

"Something's wrong with the culture," he said.

"I can tell that. What's wrong?" David demanded.

Michael shook his head grimly. The world was a real bastard sometimes.

"It's not growing fast enough. It won't be ready."

Now nothing would stop Kasprzyk from killing them all.

Thirty

"Why isn't the culture growing?" Kasprzyk thundered, his eyes flashing dangerously.

"I don't know yet," Michael shot back, feverishly scrolling through screen after screen of data. "We've had two successful transfers. All growth projections were on target. We should have been ready to transfer the cultures to the twenty-five-liter bottles for the final stage in approximately two hours, but something's happened."

"Could some oxygen have leaked in during the last transfer?" David asked.

"Doubtful," Michael replied, shaking his head in frustration. "If it had, it would have shown up immediately on the oxygen sensors."

"Could there be some kind of contaminant in the larger bottles?" Kenner tried again.

"It's possible, but the composition of the culture and the gases are monitored. If there was a contaminant, it should show up on the readouts."

Kasprzyk dropped a hand to his gun. Minutes before, he had told the Director that everything was going according to the plan. If he had to call the Director right back and tell him that the cultures weren't growing as needed. . . .

"Find out what's wrong and fix it, now!"

Beads of sweat dripped from Michael's brow as he pored over the data.

"It doesn't make sense," he muttered to himself. "There was always a very significant chance that this wasn't going to work, but all the progressions were in order. I don't understand why it would start working, then stop."

He checked for the third time that he had used the proper concentrations of phosphates and nitrates. He compared the volumes of gas aliquots siphoned off. *They're all correct. Something had to happen during this stage to slow down the growth rate, but what?*

And then it hit him.

As he examined the data on the stir rate, a cold fury engulfed him. This was not the rate he had told Julia to set. She had inputted a stir rate that was too slow to promote the growth they needed. Keeping his face as expressionless as possible, Michael approached Julia, who was bent over a stack of printouts, by all appearances desperately trying to discover what had gone wrong.

"How could you?" he whispered, his lips inches from her ear.

She started in surprise, but his hand on the back of her neck forced her back.

"I saved your life," he said, his fingers digging into the cords of her neck as he struggled to contain the fury burning through him. He wanted to break her neck. "If I don't give them what they want, if they find out what you did, they'll kill Milla and Katya."

"I was trying to buy us time," Julia whispered, her eyes darting from him to the guards, who were watching David and Kaspzryk argue at the office door, "until we could contact someone or find a way out of here."

"That's not your call," Michael hissed. "You're gambling with my family's lives."

"And you're willing to unleash chaos around the world, destroying countless lives, having our country be blamed for it, and you don't even know if that will save your family," she replied heatedly.

"It's my only chance."

Julia shifted slightly but stopped as Michael's fingers dug further into her neck.

"They'll see what you're doing any second," she said. "If they know I sabotaged the culture, they'll kill me. Is that what you want?"

Part of him wanted revenge on her, on everyone who had hurt him, but, finally, he let his hand drop. Julia relaxed and checked their captors. The guards were still watching David and Kasprzyk argue.

Michael straightened and cleared his throat.

"I've figured out the problem," he announced.

David and Kasprzyk hurried toward him. Even the two guards approached, curious.

"We've never dealt with a culture of this large volume in the lab before. The stir rate was an extrapolation of what we've done in the lab with much smaller volumes. It's too low. We need to increase the stir rate."

"Will that get us back on track?" David demanded.

"It should," Michael replied, "but we've lost a couple hours of expected growth. To be safe, I think I should also increase very slightly the amount of phosphates and nitrates to give it a boost."

"Will that work?"

"I believe so, but you have to understand that we're dealing in volumes that no one has ever handled before. Just because something works in a small sample doesn't mean more will work in a larger sample." He paused before adding quietly. "But it's the only thing we can do."

"Then do it," Kasprzyk said as he stormed off.

David peered intently at Michael, measuring him. Michael returned his former friend's gaze as calmly as he could despite the blood thudding through his temples. Finally, David shrugged and turned to follow Kasprzyk to the office.

"Thank you," Julia whispered.

"I'll fix this," Michael said, "but if you interfere again, I'll kill you myself."

Thirty-one

―∽∽∽―

"**I**s it finished?" David asked the next morning.

Michael closed his eyes and forced his exhausted brain to estimate, once more, how long it would take to reach a microbial count that could destroy the oil reserves in Saudi Arabia and Russia. He had not slept all night, unwilling to leave Julia alone with the culture; roaming the tables, ceaselessly checking and re-checking the bottles, stir rates and microbial counts. The last stage had taken longer than expected because of Julia's treachery, but it seemed to be working.

"Is it finished?" David asked again.

Michael frowned as he noticed David's flushed cheeks and watery eyes. His former friend had lost another argument with Kasprzyk and spent the past several hours drinking in the break room.

"I'd like another four or five hours to be sure."

"You don't have it," David said, loudly and belligerently.

David was drunk, and, when he was drunk, Michael knew from their days at Notre Dame, David liked to pick fights.

"How much time do I have?"

"One hour."

"There's going to be a significant failure rate when the culture is inserted into the oil reserves. Even under the best of circumstances, a significant percentage of the microbes will die. You want the culture as large as possible, which means we need as much time as possible."

"You have one hour," David replied firmly.

"Then it'll be finished in one hour."

David dropped heavily onto the stool next to Michael's. The astringent zing of scotch sweating out of his pores turned Michael's stomach.

"Tell me again what happens next," David demanded.

"We transfer the culture into the containers that we will use to transport it to the insertion point." Michael raised his hands in the air in frustration. "From there, I don't have a clue because you haven't told me how we're transporting this and, most importantly, how we're inserting the microbes into the reservoirs."

David glanced at Julia.

"Why isn't she helping you?"

Michael shrugged, a bit too nonchalantly.

"I wanted to handle this last stage myself since it's my family's life on the line."

"Her life's on the line, too."

As Michael turned back to the computer screen, David cast a hard look at Julia.

"I've been wondering about you," he said.

"You've been drinking," she replied, wrinkling her nose. "That's none of your business," David said. He cocked his head in thought.

"Michael and I have been friends a long time," he began.

Julia folded her arms and glared at him.

"I have a hard time imagining Michael being friends with you."

David jerked a thumb toward Michael.

"He's not so different from me. Neither of us trusts anyone and we both prefer to work alone," he said, wobbling slightly as he stood up too quickly. He quickly regained his balance, backing Julia into the lab table, "Which makes me wonder why he's working with you."

One of the guards sniggered as David looked the scientist up and down.

"But then, maybe the answer is obvious."

"Leave her alone," Michael said as Julia turned purple.

David turned to Michael with a look of undisguised glee.

"And this guy," he said, poking Michael in the chest, "is not the hero you think he is."

Thirty-two

"I don't need to listen to you," Julia said as she tried to wriggle past David, but he blocked her.

"Does anyone at that college of yours know what happened when he was a kid?" David asked.

"He came from a dysfunctional home," Julia replied. "He lost his family when he was young, picked himself up, got a great education, and became a success, unlike you."

David's knowing grin turned Michael cold. He'd never told David about his childhood. He'd never told anyone.

What does he think he knows?

"That's a nice, smooth story, but the truth's got a lot more sharp edges, doesn't it, Michael?" David replied.

When Michael remained silent, David began pacing. Julia's eyes followed, but Michael refused to look at him, nervously pecking at the keyboard.

"Despite how long we've known each other, despite all the times we had each other's back, Michael never told me anything. In case you hadn't noticed, he's not big on sharing his feelings," David said. The gloating in his voice set Michael's teeth on edge. The two guards had inched closer, sensing a confrontation in the offing.

"But The Global Group has intelligence assets you can't even dream of," David continued. "And they did their homework on Michael McKeon. They knew everything about Michael; things I never knew. But they made sense, completed the picture, if you know what I mean."

"I don't know and I don't care," Julia said.

"I'll start with his father," David said, ignoring her. Michael balled his hands.

"Michael's father disappeared when he was a few years old. He was killed two years later in a knife fight in a bar in Boston. A loser, like my old man, right, Michael?" When he received no response, David continued. "His mother was the real mess, though. Drug addict. Cocaine and heroin, but mostly meth."

The guards had crept closer. With Kaszpryk in the office, the only sounds were the constant whir of the stir-bars and the hum of the air conditioning. David had everyone's undivided attention, and he ate it up.

"No food or money. They lived in a filthy brick walk-up. I actually checked it out this last time in Maine. Have you ever been back, Michael?" When Michael continued to stare at the laptop, David smiled again. "I wouldn't blame you for staying away. It's still a hellhole. No father, but a string of boyfriends, or clients, for mom, none of whom stayed longer than it took to get high and have sex. She was arrested several times for prostitution, although she was doing it more for drugs than money."

Julia's eyes flicked to Michael, who had turned pale.

"Here's the first real kicker," David continued, thrusting the knife in. "When he was twelve, he found his mother dead, overdosed on the kitchen floor with a needle still hanging out of her arm."

Julia gasped and turned to Michael, who hadn't blinked or moved since David had begun speaking.

"Her boyfriend of the moment was barely conscious in the bedroom." David dropped his voice. "Now here's where things get interesting for our hero."

David's speech was clearer. The malicious pleasure he was taking from humiliating Michael had burned the alcohol from his system. Michael closed his eyes.

"It took a lot of work, but The Global Group found that boyfriend. He told one tremendous story. See, Michael knew that, with his mother dead, the state would place him in a foster home, but he didn't want to go, so he found the boyfriend's gun, jammed it into his ear, and forced the boyfriend to drive him and his mother's body to a park in Portland, where they left her body. Since she had no identification on her, they couldn't trace her back to Michael."

"He dumped his mother's dead body?" Adrian the guard asked, drawn in by the story. Julia felt sick.

"Yes, but, in Michael's defense, he was trying to protect his sister. Janie was her name, right, Michael? And Janie was already addicted to meth, too, thanks to their mother."

"Their mother gave her drugs?" the other guard asked.

"Their mother wasn't much for sharing," David replied, twisting the knife deeper. "She traded Janie for drugs. Once Janie was hooked, they made quite a pair."

Julia slumped onto a stool. Michael still gave no impression of having heard a thing, other than the slow tapping of his fingers.

"After his mother died, Michael kept that gun and warned the drug pushers who stopped by that he would kill them if they touched Janie. He tried to get her into detox, begged and pleaded and threatened her, and finally she agreed to clean herself up. She lasted a couple weeks, but, one day, Michael came back to their apartment and found his sister tied to her bed, naked. Her body was already cold. Someone had given her a lethal dose of heroin."

Michael swayed on his stool as David moved in for the kill.

"After finding his sister, Michael searched for her killer. It took him three weeks, but he found the dealer, a small-time gang-banger from Portland, a mule for a heroin smuggling ring, running drugs from Massachusetts into Maine. Michael had chased him away from Janie before. Now, I don't know for sure what happened, but the Portland police found the mule tied to his bed. Someone had taped a sock in his mouth so he couldn't scream, then smashed each of his fingers and toes with a hammer before shooting him between the eyes. The police thought it was a drug deal gone bad, but . . ."

David's voice trailed off, having claimed its victim.

Julia wiped tears as she turned away, nauseous, uncertain whether she wanted to throw her arms around Michael, or run away.

Michael continued to stare at the floor, stone-faced and silent, as his fingers typed an unknown message on his legs. David hesitated. He'd expected some kind of reaction from Michael; a fight, one he knew he could win under these circumstances. But Michael's silence unnerved him. Finally, he gave up.

"One hour. That's all you have," he said as he stomped off to the break room.

As Michael's fingers pounded out an ever-faster staccato, the two guards exchanged nervous glances, checking their weapons as they returned to their posts. They had seen faces like Michael's before, on men they had served with and against in merciless jungles and deserts around the world; desperate men who had lost everything.

It was the face of a man about to kill.

Thirty-three

━━◁∾∾▷━━

Sweat dripped from Michael's brow as he darted from container to computer, monitoring growth rates and gas outputs. Julia kept a wary distance from his feverish intensity. She could tell he was running from the ghosts David had set loose, panicked that he would add to their numbers if he failed. She checked her watch as David and Kasprzyk barged onto the floor.

"It's only been thirty minutes," she said.

"Police are back," David replied. "Time's up."

Julia cast a stricken look at Michael, who ignored the men as he continued typing on the keyboard.

"Finish the transfer, Michael," David said. "We have to go."

Michael tried to dart to the last row of containers, but David grabbed his arm. Michael wrenched it free with a violent shove, sending David stumbling backwards.

"I'm not done," he growled.

"Yes you are," Kasprzyk snapped, motioning to Adrian, who stepped toward the scientist. The guard never saw Michael's fist coming. It crashed into his nose with a sickening splat, splitting the skin and sending blood squirting into the air. Adrian roared in pain, covering the misshapen blob with his hands while Pete swung his rifle toward the back of Michael's head.

Michael ducked and kicked backwards, snapping the guard's knee sideways with an ugly tearing of cartilage and tendon. As the second guard fell to the floor, grasping his knee in agony, Kasprzyk and the bloodied Pete landed on Michael, pinning him to the concrete.

148

"I'm not done!" Michael shouted, thrashing against the man. Pete smashed his fist into the scientist's face again and again, but Michael continued yelling through a mouth filling with blood that he needed more time.

"Stop!" Julia screamed. "Stop!"

David clamped a hand over her mouth, but she stepped into him, driving her elbow into his ribs with a satisfying crunch. Then she swept his legs out, but before she could help Michael, Kasprzyk had rolled off him and drawn his Makarov.

"We don't have time for this," Kasprzyk panted. Pete and Julia froze while David picked himself up, rubbing his ribs and glaring at Julia. Several feet away, Adrian rocked sideways, holding his injured knee and groaning. A barely conscious Michael coughed up blood and several teeth. Kasprzyk grabbed his shirt and shoved him at Pete. "Take him to the break room."

Then he rose and kicked Adrian in the back.

"Get up. You and David take her." He pointed the gun at Julia. "It's time to end this."

With a baleful glare at Kasprzyk, Adrian limped toward Julia and shoved her toward the break room. Pete yanked a groggy Michael to his feet and frog-marched him behind.

"What's going on, David?" Julia demanded. "We had a deal. We provide you with the culture and you let Milla and Katya and us go free." Michael stumbled as Pete gave him a hard shove between the shoulder blades. They had almost reached the break room. "You still need us to transport and insert the culture!" she pleaded. "You can't do it without us!"

David and Kasprzyk waited by the refrigerator while the two guards propelled the scientists across the room toward the cots. Pete and Adrian stood several feet away from the scientists, guns up.

"You need us," Julia said, holding Michael upright by the arm. "Please don't do this."

"Shut up," Kasprzyk snapped.

Without warning, David and Kasprzyk opened fire.

Thirty-four

―⦿⦿⦿―

Moscow

Colonel Akhmetalin stirred in annoyance in the back seat of his armored Mercedes S600L as his cell phone rang. He recognized the number and checked to make sure that the soundproof window between him and the driver was closed before answering. Akhmetalin had the car regularly swept for eavesdropping devices and was as confident as it was possible to be in Russia that no one was listening.

The colonel was already in a bad mood. Traffic on the *Rublyovskoye Schosse*, or *Rublyovka*, as Muscovites had nicknamed it, was even worse than usual. *Rublyovka* connected Moscow to the *cottedgi*, five-story country homes belonging to the elite, including Putin himself, tucked in the birches outside the city limits. Akhmetalin had acquired one of the *cottedgi*, but had to suffer through the interminable traffic jams to reach it, unlike Putin and his allies.

"*Dobray ootra*, Vadim. Am I disturbing you?"

Akhmetalin's spine stiffened.

"No, Mr. First Deputy."

First Deputy Aleksandr Yakovlev was Akhmetalin's superior and reported to the Director of the FSB. Yakovlev was the enforcer of order and accountability at FSB Headquarters and his temper was legendary. Akhmetalin had witnessed him once nearly beat a junior officer to death with his metal waste basket.

"Are you coming to the office today?" Yakovlev asked, his voice smooth and controlled.

"Yes sir. I'm currently stuck on *Rublyovka*."

Yakovlev made a guttural noise.

"I recall that being most trying. It's much easier now that they stop traffic for the Director and for me."

Akhmetalin bit his lip.

"I was wondering if you could stop by my office when you arrive? I have a few questions."

"I am always honored to meet with you, First Deputy, but is it essential? I will be very busy all day."

"This won't take long." Yakovlev's voice suddenly dropped twenty degrees. "And, yes, it is essential."

After the First Deputy ended the call, Akhmetalin slumped in his seat, a cold sweat on his forehead. With a violent shake of his head, the colonel steeled himself. It was for precisely this situation that Akhmetalin had kept an ace up his sleeve. He had someone who could persuade even Putin to call off the dogs.

Thirty-five

———⟨❦⟩———

Approaching the Ghuweifat Checkpost on the Saudi Arabia/U.A.E. Border

"Why did you shoot the two guards?" Julia demanded as they sped toward the Saudi border in their new vehicle, a silver Range Rover.

"We didn't need them anymore," Kasprzyk replied. "Soon, the entire Saudi security system will make sure you two stay close to us."

Julia shuddered, shaken by the massacre she had just witnessed, but relieved to still be alive. David tossed a manila envelope to her and to Michael.

"That's your new identity. I burned the Canadian passports we used to enter the U.A.E."

Julia took Michael's and dumped it, along with hers, into her lap. She took a careful look at Michael, who had one ice pack pressed to the back of his neck and another to the right side of his face. Before loading the culture into the Range Rover, she had grabbed the first aid kit. After slipping past the Ruwais police, she had helped Michael clean himself as much as possible. He'd lost two teeth and the right side of his face was turning a nauseating greenish purple.

He'd been frighteningly quiet since the break room. Julia tried to catch his eye, his good eye, but Michael stared resolutely out the window. She pursed her lips in frustration. They had worked together for less than a year and, other than what Hal had told her, Michael was still a mystery. She couldn't tell what he was thinking,

but one thing was clear: hatred burned from him. He was radioac-
tive. She guessed that David felt it too, judging by the cautious looks
he kept throwing their way. And she was still thrown by what David
had revealed about Michael's past. She wondered if Hal knew what
his golden boy was capable of. She'd seen it first hand, in the way
that he had fought both guards. She had no doubt that he would
have killed them, not that she would have blamed him.

Feeling David's eyes on her, she returned to the pile of docu-
ments on her lap and picked out their two passports: American.

"The four of us work as Photo Unit Staff for Saudi Aramco's
Public Affairs Digital Image Archives, or PADIA," David explained.
"It's located in Houston and is one of the world's largest archives
specializing in contemporary images of the Middle East and the Islamic world." He pointed at Julia. "You're his wife." He shrugged
at the sharp look she shot him. "It's Saudi Arabia. A single woman
would cause problems."

"I don't know anything about photography," Julia said.

"Point and click," Kasprzyk snapped from the front seat.

David ignored both of them.

"Tonight, Aramco is throwing a huge party and retrospective
honoring the 75th anniversary of the first crude oil tanker leaving
the Kingdom. We'll be there to photograph it."

"Where's the celebration?" Julia asked.

"At Aramco's oil processing facilities at Abqaiq. Are you familiar
with it?"

"A little," Julia replied.

"One of the largest oil fields in the world is located at Abqaiq,"
David said. "It has 17 billion barrels of proven reserves. Just as important, 70 percent of all Saudi crude oil is stabilized at Abqaiq,
nearly five million barrels a day, with capacity of more than 7 million
barrels."

"What do you mean 'stabilized'?" Julia asked.

"They remove dissolved gas from the crude oil to stabilize it so
it can be stored or moved through a pipeline at simple atmospheric

pressure. The crude can then be transported. Oil goes to export terminals in *Ras Tanura, Ras al-Juaymah,* and many others. It's also connected to the *Shaybah* oil fields via a 395-mile pipeline. *Shaybah* has another 14 billion barrels in reserves."

David halted for a moment to catch his breath. The pupils in his eyes had expanded in excitement, turning his eyes black.

"With its own reserves, its pumping stations, gas–oil separator plants, and pipelines to the other fields, Abqaiq is pivotal to Saudi oil production and export capacity," David continued, his voice shaking with exhilaration. "We chose this as the insertion point because. . . ."

"Because the microbes could spread not only through Abqaiq's oil reservoir, but through the pipelines into the other reservoirs," Julia interrupted. "And, it could also contaminate any oil processed at Abqaiq. If it hits all those . . ." Her voice trailed away.

David finished the thought with undisguised glee.

"If it hits all those, it will destroy all Saudi oil."

Julia was thunderstruck by the simple audacity of their plan. The Saudi oil behemoth was a modern-day Hydra. Because of its redundant security systems and multiple oil fields, each with their own staggering capacity, Saudi Arabia could absorb almost any strike and come back stronger. Yet The Global Group had found its Achilles' heel. If they successfully inserted the microbes, they could destroy Saudi Arabia's oil.

Michael had been quiet for so long that his voice caused her to jump.

"That's why you needed such a large quantity of microbes," he whispered, more to himself than to anyone else.

"That's right."

A shocked silence filled the middle seat as Michael and Julia contemplated the unprecedented attack they were about to unleash.

"How do we do it?" Julia asked in a small, tight voice.

"Before the anniversary party begins, we'll photograph the entire installation," David explained. "We have two targets. The first target is the series of water pumps that pump deoxygenated water into the Abqaiq oil reserves to maintain enough pressure so that they can continue extracting the oil."

"What's the second target?" Michael asked as dusk settled over the desert speeding past. Julia glanced at him curiously. Wherever he had gone, he was now back.

"The pipelines from other fields empty into a giant holding tank. If we inject the inoculum into the tank, it'll contaminate the entire processing facility and also push out through the pipelines into the sending fields," David finished.

"Shut up and get ready," Kasprzyk said. He jabbed a thumb toward Julia. "There's an *abaya* and headscarf on the floor. Put them on."

"Why?"

"We're at the border."

Julia shot a murderous glance at the front seat as she pulled the black cloak from the floor and slipped it over her shoulders then covered her hair with a scarf.

"It's hot in this thing," she muttered.

The occupants of the Range Rover fell silent as Kasprzyk pulled into a line of vehicles waiting to pass through the Ghuweifat Checkpost, a narrow strip of asphalt in the middle of the desert that consisted of a few flat buildings and a mammoth parking lot.

"The last time I was here, a bureaucratic dispute between Saudi Arabia and the U.A.E. over fingerprinting requirements stranded thousands of truck drivers for days," David said.

Michael and Julia counted the ten vehicles ahead of them.

"Thank God we're not stuck in that," she replied.

As they reached the border, the other three occupants handed their passports to Kasprzyk who passed them through the open window to the border guard along with their visas. As the guard flipped through them, he motioned for them to roll down their windows. David and Kasprzyk had already prepared the necessary paperwork declaring the "photographic equipment" in the back of the Range Rover.

"What happened to your face?" the guard asked Michael.

"Fell in the bathroom," Michael replied ruefully.

Michael waited breathlessly as the border guard compared his passport to his face for a long moment before finally stamping it. He cast a quick glance at Julia, sitting rigidly as her eyes tracked the approaching guards. Suddenly, she slid next to him and took his hand. Michael started in surprise. Caramel-flecked eyes peered out of the *abaya*, locking onto his.

"We're supposed to be married," she whispered. Then, leaning closer, she said even more softly: "I'm sorry about your mother and sister and I'm sorry about what I said before. You're right. Whatever it takes to save Milla and Katya, I'm in."

The guard handed Julia's passport to Michael and smiled. Michael nodded at him and Kasprzyk raised the windows as the guard waved them on. Julia's hand lingered on his, giving a final squeeze, before she slid back to her side.

Just then, two other border guards bolted from the nearest station and raced toward the Range Rover, guns drawn.

"Stop!"

Thirty-six

Michael's heart leapt into his throat as the two guards sprinted toward them. Kasprzyk swore under his breath and tightened his hands on the steering wheel. The car in front of them had stopped also, blocking them in. Michael looked over his shoulder at the line of vehicles in back of them. They were trapped.

"Stop!" the guards yelled again.

Kasprzyk's hand dropped towards the backpack on the floor between the two front seats. Michael knew that he and Kenner had stashed their weapons in that bag. *Oh no,* he thought. *After everything I did to make the culture, is this how it's going to end? A shootout in the desert?*

As the two guards reached the Range Rover, Kasprzyk plunged his hand into the backpack and pulled out his gun. In a blink, the two guards ran past toward five men in white *thobes* sitting in a circle on the asphalt and chanting. Four other guards joined the two and began to drag the five men toward the barracks.

"I'll be damned," David breathed.

Kasprzyk hastily dropped the gun into the backpack as the first guard rapped on his window for him to move along. He slipped the Range Rover into gear and pulled ahead.

"What was that?" Michael asked.

"Protesters, I think," David replied.

"What were they protesting?" Michael asked.

"I'm not sure, but I think they were truckers protesting the fingerprinting requirements I mentioned."

The four sat in silence as the Range Rover plowed northwest on Highway 85 into the Empty Quarter, or *Rub-al-Khali*, in Saudi Arabia's Eastern Province. Julia, who had loosened the *abaya*, flashed a warm smile before closing her eyes in exhaustion. Michael drained a bottle of water as he gazed awestruck at the rippling, ochre-colored chains of sand dunes jutting hundreds of feet into the air. He realized that the four of them were unwelcome intruders in one of the most inhospitable parts of the earth, and said a silent prayer of thanks for the Range Rover's air conditioning and the cooler of bottled water at his feet. The unforgiving desert reminded him that he had cheated death several times already.

As he reached for another bottle, he prayed that his luck wouldn't run out.

Thirty-seven

―◦◦◦―

Moscow

Longfellow hung up and joined Melissa at the window of their dilapidated hotel room on *Ylitsa Obraztsova*, looking out on an old bus station that had been converted into a modern art gallery on Moscow's northern side. A rickety metal scaffolding enveloped the *Zolotaya Ptitsa*, or Golden Bird, creaking and groaning in the wind, waiting for the workers' return, a possibility the exasperated desk clerk had placed somewhere between remote and laughable. Traffic was light on the *Obraztsova* at this midday hour.

"See anything?" he asked.

"Nothing. I think we're clean."

"The desk clerk didn't bat an eye when we handed him the passports Grisha's friend procured for us," Longfellow said. "Do you think the NSA would send bulletins out for us?"

"No, they wouldn't publicize the problem," Melissa replied. "Even if they did, it's doubtful they'd reach a dive like this one."

She cracked her neck and rubbed red eyes.

"What did you find out?"

"They got Grisha away. He's awake and mad as hell. He's going after Akhmetalin."

"That's not smart," Melissa said.

"He thinks Akhematalin may be our best link to Michael's family. He told us to focus on finding Michael."

Melissa examined the mottled bedspread, then the stained chair, before deciding to remain standing.

"Which brings us back to our conversation on the way here," she said. "Michael has probably finished the culture, which means we're out of time. No one has successfully attacked the Saudi oil infrastructure. It can't be done, and if they catch him, they'll kill him."

"I'm not ready to sign off on this yet," Longfellow protested as the phone rang again. "What do you have, Jigger?"

"I analyzed the best targets in the Saudi oil infrastructure for the insertion of McKeon's microbes, like you asked," Jigger replied, a little breathlessly. "There are thousands of targets, hundreds that you might call prime."

"But?"

"But, setting aside security concerns, there's one spot that would give maximum effect; one spot with significant reserves and where nearly three-quarters of all Saudi crude oil is stabilized."

"Abqaiq," Longfellow breathed, dropping onto the bedspread in despair.

"Right, Abqaiq," Jigger continued. "If they could insert the microbes at Abqaiq, they could contaminate Abqaiq's billions of barrels of reserves, but, more importantly, they could contaminate all oil processed at that facility. And, if it spread through the pipelines to the other fields, they could destroy virtually all of Saudi Arabia's oil. But . . ."

"But Abqaiq is a death sentence," Longfellow finished.

"It's the most secure facility in the entire Saudi oil infrastructure. And it's not like they could just blast through the gates. They need up-close and personal access to insert the culture, and nobody gets that."

"Thanks, Jigger," Longfellow said, ending the call. He let the phone slip through his fingers onto the bed then covered his eyes. Melissa remained silent for several long moments before sitting next to her former mentor.

"Don't talk to me about our country's national interests, Melissa," he warned through his hands. "I don't give a shit right now."

"I won't," she said quietly.

"This is personal."

"I know."

"If I make the call, The Global Group will kill Milla and Katya."

"We don't know if they're even alive."

She held up a hand as Longfellow began to argue the point.

"If you don't make the call, Michael will die," Melissa said.

"He'd prefer that."

"That's why it's not his choice. And don't forget Julia."

"I haven't," Longfellow snapped.

After another long silence, Longfellow reached for the phone.

"He'll never forgive me."

"That's the price we pay."

Thirty-eight

—◦—

Abqaiq

As they pounded through the pitiless desert under the early after-noon sun, Michael tapped David on the shoulder.

"What do you want?" David snapped.

"My second phone call."

David shook his head.

"There's no time. We're almost to Abqaiq."

"Make time. Or I don't insert the culture."

David glared at Michael then looked to Kasprzyk, who swore loudly. Kasprzyk kept one hand on the wheel as he pulled his cell phone from his pocket and punched in a code. Michael noted which buttons he pressed. Kasprzyk held the phone to his ear.

"Director, the professor wants to speak with his wife again."

Kasprzyk placed the phone on the console between the two front seats and pressed the speaker phone button.

"Milla?"

"She's coming," Kasprzyk answered.

Michael waited impatiently as the cell phone emitted a continu-ous soft hiss. His heartbeat quickened at what sounded like uneven, stumbling footsteps followed by a sliding sound, as if someone was being frog-walked against their will. Then, the connection severed with a violent abruptness. Michael lunged for the phone, but Kasprzyk grabbed it and pocketed it.

"Get her back!" Michael demanded.

"No can do, buddy," David said, pointing a finger at the windshield. "We're here."

Thirty-nine

———⟪⟫———

Kasprzyk slid the gearshift on the Range Rover into park and the four occupants held their breath as they waited for the Abqaiq security guards to finish with the vehicle in front of them.

"The Saudi government spends more than $10 billion on security each year. Helicopters and F-15 patrols run around the clock as do heavily armed National Guard battalions," David explained quietly. "There are 25,000 to 30,000 troops protecting the Kingdom's oil infrastructure. Each terminal and platform has its own specialized security unit, made up of 5,000 Saudi Aramco security forces, and an unknown number of specialized units of the National Guard and the Ministry of Interior, but nowhere is security tighter than at Abqaiq."

David swallowed a long gulp of water. The guards were almost finished.

"There are three layers of security here at Abqaiq. The first is here at the gates and the security fence that encircles the entire compound. Then there's a second tier about one mile away from the closest facility. The Saudi Arabian National Guard operates large caliber machine guns mounted on armored personal carriers. If anyone made it past those first two layers, they would still have to get by an elite counter-terrorism squad from the Special Emergency Forces."

"Has anyone ever made it past all three layers?" Julia asked.

"No. The closest anyone's ever gotten was a few years ago, when a group of al-Qaeda affiliates we helped to fund blasted through this gate with a car filled with explosives. A second car made it through the hole in the fence opened by the first car, but exploded at the second tier."

David shot a cocky grin over his left shoulder.

"But there's always a first time for everything."

"What if they search the camera cases?" Michael asked. Kasprzyk ignored him and rolled down his window. The nearest guard motioned for the others to do the same. Scorching hot air blasted through the vehicle, overwhelming the air conditioner. Michael's and Julia's bodies had still not adjusted to the hellish heat. The back of Michael's shirt was instantly soaked with sweat. Julia gasped, desperate for the traces of oxygen not already baked out of the air.

The four handed their passports, invitations and credentials through the window. David had assured them that the Director would make certain their names were on the list for the night's celebration. *We'll find out shortly*, Michael thought grimly.

"You are here to photograph tonight's celebration?" the guard asked Kasprzyk as the other guard eyed the occupants suspiciously. Another two guards checked underneath the vehicle for explosives.

"That's right. We're from PADIA."

The guard nodded to the silver Zero Halliburton camera cases stacked in the back of the Range Rover.

"And that is your equipment?"

"Yes."

"Open it, please."

With a slightly annoyed expression, Kasprzyk pressed a button to unlock the rear door and then slowly stepped out of the vehicle. David did the same and followed Kasprzyk to the rear. The four guards formed a cautious half-circle around the rear of the vehicle, with three watching Kasprzyk and David and the fourth keeping a wary eye on Michael and Julia. Michael kept his gaze level and slightly bored as he listened to the scrape of the heat-tempered aluminum cases being removed and placed on the ground. There were sixteen in all. The lead guard stopped them after half were removed.

"Enough. Open them. Slowly."

Michael held his breath as, one after another, each camera case was opened with a double click of its draw-bolt latches. After an agonizingly long wait, the lead guard finally spoke.

"Both of you, take out a camera and take a picture of each other."

"Look, we really have to get going so we can set up," David protested.

"Do it now!"

A minor amount of grumbling reached Michael's ears before the soft shutters of the digital cameras clicked.

"Do it again, with those two cameras over there."

Footsteps shuffled. Then another set of shutters clicked.

"What is in those cases over there?"

Michael could not see what was happening behind their vehicle, but he could picture the guards inspecting each of the opened cases.

"Strobe lights," Kasprzyk answered.

"And in those?"

"Some specialized lenses."

The lead guard must have picked up a lens because David suddenly stammered: "Please be careful. Those are very delicate and very expensive. And we need it for tonight."

Michael glimpsed the other two guards positioned approximately three feet off each end of the rear bumper, weapons drawn, tense. The guard outside his window had not moved. Michael glanced at Julia, who was staring fixedly out the window. He could feel the tension radiating off her in waves. He hoped the guard wasn't picking up on her anxiety.

Finally, Michael heard the words they had been waiting for.

"Fine. Pack it back up and move on."

As quickly as possible, without appearing to hurry, Kasprzyk and David closed up the cases and replaced them in the back of the

Range Rover. With a curt nod to the guards, Kasprzyk slid into the driver's seat. As soon as David had returned, he popped the transmission into drive and pulled through the gate into Abqaiq.

"So far so good," David muttered under his breath.

But they still had to clear the National Guard and the Special Emergency Forces.

Forty

——❦——

Abqaiq and Moscow

Sa'id al-Naimi, the highest ranking security officer in the General Intelligence Presidency, or *Re'asat Al Istikhbarat Al A'amah*, looked like a man about to scream. A few inches taller than five feet and of slight build, al-Naimi's delicate features, closely trimmed beard and mustache, and small, round spectacles gave him the appearance of a nervous accountant, but the man in charge of foreign intelligence for the Saudi government, including all foreign covert networks and anti-terrorism efforts, had survived more gunfights and terrorist plots than any man had a right to.

Yet, for all of al-Naimi's control and reserve, at this moment, he *was* ready to scream. Or kill someone. He had spent months planning the security for Abqaiq's 75th Anniversary Celebration with the National Guard, Special Emergency Forces and Aramco's own personnel. He had chased down dozens of terrorist threats to the event, most of which vaporized like thin mist, but a few of which were serious. He had personally interrogated two al-Qaeda operatives, one of whom survived.

With guests from around the world wanting to tromp around Abqaiq and the Crown Prince himself coming, security was a nightmare. His phone had rung seven times in the past ten minutes, and those were the calls that his junior officers had not already screened and resolved. He glanced around the workstations jammed into the

168

Abqaiq Area Emergency Control Center, which reeked of bitter coffee and sweat. Tension radiated off the Aramco and SANG personnel monitoring the phones and computers that would indicate any emergency or supply disruption at Abqaiq or anywhere in Aramco's network. An eddy of agitated voices swirled around pockets of grim silence.

He checked his messages. Requests for further information from the SEF and the National Guard. More ominously, a message from Prince Mugrin bin Abdulaziz, his immediate superior, asking him to call immediately.

In the midst of this turmoil, his personal cell phone rang. He checked the display and froze. This could not be good news.

"*As-salaamu 'alaykum,* Agent Longfellow," al-Naimi said in a strained, hushed voice. "Peace be upon you."

"*Wa `alaykum a-salām,* Assistant Sa'id," Longfellow responded.

"Forgive my rudeness, but this is not a good time," al-Naimi said.

"I have information about an imminent threat to your country," Longfellow said.

Al-Naimi pinched the bridge of his nose.

"How imminent?"

"Before we hang up."

Al-Naimi stepped into a small office off the Control Center floor and shut the door.

"Tell me."

"Forgive my rudeness, but two friends of mine are involved against their will. They are being held hostage and I must demand a condition."

"What condition?"

"Safe passage for both to America."

"That is a condition I may not be able to grant."

"Then our conversation is finished."

"Wait."

Al-Naimi grimaced in frustration. He had known the American spy called Longfellow for many years, most recently sharing information about Iran's covert nuclear program. As much as was possible in their world, he trusted Longfellow.

"Fine. I agree."

"Your word?"

"My word."

Sitting on the stained bed in the sad, disheveled hotel room in Moscow, with his head bowed in frustration, Longfellow took a deep breath, and gave up Michael McKeon.

Forty-one

Abqaiq

"We're lucky that they didn't check the foam inserts in the cases," David exclaimed as Kasprzyk parked the Range Rover. "Hiding bladders of the culture inside the foam inserts was ingenious, if I say so myself. Five cases for each of the targets here should carry enough microbes, leaving six cases to be carried to our next target in Russia."

"Where are we?" Julia asked.

"Immediately ahead of us is the de-oxygenation facility," David replied, pointing at the windshield.

Michael leaned his cheek against the window to get a better look, then instantly pulled away. The super-heated glass had nearly burned his skin. He craned his neck, careful to avoid touching the window.

"It's huge!" Julia exclaimed.

A gunmetal gray silo thrust up into the evening sky before them. One large pipe, wide enough for a grown man to sit up in, connected the tower to a holding tank approximately a half mile away. Smaller pipes, still large enough for a grown man to crawl through, stretched out like tentacles from the tower's base in all directions.

"Water is stored in that holding tank in the distance," David explained. "That big pipe is the input from the tank. Those smaller pipes carry the de-oxygenated water out to the injection pumps scattered across this site."

"How does it work?" Michael asked.

"The water is blasted with nitrogen gas, which strips away the oxygen."

"So we need to inject the culture into the water on its way out of the facility," Michael said. "If we inject it before it's de-oxygenated, the oxygen will kill the microbes."

"Precisely," David said.

"But what happens when the inoculum hits the oil and starts to use up the nitrogen?" Michael asked. "How will it continue to grow in order to consume all the oil?"

David smiled.

"Older oil reservoirs, like the Saudi ones, have had so much oil pumped out that the pressure inside them has decreased significantly. Like many oil companies, Aramco pumps in water to increase pressure and drive out the oil. We replaced the water with nitrogen-infused seawater and have an agent inside Aramco making sure the doctored water isn't noticed."

"And as along as the nitrogen keeps pumping in, the microbes will grow and destroy the entire reservoir," Michael finished, marveling at the deviousness of it all.

"Precisely."

"Time to go," Kasprzyk barked.

As the four occupants opened their doors, the deafening roar of the pumping water immediately filled their ears. The midday sun was at its most ferocious, with searing heat radiating off the desert floor in shimmering waves. Michael's eyes watered as he fought to breathe. While Kasprzyk opened the rear hatch, David directed Michael's attention to a platform halfway up the facility.

"That's the service platform," he shouted, struggling to be heard. "There's a door they use to access the tower for maintenance. You'll enter there while the three of us take pictures and keep watch. We stole the schematics for this place. Climb the walkway to the top. There's a kill switch there to stop the inflow of water. Flip it. Then haul ass down to the bottom. You'll find a filter. The de-oxygenated water flows through that filter as it exits. There's a pressurized valve after the filter. You'll use that valve to inject the culture. Once the water is turned back on, it will carry the microbes through the smaller pipes to the injection pumps and into the reservoir."

Michael hoisted two cases. David grabbed two and Julia picked up one. Kasprzyk kept his hands free to reach for his weapon. The four set off for the building, approximately twenty yards away.

"Won't they notice that I've shut off the water?"

David nodded.

"They'll notice it in their control center, but momentary hiccups happen frequently. Anything more than two minutes trips an alarm and they'll investigate."

"Are you crazy? Two minutes to shut off the water, climb down, find the filter, empty all five bladders onto the filter, climb back up and turn the water back on?"

"Do your job," Kasprzyk barked. "You know the consequences of failure."

David and Kasprzyk waved as an armored National Guard Humvee rumbled past. For good measure, David snapped a few pictures of the Humvee. Michael shot a quick glance at Julia. Her eyes glittered like fiery jewels. Now that they had reached their first target, he felt an irresistible need to talk to her, to reassure her and himself that he had no choice, and that everything would work out. But Kasprzyk gave him no time to talk, shoving him toward the metal steps as soon as the SANG Humvee disappeared in the direction of the holding tank.

"Get going."

Michael scrambled up as quickly as possible, followed by David and Julia, with Kasprzyk behind, leaving a safe distance between him and Julia. Sweat poured out of Michael from the small exertion of climbing the stairs. As Kasprzyk stepped onto the service platform, Michael turned and spotted the access hatch. He pulled on some work gloves that David handed him and yanked the handle upwards. The door opened with a metal screech and he ducked through into the semi-darkness.

Michael took a moment to orient himself in the dim, yellow light. He was standing on a metal catwalk. To his right, a ladder ran the length of the building. Directly in front of him, an enclosed metal cylinder hummed. A blizzard of appendages connected the interior tower with the exterior shell. Michael presumed that the de-oxygenation occurred within this inner tower.

His sweat-soaked clothes clung to him in the thick, humid air inside the tower. David slipped a shoulder strap through the handles on the five cases and, with some effort, handed them to Michael, who groaned as he slipped the shoulder strap over his head. Together, the cases, loaded with camera equipment and the inoculum, weighed almost as much as he did. He stepped off the catwalk and onto the ladder. To maximize his two minutes, he planned to position the bladders near the filter, then climb back up the ladder, hand the cases to David then climb to the top to flip the kill switch.

Without warning, his foot slipped on a spot of condensation. Michael squeezed the rung with both hands, thankful for the rubberized grips on his gloves. Given how much he was sweating, if he had tried to hold on with his bare hands, he would have surely fallen.

Finally, Michael reached the bottom. With a sigh of relief, he slipped the shoulder strap off his aching shoulder and snapped open the cases, yanking out the molded foam bladders. He found the pressurized valve and, after picturing how the nipples on the bladders would fit into the valve, hoisted the strap onto his shoulder and climbed back up the ladder.

"Everything check out?" David asked as Michael dropped the cases onto the catwalk.

"So far," Michael panted. "Here goes everything."

He climbed up the ladder to the top of the tower, three stories off the ground. The air was even denser as the moisture collected on the tower's metal roof. He would not have been surprised if it had started to rain.

Michael found the kill switch right where David's stolen schematics said it would be and rested his hand on it for a long moment, trying to regulate his breathing, until he had reset his internal clock to zero. Then he pulled the switch.

Inside the Abqaiq Area Emergency Control Center, al-Naimi stared at his phone as the first beads of sweat appeared on his brow.

The phone call from Longfellow had sounded like science fiction. He was used to guns and bombs and the endlessly creative ways al-Qaeda and other terrorist organizations found to package and deliver them, but *oil-eating microbes*? Was a group of *scientists* really going to try to attack this facility? But he had known Longfellow for too many years to doubt his judgment. If he was worried, al-Naimi was worried.

He reached for the radio and flipped the comm switch.

—◈◈◈—

A red light flicked on as a giant shudder coursed through the de-oxygenation tower. Michael didn't wait, scrambling down the ladder as fast as he dared to go. He caught a glimpse of David's face framed in the access hatch, and then he was gone, on his way to the bottom. As he dropped onto the floor and reached for the first foam bladder, he stumbled and nearly fell. Black spots danced before his eyes. His heart was pumping so fast and the air was so thick that he was in danger of succumbing to hypoxia. He took several deep breaths through his nose and forced his thumping pulse to slow. He heard a scuff over his head and looked up. David had climbed part of the way down from the catwalk.

"I'm watching, Michael. Don't screw it up."

Michael turned away and grabbed the first bladder. He jabbed the nipple through the pressurized valve, relieved at the satisfying *snick* that indicated a proper seal. The bladders themselves were filled under pressure, so that once the nipple had entered the valve, the contents would gush out. Michael discarded the empty bladder and jammed another in its place.

"One minute!" David called.

Michael ground his teeth and willed the culture to flow faster. He dropped the second one and inserted the third. Then the fourth.

"One minute thirty seconds!"

"I'm not going to make it back to the top," Michael shouted. "You'll have to hit the kill switch for me."

"No can do. I'm watching you."

"You can watch me until the guards show up, or you can flip the switch when I yell to you. Your choice."

Michael dropped the fourth bladder and reached for the fifth.

"Fine!" David called. "But yell loud."

As David disappeared, Michael continued the count in his head. *One minute forty. One minute forty-five.*

"Come on," he muttered.

One minute fifty.

Done!

He dropped the last bladder and raced up the ladder.

"Pull it, David! Pull it!"

He heard no response.

"Pull it!"

Michael counted as he climbed.

One minute fifty-four. One minute fifty-five.

Finally, he felt the tower shudder as the metal cylinder began humming again. Michael collapsed on the catwalk and watched as David descended the ladder.

"You cut it awfully close," David warned.

"Shut up."

David motioned for Michael to climb through the access hatch and then followed. After the dim interior, the midday sun nearly blinded the squinting Michael.

"Did you do it?" Kasprzyk demanded.

"All five bladders with five seconds to spare," Michael panted.

"We'd better get out of here in case anyone comes to investigate," Kasprzyk said, checking his watch.

In the instant that his attention was diverted, Julia lunged.

Something flashed in her hand. It was the shard of glass she had been carrying since the airplane. Kasprzyk swung his arm to block her, a second too slow, as the shard dug a bloody trench across his forehead above his left eye. Kasprzyk's Yankees cap sailed over the railing as his head snapped back. Julia grabbed for his gun, but, snarling in pain, he back-handed her across the face, spinning her towards the access hatch. Michael moved to catch her before she fell down the tower. But as he reached for her, Kasprzyk's pistol barked.

Julia jerked in mid-air, her eyes widening in surprise. A crimson plume shot out of her chest as she slammed against the access door. As Kasprzyk shot again, David rammed a shoulder into Michael, knocking him to the floor. Michael stared in horror as the top of Julia's head exploded in a red mist of blood and bone. Without a sound, she toppled through the access door and disappeared into the dark interior.

"No!" Michael shouted.

David grabbed him and tried to wrestle him away, but Michael shoved him aside and crawled through the doorway. He couldn't see Julia. A red smear on the edge of the catwalk indicated where she had fallen. He jumped to his feet and spun angrily toward the two men, then froze, his chest heaving, as he stared down the barrels of two Makarovs.

"You killed her!"

"We warned you both not to try to escape," Kasprzyk said. A thick line of blood obscured his left eye.

"She screwed with the culture back at the lab," David added. "You covered for her, but I'm not stupid."

"I told you, if you lift one finger against any of us, I wouldn't help you."

Kasprzyk stepped forward menacingly.

"Yes you will, because you know the consequences. Now move."

Michael stood still for a long moment. He cast an angry and sorrowful glance at the tower. David and Kasprzyk had called his bluff in the most horrible way possible. They were right. He would do whatever they wanted to save his family.

"I'm sorry, Julia," he whispered. Then he stepped toward the stairs.

Forty-two

—⟨∿⟩—

A l-Naimi stepped out of the Center and surveyed his surroundings with the grim stare of a man used to looking for danger. A
desert wind had picked up unexpectedly, whipping sand into the air,
obscuring the midday sun as he lifted the radio to his lips.

"Has anyone seen a group of Americans or Europeans in any
part of the facility where they shouldn't be?" he asked all his units.

Unit after unit reported negative. Most of the guests were at the
reception hall, or visiting former homes in the *madina,* the small town
for the workers adjacent to the camp. Others were touring the elemen-
tary and middle schools, enjoying the swimming pools or tennis courts,
or getting in a few last holes on the 18-hole golf course, with its oiled-
sand fairways and greens made up of fine sand rolled flat, also known
as the "browns." One unit reported seeing a group of photographers
at the water injection pumps. Al-Naimi ordered the unit to check the
pumps then strictly instructed all units to keep their eyes open.

But for what?

If McKeon's technology was credible, and he had to assume it
was, then it posed the single gravest threat to the Kingdom in its
history. Saudi Arabia had risen out of the desert sands on a fountain
of oil. Without it, his nation would once again be nature's victim,
lost in the swirling sands, ignored and destitute.

—⟨∿⟩—

S itting in the Range Rover's driver's seat, Kasprzyk stacked three
square bandages, pressed them against the gash on his forehead,

and taped them there. He mustered all the saliva he could in this giant oven they called a country and spit on the sleeve of a shirt he had pulled from his bag. As gingerly as possible, he wiped the blood from his face and examined himself in the rearview mirror. At least he wasn't a bloody mess. There was no better way to attract the attention of jumpy security guards than to start bleeding. He closed his eyes and steadied himself. The exposed nerve endings around his wound blazed in agony and his head throbbed like a jackhammer. He permitted himself a brief moment of satisfaction at having killed the woman. He relished the thought, held it between his teeth, savored its sharp taste, then swallowed and opened his eyes.

In a few minutes, McKeon would inject the culture into the giant oil holding tank and the microbes would begin to spread out through the hundreds of miles of pipes to the other oil fields. Poison would soon course through the Kingdom's veins.

First things first.

"Get out," he ordered. They had reached the holding tank.

The desert wind had intensified. As he stepped out of the Range Rover, Michael shielded his eyes from the fine grit with one hand and cupped another against his ear, struggling to listen to David's directions.

"How do we do it?" Michael asked.

"They use valves to sample the oil for contaminants. The valves are in three spots on the tank: the oil layer, the oil/water interface, and the effluent layer. You're going to use the valve at the oil layer to inject the inoculum."

Kasprzyk placed the last camera case on the ground with a dusty thud and slammed the vehicle's rear door shut. Five camera cases. Two for Michael, two for David. Kasprzyk would have to carry one now. He caught Michael counting and pointed a finger.

"I still have one hand free and that's all I need to shoot you if you try anything. Get going."

Just then, an armored Hummer pulled to a stop and two National Guard soldiers jumped out, weapons drawn.

—ᴐᴇᴑᴤ—

A l-Naimi drummed his fingers, waiting for further word from his units. No one other than authorized personnel should be anywhere near the production or storage facilities. His men were well-trained. If anyone was out there, they would find them. The devilish detail was how did the scientists plan to deliver the bacteria?

His radio buzzed.

—ᴐᴇᴑᴤ—

" W hat are you doing?" the first guard demanded.

Kasprzyk, David and Michael all lifted their identification badges.

"We're photographers from PADIA," Kasprzyk replied, "here to photograph tonight's celebration. We're taking some shots of the entire facility before heading to the reception hall."

The guard eyed their camera cases before snapping his fingers for their badges. All three dutifully handed them over and waited while the guard stepped over to his vehicle to check on their identities. The second guard stood motionless, ten feet away, weapon raised.

After a nerve-wracking minute, the first guard returned and handed them their badges.

"You are on the list, but where is the fourth member of your group. The woman?"

"Female problems," David replied, waving vaguely in the direction of his groin. "She went to find a bathroom."

The guard nodded uncomfortably.

"You should move on to the reception hall."

"We're going to take a few pictures of the storage tank and then we'll be on our way," Kasprzyk replied.

As the SANG personnel climbed back into their armored Hummer and drove away, the three men grabbed the camera cases and hurried toward the holding tank. The wind was whipping up a sandstorm, forcing them to hunch over as they jogged the twenty feet to the tank. By the time they reached the tank, Michael's eyes were watering.

"Where's the valve?" he shouted.

"Should be over here, near the base of the steps," David replied, leading them around the tank. David stopped so abruptly that Michael bumped into him. "Here it is."

"David and I will take pictures while you work," Kasprzyk said as he dropped his case and lifted the camera around his neck. "Hurry."

Michael snapped open the five cases, then inspected the valve. He grabbed the circular handle and tried to turn it, but it wouldn't budge. He leaned into it with his shoulder, using the torque from his entire body, but no luck. Then he spotted the computer screen underneath a plastic shield. He flipped the shield up to examine it and swore loudly.

"What?" David demanded.

"It's locked. You need a computerized code to access it."

—⦿⦿⦿—

Al-Naimi's radio buzzed again.

"Assistant Sa'id?"

"Yes?"

"We just checked out the water pumps, where we saw the photographers."

"And?"

"We saw blood inside the access hatch."

Al-Naimi sat upright. Blood? There shouldn't be blood inside the water pumps.

"We climbed down and found a woman, sir."

"A woman?"

"Yes, sir. One of the photographers. We identified her from her badge."

"What was she doing there?"

"We don't know, sir."

"Did you ask her?

"No, sir."

Al-Naimi screwed his eyes shut in exasperation.

"May I ask why not?"

"Well, sir, I think she's dead. Shot in the chest and in the head."

———⟊⟊⟊———

The howling sandstorm closed in around Michael and the others, nearly obscuring the Range Rover. Kasprzyk continued shooting while David slung the camera around his neck and pulled a small device from his belt. Moving quickly, he snapped the device over the computer screen and turned it on. Numbers immediately began scrambling across its screen. Michael watched as one number after another locked in place. Finally, the device beeped and David removed it.

"Try it now!" David shouted above the whine of the storm.

Michael grabbed the wheel. With a harsh, grudging, metallic scrape, it began to turn.

Within minutes of terminating the connection with his security team, al-Naimi had raised the front gate on the radio and learned the precise time that four photographers, including the woman, had entered Abqaiq. One Polish man. Three Americans, including the woman. He then opened an email from Longfellow that contained a photograph of McKeon and an American woman named Julia Donatelli, forwarded it to the guards at the front gate and called them back.

It was them. McKeon and Donatelli were two of the photographers.

There was no time for compartmentalization or discretion. This required a full-scale alert. Al-Naimi opened a communication channel to all of his units.

"Two American men, one American woman, and a Polish man entered Abqaiq posing as photographers. The woman is dead but the three men are somewhere in the facility. They present an immediate and grave threat to the security of this facility. All units, find them and use any means necessary to stop them!"

It was only after issuing the order that he recalled his promise to Longfellow. Al-Naimi shook his head. His first duty was to stop the attack. Longfellow knew that. If he'd had another option, he wouldn't have called.

———∽∾∽———

Michael slipped the nipple from the first bladder into the draw valve then hid his face against the stiff foam. The ferocious sand had scoured raw the exposed skin on his neck, face and hands. He made the mistake of opening his mouth to take a breath and immediately choked on a mouthful of sand. He spat it out and took short, sniffling breaths through his nostrils, which were already becoming encrusted with grit. He closed his eyes against the onslaught and concentrated on the dwindling pressure against his fingertips as the bladder emptied the poison he had created into the tank.

———∽∾∽———

"Assistant Sa'id!"
The GIP Assistant snatched the radio as one of his units reported back.
"Yes?"
"We just left the photographers before your call."
"Where?"
A bark of static was his only response.
"Come in. Come in!" al-Naimi repeated urgently.
But the sandstorm had broken the connection. As al-Naimi listened in increasing frustration to the spits and stutters over his radio, his knuckles whitened around the receiver.

———∽∾∽———

Michael felt rather than saw David immediately behind him. Kasprzyk had disappeared in the darkening gyre. Michael presumed he had retreated to the vehicle. Both men had dropped the pretense of taking pictures in the middle of a sandstorm. Michael dropped the first bladder and inserted the second.
The abraded skin on his ears and cheeks screamed in agony. As the sand and winds battered him, Michael imagined that the Kingdom itself was rising up in self-defense. The land had risen. The sun was gone. All that was left was for the sky to fall.

Forty-three

———✺———

Michael dropped the fourth bladder and fumbled in the sand that had piled around his feet for the fifth.

"What are you doing?" David shouted.

"I can't find the last bladder," Michael hollered back.

Both men dropped to their knees and dug in the sand.

"Found it!" Michael declared, digging the black foam insert out of a mound. As they stood up, both men paused. Something in the wind's tone had changed. They stood still, straining to listen.

Voices! Men shouting in Arabic. Behind the voices, Michael could hear the loud roar of several engines close by.

"The SEF!" David shouted. He spun at Michael, a look of panic in his eyes. "Dump that thing as quickly as you can. Maybe they won't spot us. If they do, I'll tell them that we got trapped in the sandstorm. Hurry!"

With that, he disappeared into the churning grit. Michael turned back to the tank and jammed the last bladder into the valve as his heart thudded in his chest. Despite the wind whipping around him, he started to sweat again. Where was Kasprzyk? The sandstorm was so disorienting that if Michael had to run for the Range Rover, he wasn't sure he could find it. Of course, if he had to run, he and his family were dead anyway.

A shot rang out, loud and clear. Michael jerked and looked wildly about, but he was blind. He could hear men shouting in Arabic nearby. He squeezed his fingers against the bladder, pleading with it to empty faster. Then the quick, triple-tap of semi-automatic fire sounded, followed by the lonesome howl of the wind. He dropped the final bladder and backed against the steel tank. He looked left, then right, through the striations of umber whirling around him, unsure where the shots had come from. Where were David and Kasprzyk? He couldn't leave them even though he wanted to. They were his only connection to the Director, and to his family.

Michael kept his back to the steel tank as he inched his way right, in the direction he believed the vehicle was parked, as hundreds of shadows hurtled around him, each one a possible National Guardsman. Each one bringing capture, torture and death. Finally, as the tank circled away, he had to leave its security and strike out blindly toward the vehicle.

One step. Another. His feet sunk into the sand that had accumulated around the tank. A third step. A fourth. With no fixed marking, it was impossible to tell if he was moving in a straight line. He strained to hear anything over the wind, but the voices had gone silent. No more shots rang out. A fifth step, then a sixth. The sand shifted under his feet and he stepped into a hole.

Michael's leg buckled as a searing pain lanced through his ankle. He fell to the ground and choked down a scream, grabbing his ankle, which was already throbbing. As he struggled to stand, he failed to notice the dark shadow that remained static behind him. Gradually, the shadow coalesced into a figure as it stepped forward. A cloth was wrapped around the figure's face. Goggles covered his eyes. In his hand was a Makarov pistol. He raised the pistol and pointed it at the back of Michael's head.

Lost amidst the sandy maelstrom, deafened by the howling winds, blinded by the flying grit, his leg wracked with pain, Michael somehow sensed the threat from behind. He turned slightly, as much as his ankle would allow, enough to spot the man. Then again, the man had let him turn. He wanted Michael to see the bullet come.

"Kasprzyk!" Michael shouted, not a plea, but an epithet.

The man said nothing.

Michael struggled to stand, letting all of his weight rest on his left foot.

"I did what you asked me to do," he bellowed into the howling wind. "We're not done yet. You still need me for Russia."

Another figure materialized out of the swirling sands. It was David, breathing hard and bleeding from a bullet wound to the shoulder. He nearly ran over Michael before spotting him and spat sand when he spied Kasprzyk's Makarov.

"What the hell are you doing?" David shouted, his face contorted in agony. "We have to get out of here!"

Kasprzyk's voice, muffled by the scarf and tossed by the wind, was barely audible.

"It ends here."

"No! That's not what the Director ordered. We have to get to Sakhalin. You can't kill him now."

The shot came.

Michael's head snapped back. But the shot was immediately followed by two more. *Tap-tap-tap.* Not the single shot of a Makarov. A triple-tap from a semi-automatic rifle. Then another. Michael opened his eyes. The first three bullets had chewed a hole through Kasprzyk's rib cage, under his left arm. The Makarov had fallen, already lost in the shifting sands. Slowly, like a felled tree, Kasprzyk toppled over, lifeless. The second triple-tap had exploded the top of David's head. Dark, blood-soaked sand clotted around the gray brain matter leaking from his open skull.

From the left, right and center, three SEF soldiers stepped into Michael's limited field of vision, rifles raised. The hard, round barrel of another semi-automatic pressed against the back of his skull.

He was surrounded.

He had prepared an unfathomable amount of microbes in unprecedented time and had successfully injected them into the most heavily guarded oil site in the world, but he had still failed. Julia was dead. David and Kasprzyk, his only two links to the Director and to his family, were dead. As Michael raised his hands in surrender, he knew with bitter certainty one more thing.

He, Milla, and Katya were dead too.

Forty-four

━━⚮⚭⚮━━

Mahabith Detention Facility
Undisclosed Location
Empty Quarter, Saudi Arabia

They came before Michael was ready, the three men in black. Tight-fitting black turtle-necks tucked into black trousers, in turn tucked into high, black, military-style boots. Skin-formed black gloves covered their hands, and black fleece ski masks hid their faces. Not that it mattered. Michael knew he was never going to escape this prison to identify anyone. The gash above his eye, opened by the taller one's walnut-sized knuckles, had not had time to clot. The knife-like pain in his side, undoubtedly a broken rib, sustained when they had thrown him down the cement stairs into this pit, had not subsided. He could breathe only in short, painful gasps.

They stood inside the door, silent, as before. The puckered vents over their mouths moved in sync with the rise and fall of their well-muscled chests. Slow and easy. Michael could not tell if their eyes were black, or if it was just a trick of the shadows. Either way, they were demons from a nightmare. Most frightening was the bored, business-like approach they had taken to beating him. In Michael's life, beatings had always been fueled by rage, jealousy or fear. These men were doing a job. As he blinked away his own blood, Michael knew they were good at their job, and that they weren't finished, not by a long shot.

He hadn't even had time to figure out where he was. There were no windows and no opening in the single, steel door. Clearly, no one was supposed to see what happened in this room. He was fairly certain he was underground. The room was cool, like a basement, with no discernible air flow. The floor was concrete. It had a sterile, antiseptic smell of industrial solvents. Underneath it, though, the stench of sweat, blood and fear was unmistakable. They had left him in pitch darkness, but, now that they had returned, a light in the ceiling glowed dimly. *So they can do their work*, Michael thought grimly. In that dim light, he noticed that the walls were bare, gray concrete. Rough. The kind that would rip your skin if you rubbed against it.

What stopped his heart was the drain in the middle of the room. The concrete floor sloped down to it, and something black was encrusted around its edges. The drain was at his feet, directly in front of the metal chair to which he was tied. The chair was bolted to the floor, to hold him in place while they hit and kicked him. The blood from his forehead continued to run down his face and had begun to pool in his collar. He lifted his head and opened his one good eye.

The man in the center, the largest one with the walnut knuckles, snapped his right fist forward. Michael's brain barely had time to register the movement before the man's fist crashed into his right eye socket. His entire body slammed into the chair. The restraints dug into his arms and legs, but the bolts did their job. His head snapped back as fireworks exploded behind his eye. The room winked out, then came back into view, hazy and unfocused.

The men in black moved in. Just doing their job.

—*ᴥᴥᴥ*—

Michael woke. It could have been hours later, or minutes, or days. He had no way of knowing. It was longer than the first time because his right eye was crusted shut. He couldn't hear anything out of his right ear and, now, both sides of his rib cage screamed every time he tried to breathe. He moved his fingers and wiggled his toes. Those weren't broken yet, and his neurological pathways were still able to communicate those commands. That was something, at least. He ran his tongue around inside his mouth and winced. Several teeth were loose. The coppery taste of his own blood was so overwhelming that he gagged. His head had whip-sawed so viciously during the beating that his neck muscles were overstretched and useless. Staring at the floor, he noticed that they had not washed his blood down the drain. Yet.

The men in black had done their job, but they had not killed him. They were keeping him alive, for now. It didn't take a genius to figure out why. He knew what would come next, and wasn't surprised when the door opened.

Michael didn't recognize the man who stepped through the door, but he couldn't have been more different from the three men in black. To start with, this man was dressed in white, the traditional *thobe*. He was smaller and thinner than the three men, and his face was not covered. Round spectacles flashed in the overhead light, turning opaque, hiding his eyes. Something in the heavy way the man dragged a chair across the floor frightened Michael even more than the beatings from the masked thugs.

Michael's right hand had started shaking. He ignored it and waited for the man to speak.

"Professor Michael McKeon," the man began in a quiet voice.

Michael couldn't hide his shock.

"Yes, I know your name," the man continued wearily. "I've learned a lot about you in a rather short period of time."

He removed his glasses and pinched the bridge of his nose before replacing them, dropping his hands into his lap with dreadful finality. The man's mustache twitched once. Then he cocked his head slightly, like a professor who was about to repeat a lesson for an exceptionally dimwitted student.

"Let me tell you what I know and then you will tell me what you know." He didn't wait for a response from Michael. "I know that you developed a process for accelerating the growth of certain strains of microbes that can destroy oil. I know that you have successfully tested this process in the lab and in the field under limited conditions. I know that you were kidnapped by an organization calling itself The Global Group. I also know that this group kidnapped your wife and adopted daughter to force you to cooperate. I know that you and three others infiltrated Abqaiq, pretending to be photographers. I know that we found five empty containers next to the water injection pumps that contained the microbial solution. I know that we found five empty containers next to the oil storage tank and an additional six filled ones in the rear of your vehicle. I know that the woman and your two kidnappers are dead, and you are alone. Finally, I know that you will tell me how to stop the microbes."

With that, the man sat back in his chair and waited.

A grim silence settled in the room. Neither man moved; Michael, because he couldn't, and the other man because he chose not to. Michael judged from the deathly stillness in the room that it was soundproof. *They don't want anyone to hear what happens in here, either.* Finally, with great effort, Michael forced his overtaxed neck muscles to lift his head and squinted his left eye until the man came into focus. He opened his battered mouth and rolled his swollen tongue, trying to find enough moisture to speak, but he couldn't stop his hand from shaking.

"I'll tell you what I know," Michael croaked. The first words he had uttered since his capture. "I know that I'll never tell you a goddamned thing. Go to hell."

The man shrugged his shoulders in apparent resignation. He stood up slowly and shuffled to the door, which opened before he touched it. As the man disappeared up the stairs, the three men in black filed through the doorway. Silently. Effortlessly. Business-like. Two of them approached Michael on either side. He tensed, waiting for the beating to begin, but was surprised when they unlocked the chain binding him to the chair and lifted him off the floor, his arms pinned to his sides. Michael gasped as his elbows were forced into his broken ribs. His head lolled side to side with each step. They stopped in front of the man with walnut knuckles, who stood in front of the door.

Without a word, they dropped Michael to his knees. His brain was too battered to engage his reflexes, and his knees cracked against the concrete floor like twin rifle shots. His lower legs and feet immediately went numb. Then the two men grabbed his wrists and yanked him off his knees. Michael ground his teeth into his lips as his ribs blazed in agony. Through the scarlet haze that had enveloped him, Michael heard two metal clicks then felt the men release his wrists.

He didn't fall. His wrists were chained to a metal bar fastened to the ceiling. The bar was high enough so that he had to stretch to touch the floor with the balls of his feet. The man with walnut knuckles stepped toward him and drilled his giant fist into Michael's solar plexus, knocking the wind out of him in a painful rush. Then the three men went back to work. Fists. Forearms. Elbows. Knees. Feet.

As the beating continued, Michael dug inward. Dug with the panic he had felt when Milla and Katya went missing. Dug with the rage he had felt when he found his sister dead. Dug with the desperation he had felt when his father and then his mother had attacked him.

He dug until he found what he was looking for, the cave inside him where he had crawled for the first time when his father beat him. It was a dark and angry place, but completely impregnable. He had lived there every time his mother brought a dealer or a client to their apartment. He had dug even father inside it when he tracked down his sister's killer and shot him between the eyes. He had continued to live there until Longfellow first enticed him out with equations and algorithms that wormed their way into his brain and wouldn't let him rest. But it was still there, as he knew it would be. Waiting for him. *Come inside. No one can touch you in here.*

He crawled inside.

Forty-five

Moscow

Longfellow was wild, pacing around the cramped hotel room like a madman while Melissa tried to hear Jigger over Longfellow's curses and mutterings.

"What do you mean you can't see anything?" she demanded angrily. "How could you not see anything?"

Jigger's voice was clearly audible in the room.

"I hacked into a satellite that was positioned over Saudi Arabia, but a gigantic sandstorm blew up just as it was focusing on Abqaiq. I backed up the video feed and, just prior to the storm, I identified McKeon and Donatelli outside a de-oxygenation tower, so they made it inside the facility, but that's it. After the storm blew over, I can't find them anywhere."

Longfellow continued pacing, ignoring the wave of nausea that rolled over him. He dialed Sa'id's number then let loose a blistering stream of invectives when the voice mail picked up again. Sa'id was ignoring his phone calls, there was no other explanation. The Saudi had promised safe passage, but, if Michael had actually introduced the microbe before being caught, then all bets were off.

Either Michael and Julia were dead, or captured, and Longfellow wasn't sure which would be worse.

Forty-six

⸺ꙮ⸺

Mahabith Detention Facility
Undisclosed Location
Empty Quarter, Saudi Arabia

From deep inside the cave, Michael heard someone calling his name.

Michael. Michael.

It was too dark to see.

Michael.

No. It hurt too much to answer. It was better to stay in the cave.

Michael.

Something flittered before his eyes, like shadows before the flame. He could not discern who, or what, it was, but it was hateful. Michael knew that much. And dangerous. It needed to be killed.

Slowly, painstakingly, Michael crawled toward the entrance, ready to kill the shadow outside.

He opened his left eye. He was still hanging from the ceiling. His shoulders burned as if the tendons had been ripped from the bones. His head rested on his left shoulder. He couldn't breathe out of his nose. Every inch of him screamed in agony.

"There you are," the man in the *thobe* said. "I've been waiting for you. Those men, they're very talented. They know how to take you to the edge of death and stop you from falling over." He removed his spectacles, dark eyes glittering in the dim light. "Know this, Michael, we will not kill you. Not for a very long time. These men are that talented."

Michael wished he could kick the man, could wrap his legs around the man's neck and break it, but he could not even move his feet. He stared balefully at the man. There was nothing he could do. Michael moved his lips. A bubble of frothy blood formed and popped. The man took another step closer.

"Tell me," al-Naimi said softly, like a parent asking where it hurts. "This serves no useful purpose. Tell me and it all ends."

"They made me," Michael whispered.

"I know."

"They said they'd kill Milla and Katya if I didn't destroy your oil."

"Yes."

Al-Naimi's eyes had begun to burn with an inner fire. He wanted answers.

"Another target."

The Saudi's brow creased in puzzlement.

"There's another target in the Kingdom?"

A racking cough caused Michael to groan.

"Not here."

"Where?"

"Russia." Michael's breath rattled in his throat. "The Sakhalin Islands. You've caught me, so I can't complete the mission. They must know that by now. That means my wife and daughter are dead." Michael fixed the man with a frigid, lifeless stare out of his one working eye. "That means, those assholes can take all the time with me that they want. I'm already dead."

Michael slumped, letting all his weight hang from his shackled wrists. His fingers twitched, trying to type Milla's and Katya's names, but they lacked the strength. He watched the man's boots for a long time. Finally, they turned and disappeared out of Michael's vision. He waited for the three pairs of black boots to reappear.

Then, somewhere in his bruised and battered brain, a synapse fired. Then another, and another. He had an idea.

"Wait."

Forty-seven

Al-Naimi had agreed to return Michael to the chair. After hanging from the ceiling, being chained to the chair felt like a vacation. The Saudi sat facing Michael.

"Tell me."

"Water."

"No."

Michael closed his eye and waited. After several minutes, the man must have decided to let him win this point because Michael heard him snap his fingers. One of the black-clad henchmen entered with a glass of water. With a practiced hand, he tilted Michael's chin back to open his throat, and slowly dribbled the water in.

The water washed away the noxious taste of dried blood and mucus. Michael also regained better control of his tongue. He could speak, slowly and painfully, but he nodded thanks at the Saudi after they were alone again.

"Tell me."

"Right now, the culture I prepared is coursing through the reservoir and facilities at Abqaiq, and out through the pipelines to all the other reservoirs in the Kingdom. You can't isolate Abqaiq by closing off the pipelines. It's already too late."

"How do I know that this microbial threat is real?"

"It's real, and you know it. Right about now, your methane, hydrogen, and carbon dioxide readings are off the charts. Those are produced by the breakdown of the hydrocarbons in the oil. I'm sure you checked them. You wouldn't be sitting here and I wouldn't still be alive otherwise."

"How long?"

"Until it spreads through all your reservoirs? Four, maybe five days."

"Can it be stopped?"

This was the moment of maximum danger. The answer would seal Michael's fate.

"Yes."

Michael saw the man's chest swell with oxygen as he took a deep, relieved breath.

"How?"

"That I won't tell you."

Al-Naimi glowered at him and raised his hand to snap for the men in black, but Michael interrupted him.

"Yet."

Al-Naimi paused, his hand in mid-air. Then he returned it to his lap.

"What do you mean, yet?"

Michael shifted against his restraints. He wanted another glass of water, but decided not to press his luck.

"Every second you spend with me, you lose more oil. I'm sorry for that. I had no choice. I can't restore the oil you've lost, but I can stop the microbes. You'll never beat the answer out of me, but I'll give it to you on three conditions."

"You are not in a position to set conditions."

"You're not in a position to refuse them, unless you want to become known as the man who watched the Kingdom lose its oil."

An angry silence crackled between the two men. Michael waited. He knew the man would relent. He wanted the answer too badly. That much was clear.

"Name them and I will consider them," al-Naimi spat.

"First, I want confirmation that my wife and daughter are still alive."

"How am I supposed to provide that?"

"Find Kasprzyk's cell phone and you'll find a number he dialed to reach the Director. It's probably the last number he called. Find me the phone and I'll make the call. The Global Group owed me a third call with my wife and daughter. I'll tell the Director that I'm ready for Phase Two once I hear them on the line."

"What if he already knows you have been captured? What if your group was supposed to have reported in by a certain time?"

"If he's already killed them for any reason, then you can toss me back in here for the rest of eternity, but I won't tell you anything, so you better find that goddamn cell phone fast and hope we're in time."

The man nodded slightly, which Michael took as permission to continue.

"The second condition is that you deliver me safely to the Sakhalin Islands."

"Why would I have any interest in sending you there? Once you are released, you will disappear. Do you think me stupid?"

"No, I don't think you're stupid. In fact, I'm hoping that you're highly intelligent. That way, you'll understand that you have two things to gain. The first is that I'll come back and stop the microbes as soon as I have my wife and child. And the second is that your biggest oil competitor, Russia, will be mortally wounded, leaving Saudi Arabia as the single energy superpower in the world."

"I have no interest in starting a war between the Kingdom and Russia."

"You're supposed to be highly intelligent, remember? You wouldn't be the one starting a war. If I was captured, who would believe that Saudi Arabia would send some crazy American scientist to destroy Russia's largest oil reserves? If anyone was blamed, it'd be America, which only helps the Kingdom, too."

Al-Naimi's eyes narrowed shrewdly as he evaluated Michael's proposal.

"You have forgotten one thing."

"What's that?"

"Your third condition."

Michael smiled as much as his damaged face would allow.

"You leave me and my family alone."

The man sat still for several more minutes, pinching the bridge of his nose. Finally, he shifted forward. Michael waited for his decision.

"I have three conditions of my own."

"What are they?"

"First, you take an assistant of mine with you."

"Fine."

"Second, you finish the job within two days. Any longer than that, and I will put a bullet in your head."

"Any longer than that and my wife and daughter will undoubtedly be dead and I'll welcome the bullet. What's your third condition?"

"It was the Director who targeted my country?"

"Yes."

"Then you must kill him."

The right side of Michael's face was so bruised and battered that he couldn't feel it move, but the left side slid into a hungry grin.

"It would be my pleasure."

Forty-eight

Moscow

In his suite at the Ritz Carlton, NSA Director Billings slid the latest report on the Middle East into the shredder, relying upon his storied self-restraint to keep from throwing the shredder through the window. To try to keep the talks on track, the President had him scuttling back and forth between the Saudi and Russian delegations. It felt like begging, Billings thought distastefully.

Stark was alive and missing, so still a threat. Viktor had tracked her to a cottage outside Moscow, but, by the time he'd arrived, she was gone. Longfellow, too.

"What?" Billings barked impatiently at an analyst who had quietly approached.

"I may have located Stark, sir," said the analyst, a mousy woman in her late twenties with thick glasses.

An electric jolt coursed through the NSA Director as he jumped out of his chair.

"Where?"

"Well, sir, our listening post in Moscow has been monitoring all communications for mention of Michael McKeon, as instructed. Several hours ago, a single cell phone left repeated voice messages at a number in Saudi Arabia. Each mentioned McKeon."

"Where's that phone now?"

"The phone isn't registered anywhere, but it's an i-Phone." The analyst, flustered by Billings' impatient scowl, spilled the words out as quickly as she could.

"So?"

"Most people don't know that the i-Phone operating system secretly logs the user's precise location, down to the latitude and longitude, up to one hundred times a day. I was able to trace the signal back and upload the coordinates. They've been in one location for a couple hours now."

"Where are they?"

"In a hotel on the northern side of Moscow, near the Third Ring."

Billings slammed his palm on the desk in jubilation.

"Come with me and bring your laptop so you can keep tracing that signal." Billings dialed Viktor's number. "We have them." He gave the Russian the location. "Bring your crew and meet us there. Come armed. You're going in heavy."

He breathed a sigh of relief as he raced down the hall toward the elevator, with the analyst on his heels. *Now we've got them.*

———

Across Moscow, in the *Zolotaya Ptitsa*, Melissa Stark checked her watch and made a decision.

"I'm going out," she said.

"Where?" Longfellow replied.

"I want to find my assistant and ask her to do some digging to find out why I'm in this mess. If someone accessed my computer or my office, she'd know."

"They're probably monitoring her email and phone. How are you going to reach her?"

"On the flight over here, my assistant asked permission to see *Boris Godunov* at the Bolshoi." Melissa checked her watch. "The late evening performance starts in one hour. If I can spot her before she enters the theater, I'll ask her to help."

Longfellow pulled a doubtful face.

"I don't think that's a good idea."

"I need to know who did this to me," Melissa replied heatedly.

"The more you move about the city, the more likely you'll be caught, especially around the Bolshoi."

"I'll be careful."

"I'll go with you."

"No, we're even more conspicuous traveling together. It's better that we separate. If I'm not back in three hours, clear out of here."

"If we don't meet here in three hours, come to *Respublica*. It's an all-night bookstore, a mile up from the Kremlin. I'll find you."

———

Billings' phone chirped as he jumped into the back seat of his SUV, signaling an incoming text message. Seeing his face darken, the analyst scrunched into the corner of the back seat with her laptop. The NSA Director punched a number into his phone and signaled impatiently for his driver to head out.

"Frank, there's someone else your agents need to find and hold: Stark's assistant, Dani. I have a report that they pulled video footage and it was her sitting at Stark's keyboard when the offshore account was opened. Either she's working with Stark, or framing her. Either way, try to make sure your agents actually hold onto her until I get back."

Billings terminated the call and sat back against the leather seat, drumming his fingers relentlessly on the arm rest while the Moscow cityscape whizzed past.

"You said they were making calls," he said suddenly to the analyst.

"Yes sir."

"Who were they calling?"

"Three numbers. One is a cell phone in Saudi Arabia."

Billings' expression darkened further, the creases on his face as deep and permanent as the Rocky Mountains of his birth. "Name?"

"No name, sir. I tried everything."

"Did you call it?"

"No, sir," said the shocked analyst. "I didn't think anyone would want, I mean, that didn't seem like something I'm trained . . ."

"Give it to me," Billings interrupted, snapping an impatient hand in her face. "The other two numbers?"

The analyst blanched, afraid to answer.

"The other two?" Billings demanded.

"One is to the NSA."

Billings' storied self-control was about to snap. Who the hell was Stark or Longfellow calling in the NSA? If someone was helping them despite his orders, that person would find themselves on the next plane to Guantanamo if they were lucky.

"Who?"

"It's a personal cell phone listed to a computer analyst. His name is Edward Tellerman. Everyone calls him Jigger."

Billings made a fist and stared, unseeing, out the window while he contemplated this betrayal. "The other number?"

"It's an American cell phone, but I can't trace it yet. And I didn't call that one, either, sir," she added hastily.

Billings let a slow breath hiss through his teeth as he called a number back at the NSA. "Jack? There's a computer analyst who has been helping Melissa Stark. His name's Edward Tellerman."

"Jigger," the analyst added, then quailed under Billings' withering stare.

"Apparently people call him Jigger." Billings closed his eyes as if in pain while he listened. "You had him and you let him go? Find him, toss him in a room, and find out what he's been doing with Stark and Longfellow! And nobody lets him go until I say so!"

———※———

After Melissa left, Longfellow locked the door and began poring over the information Jigger had provided about the Russian oil reservoirs and distribution system, trying to identify likely targets of The Global Group while he waited to hear from al-Naimi.

Concentrating was difficult as his mind kept returning to Michael and Julia. And he was anxious to hear again from Grisha, to see if he was making any progress finding Michael's family. Longfellow paused as a wave of sadness washed over him. He still hadn't had time to grieve Fouad and Dmitry.

Longfellow glanced bleakly around the empty room. This was the life they had chosen. Their clandestine, violent work left them isolated, unable to function outside the shadows. Sooner or later, it broke them all. He'd been more fortunate than most. He'd had Laura until her cancer claimed her. But now, he had no one.

That wasn't true. He had Michael. At least, he hoped he still had Michael.

Forty-nine

—ew—

Melissa exited the *Teatralnaya* metro stop and quickly submerged herself into the crowds milling around Theater Square as she made her way toward the grand, pink and white Bolshoi Theater. She felt naked, exposed as she swept her eyes back and forth, looking for Dani, but on guard for any police or Secret Service.

There's no reason they should be looking for me here, but still. . . .

Suddenly, there she was in a short black dress, wrap and heels, hair pulled back in a bun. Melissa pushed through the current of gawking tourists toward her assistant, afraid to draw attention to herself by calling out. After being momentarily blocked by a street vendor, Melissa had closed the gap to ten feet when Dani stopped in front of the theater's eight-columned portico. As her assistant craned her neck to gaze at the sculpture of Apollo's chariot, a man stopped behind her. At first, Melissa assumed he was admiring the theater, or her assistant. Then she saw the gun.

As the long barrel of the silencer reached toward the small of Dani's back, Melissa shouted: "Dani!"

Dani turned her head in surprise then her mouth and eyes opened wider as the first shot severed her spinal cord, dropping her to the ground like someone had cut her strings.

"No!" Melissa screamed.

The man aimed and fired again at the downed woman, leaving a hole in her forehead, before turning toward Melissa. He was tall and gaunt, with the hollow cheeks and dead eyes of a heroin addict.

Time slowed to an imperceptible crawl as the gun tracked toward her. Melissa couldn't take her eyes off Dani's crumpled body and the expanding crimson pool around it. She didn't even notice as the gun stopped its arc, pointing at her heart. As the gunman pulled the trigger, the surging, panicked crowd knocked Melissa sideways. A woman screamed and fell as the bullet meant for Melissa tore through her shoulder.

Melissa turned and ran, tears streaming down her face. She never looked back. She didn't have to. She'd never forget Dani's shocked expression as the bullet ripped into her.

—❧—

Longfellow grabbed the phone from the nightstand as soon as it buzzed.

"Finally!" he exclaimed, seeing the text was from al-Naimi.

Package arrived slightly damaged.

"Yes!"

Michael was hurt, but alive. Longfellow's grin evaporated as he continued reading.

Contents spilled. Can't return yet. Will forward to next destination.

Outside the *Zolotaya Ptitsa*, the car doors on several black SUVs slammed.

Fifty

———

Too furious with al-Naimi to sit still, Longfellow stomped toward the window. He was about to continue pacing when he noticed the two black SUVs parked in front of the hotel.

"They've found us," he breathed.

He raced to the door, listened for a moment then cracked it open. The dingy, yellow-lit hall was empty. He quickly shut his door and darted across the hall to the opposing room, lockpick in hand. Ten seconds later, he was inside the next room.

The men were good. They didn't make a sound until their dark forms flashed by Longfellow's peephole. With a crash, they kicked the door in to his room while Longfellow watched from across the hall. A minute later, the leader was back in the hallway, on his phone.

"They're gone. I don't care if their phone signal's still here, they're not."

A foot away, Longfellow swore softly, opened the back of his phone, and removed the battery.

"The signal just disappeared?" the leader repeated.

Longfellow returned to the peephole in time to see the leader cast a long look at the room where he was hiding, then beckon quietly to the other members of his team. Without waiting further, Longfellow raced for the window on the far side of the room. Thanking his stars that the *Zolotaya Ptitsa* was old enough to have windows that actually opened, Longfellow threw open the window. The rusty staging was two feet away.

"I'm getting too old for this," he muttered, draping a leg over the sill.

Praying that the staging would hold, he leaned out the window and leapt. His bandaged shoulder and hand blazed in agony as he grabbed the nearest bar and hung, scrambling to find a hold for his feet as the rickety scaffolding shook and swayed from the force of his jump. Longfellow had just begun to climb down, hand over hand, when he heard the door crash inward. Two more handholds, then he dropped the ground and pressed against the side of the building as a shot pinged off the scaffolding.

"There he is!" one of the assailants shouted.

With the scaffolding as cover, Longfellow turned and raced toward the rear of the hotel, jumping over piles of debris and abandoned tools. As he reached the corner, a figure in jeans and black jacket spun into view holding an assault rifle. Reacting instantly, Longfellow grabbed a rusted shovel by his foot and swung before the assailant could aim. The shovel collided with the man's skull with a dull *thwang*, knocking him unconscious. Longfellow scooped up the rifle and raced across the parking lot to the back of the art gallery, slipping through an opening in the corrugated metal fence just as the assault team spilled out of the hotel. Breathing heavily, Longfellow slipped the strap for the rifle over his shoulder and decided to watch the attackers as long as he could, to learn who was after him.

He narrowed his eyes and raised the rifle as one of the SUVs pulled into the parking lot. The team leader hurried over to the rear door. As the window rolled down, Longfellow raised the sight and centered the magnified crosshairs on the passenger.

Billings!

Longfellow watched as the window rolled back up and the SUV pulled away. The team leader then directed two of his team back into the building while he and the other member carried the unconscious assailant toward the other SUV on the street.

Longfellow dropped his phone onto the pavement and crushed it with his heel. With two guards remaining, he had to find a way to stop Melissa before she entered the hotel. Then they needed to get out of Moscow, because he now knew where Michael was headed.

Thirty-five minutes later, Longfellow had completed a hasty reconnaissance of the area around the hotel. Two metro stations and a bus station were clustered several blocks southwest on *Ylitsa Novoslobodskaya*, but there were too many routes Melissa might take in returning to the *Zolotaya Ptitsa* and too great a risk he would miss her. He needed to find a spot closer to the hotel. Heading north on *Obraztsova* toward the hotel, Longfellow eyed the pink and white buildings of the State University of Communications, but none had a clear line of sight. His skin prickled as he approached the hotel, dark and ominous behind its abandoned scaffolding, one of the few reminders of Soviet decay in this *Novaya Sloboda*, or "New Suburb."

Longfellow ducked into a doorway as several black SUVs approached then breathed a sigh of relief as they continued past. He surveyed the street, but found no signs of surveillance. With only two guards, they were most likely placed inside the hotel, possibly in their room. Taking no chances, Longfellow used a nearby alley to circumvent the hotel, returning him to *Obraztsova,* facing the converted bus station just north of the hotel. The mammoth red and white station, originally constructed so more than one hundred buses could drive in and out without having to turn around, had been turned into a contemporary art gallery by a millionaire Russian model and her billionaire boyfriend. Enormous numbered hangar doors lined the front of its façade, but its café had views of the front and back of the hotel next door. Judging from the crowd milling outside, the art gallery's glamorous owner was throwing some sort of reception.

Longfellow checked his watch. Melissa had been gone for almost two hours. He had no idea when she would return, but he needed to get off the street and in place. The problem was that the path to the café would take him underneath the window to their room, where the black-clad gunmen might very well be watching.

To his right, Longfellow spotted two university students sipping coffee and chatting animatedly on the sidewalk, one with a backpack slung over his shoulder. The zipper was open and something was sticking out. Longfellow smiled and strode past, slipping the knit hat out with a practiced hand. He covered his gray hair with the hat and slipped into a group of middle-aged, over-dressed Muscovites crossing the street toward the old bus station. He casually worked his way into the middle of the small throng, asking innocuous questions about the building. A stick-thin woman in skin-tight blue jeans, brown suede boots and an amorphous, iridescent jacket that floated around her like a jellyfish was particularly ready to talk. As she jabbered about an exhibition on "faux-utopian Soviet dis-reality" and the European soccer club owned by the model's boyfriend, Longfellow kept a wary eye on the hotel and his window.

With a grateful thanks, Longfellow begged leave from the woman as they entered the center, slipping instead onto a couch next to the café's window overlooking the hotel. He had just raised his hand to order a coffee when something outside caught his attention. A woman, her hair tucked into a baseball cap pulled low over her forehead, had darted across the street toward the front entrance of the hotel. The face was obscured, but Longfellow had no doubt who it was. He jumped to his feet, but he was already too late.

Melissa Stark had just entered the *Zolotaya Ptitsa*.

Fifty-one

⁓⁓⁓

Longfellow raced out of the former bus station. Halfway across the parking lot, he heard the first tinkle of breaking glass. Then a clump of asphalt by his foot exploded into the air. He ducked behind a parked sedan and kept running as its windshield shattered from another shot. He yanked the Sig Sauer from his belt and fired once at the dark figure barely visible through his room's window then ducked around the front corner of the hotel.

The desk clerk dropped the phone and raised his hands in surrender as Longfellow burst into the lobby, gun drawn.

"Where is she?" Longfellow demanded. "The woman who came with me."

When the man hesitated, Longfellow ground the gun into his temple.

"Where is she?"

"In the bar," the man groaned, pointing to the door leading off the lobby.

"Did you call them, the men who are looking for us, and tell them she's here?" When the man hesitated, Longfellow cracked the gun against his skull.

"I tried, but you arrived before I could."

Longfellow glanced grimly at the stairs. The gunmen could reach the lobby any second.

"You're coming with me," he said, grabbing the desk clerk by the collar and shoving him toward the door. The bar was a dark, depressing place, its only redeeming factor that its dim lighting almost entirely hid the cracked and stained vinyl booths.

Melissa was slumped at the bar, her head in her hands.

"Melissa!"

She jumped, turning a tear-stained face toward Longfellow.

"What—?"

"There are two gunmen here. We've got to go now!"

Longfellow could see that she was upset, but, like a true professional, Melissa responded immediately, racing after him as he pushed the desk clerk into the kitchen.

"This way," Longfellow shouted as he spotted the door in the far wall. Ignoring the frightened screams of a babyshka stirring a pot of boiled beets, Longfellow shoved the desk clerk toward the door. When he made a feeble attempt to grab a fry pan and swing it toward Longfellow, the spy crunched his gun against the man's temple, dropping him on the spot and eliciting a stream of angry wails from the babyshka to God and to the State, whoever might answer first.

Longfellow and Melissa burst into a back alley, weapons raised, searching for any threat. When none appeared, the two spies raced down the alley, turning left and right, snaking their way through the labyrinth of alleys and small lanes until they reached the columned *Novoslobodskaya* Metro station. As they collapsed into an empty car moments before the train pulled away, chests heaving from the exertion, Longfellow noticed that Melissa was still crying. He took her hand. After a moment's hesitation, she crumpled against him.

"They killed Dani," she hiccupped through gasps for breath.

"Your assistant?"

Melissa nodded. "They shot her right in front of the Bolshoi. I saw it."

"Who?"

"I don't know," she wailed, digging her fists into her eyes. "I saw her face when they shot her. She was so young. This is all my fault."

"You don't know that."

Melissa cast a scornful look at Longfellow as she wiped her eyes.

"Of course I do. It's not an accident someone executed my assistant. He tried to shoot me, but I got away."

Melissa fell silent as the train bumped and thumped along. By the time she spoke, she had regained control of her emotions.

"I can't do this any more. I've been behind a desk too long. I've forgotten what it's like to be in the field. The fear, the violence." She tossed her hands into the air. "What are we doing?"

She turned angrily to Longfellow.

"What are we doing?" she demanded again.

"What do you mean?"

"We haven't accomplished anything except getting shot at and we don't even know who is shooting at us. Dani's dead. Michael and Julia are still missing. Milla and Katya are still hostages, if they're even still alive. And we're on the run, with no hope of saving ourselves or anyone else."

Melissa collapsed into morose silence, her head resting against the window. Longfellow sighed and pulled out the new prepaid phone he had purchased during his reconnaissance and dialed Jigger's number. When the analyst answered, he was breathless and whispering.

"Dude, I can't talk any more. They found me. I don't know how, but they found me. My sister's going to be pissed. I got to go. You guys are on your own. Sorry!"

Longfellow stared at the phone for a long moment as Melissa closed her eyes, having overheard the conversation.

"I have one bit of good news," he said quietly.

"I need it."

"I finally heard from al-Naimi. Michael's alive."

Melissa turned excitedly to Longfellow. "Thank God! Is Julia okay too?"

"I assume so, but . . ."

Melissa slumped into her seat and groaned.

"But what?"

"But he's not turning Michael over. He's making him complete the mission."

"Attack Russia? Why?"

Longfellow shrugged.

"So where does that leave us?" Stark asked as the train slowed for its next station.

Longfellow waved the phone. "I need to call Grisha's friend about a plane."

"Why?"

He grinned.

"Because I think I know where Michael and Julia are going next."

Fifty-two

—◦◦◦—

Molodaya Guardiya Industrial
Storage Facility, Moscow

The industrial storage facility off the Dmitrovskoye Highway was an unprepossessing structure of weathered brick, dark windows and quiet loading ramps with dented HVAC piping snaking up and down the building's exterior. It appeared to promise nothing more than the other Soviet industrial remnants littering Moscow: cavernous spaces of crumbling concrete, cargo elevators that didn't work, and nasty chemical surprises seeping from clogged catch basins. But the storage facility's anonymous, dilapidated exterior was part of its allure. Like Colonel Akhmetalin, it presented one face to the public and another, turned inward.

Akhmetalin had needed a place to hide from the ever-present eyes and ears of his own agency, the FSB, so he had purchased the facility through a front corporation. The term always made him smile. Such a western idea, but one that Russian intelligence services, and Akhmetalin, had embraced with open arms.

He left the first two floors in their state of disrepair, but the third floor was his private control center for any personal operations he wanted to keep away from the piggish eyes of that red-bearded bastard, Yakovlev. The southern side was his office, equipped with wireless technology and a full electrical upgrade, and decorated to his own tastes. His only complaint was that the workman had laid the wood flooring improperly and it tended to jiggle and creak when he paced, as he was currently doing. The Calamander wood he had flown in from Sri Lanka—the same flooring he had used in his dacha in Razdori—was beautiful, with its streaks of orange and gold contrasting with the ebony. But it jiggled. He would have forced the workman to fix the problem, if he hadn't shot him. Tradespeople tended to gossip and he couldn't have anyone knowing about this location.

The brass samovar on his bureau rattled with each step. He had worn a circuitous groove in the nap of the Persian rug on his floor, but, like a restless, caged animal, he couldn't stop moving. The last coded burst transmission he had received from Yuri, or Kasprzyk as he was known to the other members of The Global Group, had said that the team had arrived at Abqaiq at 6:27 p.m. local time the previous night, had cleared the gate, and was approaching the first target.

Then all had gone silent. Yuri should have reported in by eight or nine at the latest, but Akhmetalin had heard nothing. He had trained all the eyes and ears he could muster towards Abqaiq without alerting his superiors. There had been a small flurry of activity, but a dust storm had brewed suddenly and obscured everything. When the storm abated one hour later, the anniversary celebration was in full swing, the guards were at their regular posts, and nothing looked amiss. Akhmetalin had stolen some time on a Russian satellite passing the area with imaging so powerful it could spot a quarter on a beach, but there had been no sign of the team or of their vehicle.

They had disappeared.

The FSB Colonel eyed the bottle of vodka perched next to the samovar. He never touched the poison, but he wanted some now. He stomped toward the bottle and grabbed it roughly, angry at himself for this most Russian of weaknesses. His thick, callused fingers fumbled with the cap and the glass trembled in his left hand as he poured. He downed the shot in one mouthful and quickly poured another and swallowed, gritting his teeth and closing his eyes, enjoying the explosive burn in his chest from the caustic liquor. It had been a long time.

Akhmetalin sighed and collapsed into his leather-backed chair behind the ornate, mahogany desk that curved across his office in a half-circle. He rubbed his bleary eyes, red-rimmed with exhaustion, and tightened the tie he had jerked loose at midnight. His suit coat hung, crisp and fresh, on the tree in the corner, but his pants and shirt were rumpled and sweat-stained from the past twenty-four hours. He needed a shower, a fresh change of clothes, some strong tea and a mammoth stack of blini, the paper-thin Russian pancakes he loved.

But first, he needed to decide where he stood. Option A, the team had successfully completed the operation but Yuri was unable to communicate either because of technical problems or because it wasn't safe. Possible, but unlikely. Safety was not a troubling concern because the coded burst they had planned was extremely difficult to track. If there had been technical problems, Yuri would have found an alternative way to get word to Akhmetalin. The Colonel's brow furrowed as he pondered a third reason for the lack of communication. Yuri could be dead, but Akhmetalin had planned for that possibility. The American, Kenner, had been instructed to call an apartment in London and leave a message on the answering machine if Yuri had been killed. There was no message. If Yuri and Kenner were both dead, then undoubtedly, the entire team had been killed. The question still remained, however, had they completed the mission before being killed? If not, then that left him with Option B.

Option B meant either containable failure, or unmitigated disaster. If the team had failed to inject the inoculum and been killed in the attempt, that was disappointing. This had been his best chance to eliminate the Saudi threat, but, if word of the attack leaked out, the Americans would be blamed. That would, at least, be a partial success.

But if the Saudis had captured his team, that would be a disaster. The Saudis were as brutal as the Russians, perhaps even more so.

McKeon and the female professor would crack immediately. Kenner, too. But they would blame The Global Group. They could not tie him to the operation. Yuri could, though.

Akhmetalin swiveled in his chair and glanced out the window at the cold, gray Moscow evening. Another long, hard winter was coming. Akhmetalin had always sneered at the Europeans who played in the snow. Riding their silly ski lifts. Laughing on their toboggans. They knew nothing of a true winter. A Russian winter was not a plaything. It howled off the steppes, punishing all who sought succor in a barren land. One day soon, the hard, pitiless Russian winter would scour the rest of the world clean. Only the icy Russian spirit would survive.

Yuri, like Akhmetalin, knew how to survive the winter, but could the Saudis force him to talk? The Colonel pondered this question for a long time before concluding that his agent would never talk. One of Yuri's teeth had been fitted with a false cap, hiding a cyanide pill. Akhmetalin had trained the agent to loosen the cap with his tongue in case his hands were tied, or missing. If captured, Yuri would do his duty and die, of that Akhmetalin was certain.

Akhmetalin decided to order one of his subordinates to continue surreptitiously monitoring Abqaiq while he headed to his apartment for a shower and change of clothes before a very hearty dinner. All in all, he thought he had handled a difficult day well. And there was still the chance that the Saudi oil reserves were dying by the moment. At the very least, he might still be able to sow discord between the Americans and Saudis. It wasn't everything, but it was something.

He stepped toward the door, confident that he had weathered the worst.

Then his phone rang.

Fifty-three

Akhmetalin barked a short laugh of relief when he recognized Yuri's number on the display and quickly thumbed his phone on.

"*Na-kon-nets.*" Finally. "*Operatseya oo-dalass?*"

"Yes, Director," Michael replied coolly. "The operation was a success."

The Colonel froze. His eyes darted around his office as if he expected to see McKeon materialize out of thin air. Why did he have Yuri's phone? How did he find this number? Akhmetalin's number was password-protected with a failsafe device that erased the phone after a third unsuccessful attempt to guess the password.

"Kasprzyk didn't hide his password very well," Michael continued.

Akhmetalin still had not responded when McKeon's disembodied voice returned to assault his eardrum.

"You're awfully quiet, Director. I expected you to be happy. I've kept up my end of the bargain. You better have kept yours."

Akhmetalin struggled to recover from his shock.

"Where is . . ."

He almost spoke Yuri's real name, but caught himself.

". . . Kasprzyk?"

"That's not his real name is it? I can hear it in your voice. He's not Polish, either, is he? He's Russian and so are you. So let me ask you this: I can understand why two Russians would want to destroy Saudi Arabia's oil, but why attack your own country's oil?"

This was bad. Terrible. McKeon was never supposed to hear his voice. Now he knew one significant part of Akhmetalin's identity. He was Russian. Akhmetalin shook himself. It was a momentary lapse. Time to regain control. He hardened his voice.

"You didn't answer my question."

"Kasprzyk? He's dead. Everyone's dead, except me."

"How did you escape?"

"You didn't answer *my* question. Why do two Russians want to destroy Russian oil?"

Akhmetalin regained his footing.

"We have our reasons, which don't concern you. What concerns you is that I still have Milla and Katya and you haven't finished your mission. Since everyone else is dead, I shall take your report. Tell me what happened. Do not leave anything out. I will know and the repercussions will be severe."

Akhmetalin heard McKeon sigh.

"I should've figured Kasprzyk and you for Russians long ago. You don't shut up with the threats." McKeon's voice turned frigid. "Believe me, I haven't forgotten that you have my wife and daughter."

"So tell me what happened."

"I successfully injected the culture at the water pumps and at the oil holding tank. While we were at the water pumps, Julia attacked Kasprzyk and he killed her." Michael, his voice flat and even, tried to stay as close to the truth as possible.

"That must have been upsetting to you."

Michael ignored the satisfaction in the Director's voice and continued with his report.

"Kasprzyk, David and I drove to the oil holding tank. A sandstorm kicked up just as we arrived."

The Director nodded silently. The sandstorm had prevented him from monitoring the facility via satellite.

"Saudi security forces arrived as I was finishing the last bag of inoculum. They killed David and Kasprzyk."

"How did you escape?" Akhmetalin let the suspicion pour into his voice.

"I slipped away in the sandstorm. I found our truck and carried five camera cases with me on a strap we rigged. I wandered blind for ten, twenty minutes until I found the reception hall. Then I found the gym, stole some clothes, car keys, and an ID badge from a locker, and escaped."

"If you have the cases, that means you have the culture?"

"Yes."

"Where are you?"

"I'll keep that to myself for now."

Akhmetalin wanted to shout in relief. This couldn't have worked out better. It was unfortunate about Yuri, but he had known the risks. With Yuri dead, no one could point the finger at Akhmetalin. The Colonel eyed the opened bottle of vodka. Perhaps one more shot to celebrate? History rewarded the bold. Soon, Akhmetalin would receive his rewards.

"I need to arrange a flight for you to the next target."

"Sakhalin?"

Akhmetalin pursed his lips, annoyed. Yuri, or, more likely, that idiot Kenner must have revealed the next target. Information was a precious commodity that should be doled out in small drops. He sighed inwardly. No matter. Everything was falling into place.

"Where shall it meet you?"

"Not until I get my third phone call."

"You're not in a position . . ."

"Shut up. You have five minutes to have Milla call back on this phone or I turn myself in to the Saudi security forces and give them this phone. After I talk to Milla, I'll tell you where to send the plane."

Michael terminated the call. Akhmetalin stared at his phone for a long moment. *So McKeon's still in Saudi Arabia. Interesting.* He walked over to the bureau and poured himself a generous portion of vodka. He banged it down his throat in a single shot and gritted his teeth against the burn. *This is all working out better than I could have hoped.*

But then a troubling thought hit him. McKeon wanted to talk to his wife. He tapped the glass against his chin, weighing how he could possibly respond to that request.

—◦◦◦—

Mahabith Detention Facility
Undisclosed Location
Empty Quarter, Saudi Arabia

Michael's hand trembled with rage as he placed the phone on the table between him and his interrogator. Al-Naimi stared at him with a strange mixture of compassion and calculation.

"I can see why you want to kill this man called the Director."

Michael nodded silently. He ignored the plate of dates the man had brought. His stomach was too twisted to handle food. Instead, he reached for a glass of water. His mouth still tasted of blood and sand.

"Will he call back?" al-Naimi asked.

Michael nodded again.

"I was right. He wants me to go to Sakhalin."

"A Russian wants to destroy Russian oil?" The interrogator patted his beard. "Curious."

Michael finished the water, which gurgled painfully in his empty stomach, and looked around the small conference room. It was small and nondescript with beige walls and no windows. His head throbbed and his ribs ached from the beating he had received but he had refused the offer of painkillers. He needed a clear head. A Saudi doctor had cleaned and bandaged his wounds and wrapped his ribs and ankle. His right eye was swollen shut, which was slightly disorienting. Someone had mercifully brought him a change of clothes, taking away his old clothes, which stunk of blood and sweat and were encased in layers of grit and grime. The long-sleeved, white cotton shirt and thin, tan linen pants felt cool, almost chilly, in the air-conditioned room.

"I hope you can trace these phone calls and find that son of a bitch," Michael muttered.

"We will." The man shifted. "Perhaps it's time for introductions. I am Sa'id al-Naimi, of the *Re'asat Al Istikhbarat Al A'amah*, the General Intelligence Presidency."

"I'm honored," Michael replied sardonically.

"Thank you, but you should know that most people who meet me don't survive."

The same is true for me, Michael thought.

"The GIP handles all foreign intelligence for the Saudi government. We are also in charge of anti-terrorism."

"I'm a terrorist?"

"What else would you call yourself?"

Michael accepted the appellation with a nod.

"A reluctant one, though," Michael said.

Al-Naimi splayed his hands in a gesture of helplessness.

"Reluctant or not, you have attacked my country on my watch. You have resisted our interrogation longer than most, but, understand this, if the Director doesn't call you back within the remaining two minutes, I will take you back downstairs, and conduct the rest of the questioning *personally*."

Michael simply shrugged. The Director would call. He had to.

Fifty-four

Twenty seconds . . . fifteen . . . ten. . . .
The two men watched the hand on the wall clock tick away the remaining seconds.

Five seconds.

The phone rang. Michael let out a slow breath and picked it up.

"You were almost out of time," he said, speaking as much to himself as to the Director. But the Director was not on the phone.

"Michael?"

"Milla!"

"Michael! Thank God! They said you were dead."

"How's Katya?"

"She's scared, but we're alive."

Michael heard the sounds of a struggle, and then the Director came on the line.

"Where shall I send the plane?"

Michael took a long breath and looked at al-Naimi.

"Riyadh."

Michael could hear the smugness in the Director's voice.

"It's on its way. When you land in Yuzhno-Sakhalinsk, go to this address."

Michael scribbled the address on a notepad al-Naimi slid across the table to him.

"There will be a man waiting for you there. He will take you to Nogliki and then to Molikpaq. That's your target. He will stay with you and show you where to insert the inoculum. When you're done, he will notify me and we will make arrangements for the release of your wife and daughter."

After the Director terminated the phone call, Michael slipped the phone into his pocket and made to stand up. He caught his breath as a red hot bolt of pain lanced through his ribs.

"Please sit down," al-Naimi said quietly.

"I'm fine."

"I'm not concerned with how you feel."

Michael looked at the man's stony face and slowly sank back into his chair. A queasy feeling stirred in his stomach.

"What's going on?" Michael asked.

Al-Naimi answered. "You are not getting on that plane."

——⌇∾⌇——

FSB Headquarters, Lubyanka Square, Moscow

In a darkened, closet-sized room deep within the bowels of the FSB Headquarters, First Deputy Aleksandr Yakovlev tapped on the shoulder of an audio technician and signaled to him to stop recording. The glow of the computer console and winking lights cast a greenish glow across the man's puffy face. In the flickering light, Yakovlev's goatee made him look more like the devil instead of Lenin, although the technician would never think of pointing that out. He kept his eyes glued to the computer screen and tried to ignore the sweat running down his temples.

"Good work, Dmitri," Yakovlev said to the tech. The man's name was actually Mikhail, but the technician would never think of pointing that out either. "Alert our agents in Yuzhno-Sakhalinsk. Have them waiting at the airport."

After meeting with "Viktor," Yakovlev had ordered Akhmetalin to his office. He hadn't expected to glean any information from his subordinate, but wanted to turn up the heat and see what bubbled to the surface. Around midnight, his agents had discovered an industrial storage facility off the Dmitrovskoye Highway and the Third Transport Ring leased to a front company for the FSB colonel. The building was not on the list of properties the FSB maintained, nor was it connected to any active operation. Akhmetalin had gone rogue. Yakovlev's team had just finished setting up surveillance this evening when Akhmetalin had burst out of his office. He had been in such a hurry that he had not noticed the team tailing him to the factory. The FSB officers spotted Akhmetalin through a window on the second floor and picked up the sound vibrations from the window, relaying them to the sound tech.

As Yakovlev left the tech in the closet-sized room and stalked down the hallway as fast as his stumpy legs would carry him, his eyes squinted intently at an unseen target. His red, bushy eyebrows nearly touched his cheeks. He had never liked Akhmetalin. The man was taller than him by a good forty-five centimeters, and was an arrogant bastard to boot. Yakovlev danced on the balls of his feet in anticipation of hunting his subordinate. He would give Akhmetalin just enough rope to hang himself. And Yakovlev would enjoy watching him dangle.

Fifty-five

―᠍᠍᠍᠍᠍᠍᠍᠍ᨌᨌᨌ᠍᠍᠍―

King Khalid International Airport, Riyadh

"You should have told me you weren't going to let me fly on the Director's plane," Michael said angrily as the GIP agents loaded the cases containing the last of the microbes onto the waiting plane, a small eight-passenger Citation Encore.

Al-Naimi sat across from Michael.

"We have left a message for the Director's pilot saying that you have arranged your own transportation to Sakhalin."

"You're playing games with my family's lives."

"It was necessary. Never do what your enemy expects," al-Naimi cautioned. "Believe everything is a trap. That is how you survive."

He gestured wearily around the plane.

"This aircraft has a top speed of almost 800 kilometers per hour," he explained. "You'll fly to Bangkok, then to Seoul, then to Yuzho-Sakhalinsk. Khalid will travel with you and will keep you under surveillance after you arrive."

One of the agents stepped forward and nodded as al-Naimi watched Michael from under heavy lids.

"I'm taking an awful chance, letting you leave. I don't believe threats are necessary here. You've been threatened enough and understand the consequences. My position, however, requires that I remind you that we will be watching you constantly. Consider that a promise instead of a threat."

Michael touched his still-throbbing eye and nodded.

"I understand."

Fifty-six

—◦◦◦—

Ritz Carlton, Moscow

Billings flashed his key card and yanked open the door to his suite, still incensed that they had missed Stark and Longfellow. Viktor's men would keep watch on the *Zolotaya Ptitsa*, but Longfellow and Stark were too smart to return. And the iPhone was no longer transmitting so he had no idea where they were. To make matters even worse, that damned computer analyst, Tigger or whatever his name was, had disappeared also. Billings shoved the key card back into his pocket. What were things coming to when the NSA, with all of its resources, couldn't find a fucking computer analyst?

It was the smell of after-shave that first told Billings that he wasn't alone.

He recognized it, some vulgar, cheap after-shave with cowboys in its commercials, like Rawhide or Round-Up or some ridiculous thing like that. He had to smell that disgusting stench every day at work, so he wasn't surprised to see who was sitting on the couch in his living room, cowboy boots on the coffee table.

"To what do I owe this unexpected pleasure, Jack?" Billings asked, making a show of checking his watch. It was almost midnight.

White House Chief of Staff Jack Rafferty peered sourly over the tips of his boots at Billings.

"It's a right godawful mess, Stan, a mess!" he drawled in a thick, West Texas accent.

229

Billings steeled himself. Born and bred in Colorado, the NSA Director considered himself a true Westerner, unlike the silver-buckled former cowhands constantly bragging "Don't mess with Texas!" He had always found the Chief of Staff embarrassing and had no idea how the famously self-controlled, Catholic President from Massachusetts abided the man. But here he was.

"What is, Jack?"

"Everything," Rafferty replied with a disgusted wave of his hand toward the world in general. "Some renegade general in Libya is trying to seize the parliament building. ISIS just released another beheading video. And the fucking Iranian National Guard is in Iraq."

Billings noted with displeasure that Rafferty had gotten into the bottle of eighteen-year-old Glenlivet he had ordered from O2 upon his arrival. The man knew no boundaries.

The Chief of Staff drained the scotch from his glass, slammed the crystal tumbler onto the coffee table with a sharp crack that made the NSA Director wince and heaved himself off the couch with an angry grunt. Rafferty was Billings' opposite in almost every way: rotund, almost slovenly, to Billings' ascetic trimness; voluble to Billings' terseness; unbridled to Billings' desperate need for control. But they did share two things in common: both detested the other and, at the moment, both were furious.

"As much as I'd like to commiserate, I have work to do before I meet with the President in an hour, so," Billings said, waving a hand toward the door.

Rafferty stepped closer, ignoring the gesture.

"And, at the most critical moment of this presidency, when the fate of most of the world, and certainly of this presidency, hangs in the balance, I discover that our Deputy NSA Director has gone missing!" The red-faced Chief of Staff planted himself uncomfortably close to Billings. The NSA Director recalled stories of President Johnson berating staffers while sitting on the toilet just off the Oval Office with the door open and his trousers around his ankles. What was it about Texans and a lack of respect for personal space? Billings forced himself to stand his ground.

"Not only that," Rafferty continued, "but I discover that you have issued an arrest warrant for her and for one of our most senior NSA agents. How do I find this out? Not from my NSA Director, but from the CIA who learned it from the fucking Russians!"

Billings blinked once, but otherwise gave no indication that the fact that the Russians knew about the arrest warrants surprised him.

"Cell phone intercepts of First Deputy of the FSB Aleksandr Yakovlev," Rafferty said, by way of explanation.

"Which is the reason I didn't involve the local authorities in the first place," Billings said, trying to keep his temper in check. "And I'm not *your* NSA Director, Jack. I report to the President."

"The President speaks through me and he's pissed."

A flicker of a smile danced across Billings' face at the thought of this President actually saying he was *pissed*.

"She wasn't my hire," the NSA Director protested.

"She's your responsibility."

"She's a traitor."

"Bullshit!" Rafferty thundered. "She's former Secret Service and a field op. She was nearly killed in the line of duty. She's been instrumental in responding to this mess in the Middle East and Northern Africa. Her record is spotless. The Joint Chiefs love her. Our allies love her. The President loves her. And this fiasco over your arrest warrant is threatening to derail these talks!"

The last thin strand of Billings' self-control snapped.

"We're in this mess because this administration has ignored my advice. If we had taken a stronger, more pro-active and resolute response to the terrorists, to the petro-dictators, to everyone who opposes us, we would be a force to be feared and we wouldn't have to come, hat in hand, begging the Russians and the Saudis to help us."

"Watch yourself."

"We're the United States of America. We act whenever, wherever it is in our interest to do so, and the rest of the world can get in line."

Rafferty took another step closer, beady eyes glaring out of fleshy folds. Billings, taking full advantage of the four inch difference in their heights, stared imperiously down his nose.

"If this President doesn't have your full, unwavering support for his policies, then we'll deal with that situation pretty damn quick," Rafferty said. The Chief of Staff bent over and picked up a manila folder from the coffee table, flipped it open, and slid out a picture, which he held in front of Billings' face. "Mind telling me who this is?"

Billings ground his teeth. It was a picture of the parking lot next to the *Zolotaya Ptitsa*. Viktor, submachine gun slung over his shoulder, stood next to Billings' SUV. And Billings was clearly visible through the open window.

"Were you following me?"

"The CIA was following him," Rafferty said, jabbing a stubby finger at Viktor's face. "What the hell's he doing meeting with you?"

Billings batted the photograph away and stepped around Rafferty. "He's one of my off-the-book operatives." He raised a hand. "Don't lecture me, Jack. We all have them. I was using him to find Melissa to try to avoid the mess we're in."

Rafferty held the photo up again. "He's an active FSB agent. Everything you've told him, he's told his boss, First Deputy Yakovlev. The CIA has the intercepts to prove it."

Billings paled slightly, but held firm.

"Regardless, he's been a serviceable asset. Nothing I've told him has compromised our security."

The Chief of Staff stuffed the photo back into the manila folder and glared at Billings.

"You better hope not. But you are to have no further contact with him."

Billings accepted the order with a clipped nod.

"And when were you going to bother telling us about Stark's assistant?"

Billings blinked slowly at Rafferty.

"What about her assistant?"

Rafferty shot him a look of disgust.

"You know, Stanley, I always knew you were a cold-blooded son of a bitch, but I thought some ounce of humanity flowed through those veins of yours."

Billings could take no more. "What the fuck are you talking about?"

"I'm talking about the fact that her assistant was gunned down outside the Bolshoi earlier today. One of ours. One of yours. I've been on the phone with the Moscow police for an hour." Rafferty jabbed a finger into Billings' chest. "And if her murder is in any way connected to this crap with Stark, I and the President will hold you personally responsible." The Chief of Staff gave a final shove with his finger then stepped to the door. Before leaving, he cast one last scornful glare at Billings. "You're benched. President's orders. We'll deal with you back in Washington. Don't leave this hotel."

After Rafferty had gone, the always grim and measured Billings stepped to the coffee table, grabbed the crystal tumbler the Chief of Staff had used, and hurled it against the mirror, shattering both. Unsatisfied, he threw the opened bottle of scotch after it. Breathing heavy, his eyes closed in fury, the NSA Director pulled an encrypted cell phone from his pocket, one he had never shared with the NSA, and dialed.

Fifty-seven

———

Molodaya Guardiya Industrial Storage Facility, Moscow

Akhmetalin eagerly grabbed the phone. It was the agent he had sent to Riyadh to collect McKeon.

"Do you have him?" Akhmetalin demanded.

"He didn't show, sir."

The FSB colonel hung up on his agent and resumed pacing until the squeaking wood threatened to drive him insane. *No matter*, he told himself. *McKeon may have slipped out of my grasp for the moment, but my people will be waiting for him in Yuzho-Sakhalinsk.*

———

En Route to Yuzhno-Sakhalinsk

The table between Michael and Khalid Nazer, the GIP agent, was covered with all the photographs and plans for the Vityaz Production Complex, more commonly referred to as Sakhalin II, that al-Naimi had been able to produce before the Citation Encore lifted off for Yuzho-Sakhalinsk by way of Bangkok and Seoul. Michael peered at the dagger-shaped island, the farthest east point of Russia's Far East. Jutting out of the Sea of Okhotsk, separated from the northeastern coast of Russia by the Strait of Tartary and from Japan by the Strait of La Perouse, the six-hundred-mile-long island was rough, remote and ice-bound six months of the year.

"In the winter, offshore temperatures drop to seventy degrees below zero. Even now, in April, heavy snows are not uncommon," Nazer said. "The Russian writer Chekhov referred to Sakhalin as 'hell.'"

"That's seems to be where I'm spending most of my time these days," Michael muttered, tracing a finger along the map of the Sakhalin II facilities. "There are three rigs off Sakhalin's northeast coast: Piltun-Astokhskoye-A, Piltun-Astokhskoye-B, and Lunskoye."

"PA-A is Molikpaq?" Nazer asked.

"Right. Molikpaq is Inuit for big wave. It was first used in Arctic waters offshore Canada before being towed to Sakhalin and retrofitted for the much harsher climate. Then they filled its substructure with sand and permanently anchored it to the seabed. PA-A, or Molikpaq, is anchored about ten miles offshore. More than 150 people live and work on it. With fourteen oil wells, four water injection wells and two re-injection wells, Molikpaq is the heart of Sakhalin II. That must be why The Global Group targeted it."

"How much oil is beneath Sakhalin?" Nazer asked.

"An estimated forty-five billion barrels," Michael replied. He turned back to the map he had been examining. "Gas and oil are pumped from the three rigs through giant pipes embedded in the seabed to the onshore processing facility located between Nogliki and Nysh." Michael placed a finger on the OPF then continued tracing south. "They separate the oil and gas at the OPF, add antifreeze then pump it more than five hundred miles south, over mountains, under rivers, and through swamps to the liquid natural gas and oil export terminals at Prigorodnoye in Aniva Bay, the southernmost part of Sakhalin, facing Japan."

Nazer placed several satellite photos of Aniva Bay on top of the map and pointed out the two giant geodesic domes. "Those tanks can store 1.2 million barrels of oil. Subsea pipelines connect them to a tanker loading facility just offshore. Up to 50,000 barrels of oil can be loaded an hour."

"Almost as impressive as your country's operations," Michael said with a slight smile.

Nazer acknowledged the jab with a somber nod. "What about security?" he asked.

Michael flipped open a manila folder and scanned its contents. "With so many of its facilities in incredibly remote locations, Sakhalin II has invested heavily in video surveillance, virtual tripwires and local satellite control rooms." He handed Nazer an internal security plan al-Naimi had somehow obtained. Judging by the contents of the file al-Naimi possessed, the GIP was clearly already aware of the threat Sakhalin II posed to Saudi oil dominance. "In what's described here as the world's largest closed circuit television system, more than six hundred cameras monitor Sakhalin II's infrastructure from start to finish, north to south. The system uses real-time analytics to trigger alarms for any threats or potential threats. Strategically located monitoring stations can respond and dispatch security." Michael closed the file. "Obviously, many of the facilities, like the rigs, the OPF, and the export terminals also have constant, boots-on-the-ground, security."

"And the Director plans to hit Molikpaq?" Nazer asked. "Do we know where?"

Michael shook his head. "Other than the target, he didn't tell us anything, including how I'm supposed to have access to the rig."

Nazer grinned as he stuffed the files back into the backpack. He patted the front zipper pocket. "Assistant Sa'id has arranged for transport to Nogliki and has also secured two passes on the helicopter to Molikpaq. Usually visitors wait weeks for the helicopter, but he was able to yank some strings."

"You mean 'pull some strings.'"

"I think he probably yanked them," Nazer said with a short laugh.

"You have a good grasp of American slang."

"I studied at Yale before joining the GIP."

"Very impressive. What's our cover?"

"We're environmental reporters covering the potential harm to the Steller Sea Eagle caused by Sakhalin II."

"Is Sakhalin II a threat to the Steller Sea Eagle?"

"Depending on whom you ask, very much so, or not at all. There is a colony of them in northern Sakhalin and local environmental groups are concerned that they could be harmed. The oil companies have agreed to monitor and take certain steps to minimize their impact. We're checking up on those steps."

"Very good." Michael stood up. "I'm going to grab a Coke from the back. I saw that you folks were kind enough to stock the fridge."

Nazer followed Michael to the rear of the plane and took an apple juice. He regarded Michael quietly while sipping the juice, and Michael let him. He had become used to being analyzed and measured, and took the opportunity to examine the Saudi operative. Nazer was about six inches shorter than him, broad in the shoulders and narrow in the waist with short, powerful legs. A sprinter's build. His beard was closely trimmed and well-kept. Dark, intelligent eyes glittered out of an angular, but not unpleasant, face. Michael finished his Coke and waited.

"Is there something you want to ask me?"

When Nazer hesitated, Michael pressed.

"About my microbe? I didn't create it as a weapon."

"No, I know that. I read your work while they were, well, while you were with Assistant Sa'id. It's incredibly impressive work. You're brilliant."

Michael shifted uncomfortably. "I'm not very good with compliments. What is it you want to know?"

"Assistant Sa'id said that The Global Group kidnapped your wife and daughter."

"That's right."

"Your daughter is five years old?"

Michael nodded once, his face tightening.

"It's not right," Nazer continued quietly. "Taking a man's wife and daughter, it's not right."

Michael turned away, but Nazer grabbed his elbows, the Saudi's black eyes locking onto his.

"I will help you."

"I know," Michael said as he tried to slip away, but the man tightened his grip. "That's why Al-Naimi sent you with me."

"I mean, beyond Sakhalin."

Michel stopped squirming and stared at the Saudi in surprise.

"The kind of people who would target a little girl don't deserve to live. I will help you find them and kill them."

Michael stumbled over his response and swallowed hard.

"Not many people have ever offered to help me," he said quietly.

Nazer raised his chin and pointed to his chest. "This one is."

Michael grabbed the man's forearm and shook it once, almost shyly, then a second time, more assured. "Thank you."

Fifty-eight

—⟋⟍—

Yuzhno-Sakhalinsk, Sakhalin Island

Melissa Stark stepped out of the shower and dried herself with an over-starched, scratchy towel that smelled vaguely of stale cigarette smoke. She hurried to the bed in her room at the Hotel Gagarin, and slipped on the same pair of jeans she had purchased in Moscow, wrinkling her nose in disgust. Her jeans were filthy from the explosion in Moscow and desperately needed a washing, but there was no time. And they were preferable to the knock off jeans for sale in Yuzhno-Sakhalinsk that were either skin-tight and stiff, or could double as a tent. Their cheap dye would also probably turn her legs blue.

She cast a doubtful eye at the bra and heavy sweater she had purchased. No doubt they would itch, but she had had no choice. Her old bra was too sweat-stained to even contemplate putting back on, and the fleece she had worn in Moscow had no place in Sakhalin's cold air.

With an exasperated sigh, she pulled them on and rotated her shoulders several times to adjust the bra and the sweater. She'd never been to this frigid, former penal colony before, and the sooner she could escape it, the better. A knock on the door caused Melissa to spin and snatch the pistol from her bed. She checked the peephole then unlocked the door.

"Anything more from Sa'id?" she asked Longfellow as he entered the room.

Longfellow had been trying to raise the Saudi since Moscow. "Nothing."

"Are you sure Michael is coming here? What if his target is Siberia?"

Hal leaned against the door, gray from exhaustion. They'd had this argument the entire flight from Moscow aboard the Hawker 1000 Grisha's friend had provided. Why his friend had such a luxurious jet available at a moment's notice and how he had gotten them past customs and air traffic control, Longfellow would rather not know.

"Siberia is dying. Siberia is the past. Sakhalin Island is the future. Sakhalin is Russia's greatest hope, perhaps its last. It has billions of barrels of untapped reserves. Russia has pinned its plans for global energy dominance squarely on Sakhalin. If The Global Group wanted to devastate Russia not only economically, but psychologically, they will hit Sakhalin. Destroy Siberia and Russia will turn its face eastward to Sakhalin. Destroy Sakhalin and you destroy Russia." Longfellow shrugged. "And coming here is better than sitting in Moscow, waiting for Billings or the FSB to find us."

Melissa nodded, as she had the entire flight from Moscow.

"And, if it makes you feel better," Longfellow continued, "I was able to charm some information out of an air traffic controller at the airport. There's a private flight expected today that originated in Riyadh. They don't get many of those here, so I'm betting that's Michael and Julia."

Melissa grinned.

"That's the best news I've heard in days. Let's go."

⚯

Down the street, in a dented, blue van with tinted windows, two men with hard eyes watched Longfellow and Melissa exit the Gagarin.

⚯

The Citation Encore's wheels touched down with a jarring bump on the runway at the Yuzhno-Sakhalinsk International Airport before taxiing to a stop near the industrial-looking, gray terminal. Michael waited as Nazer opened the cabin door. The icy blast that struck him was as jarring as Saudi Arabia's heat had been. He shivered and zipped the down jacket Nazer had supplied. The wind sliced through his linen pants as if he were naked. The two men split the camera cases between them and hurried across the tarmac to the customs door.

"What time is it?" Michael asked.

"Just before one in the afternoon, local time," Nazer replied.

Only a bored official waited at the customs desk. Michael braced himself for another maddening dance with Russian bureaucracy, but the official, a short, wispy-haired man stuffed into his uniform, gave their camera cases a cursory examination before waving them through. As Michael and Nazer disappeared around the corner, a tall, dark-haired, sallow-faced man in a leather trench coat and high, black boots, stepped up to the official and slipped him a stack of rubles.

"*Horoshaya rabota*," the dark-haired man said in a raspy voice. *Good job.*

Around the corner, Michael pointed at a sign for the bus, but Nazer kept walking.

"Wait, where are we going?" Michael asked. "This is the bus to the city center. The Korean restaurant is in the city center."

Nazer paused and cast a patient look at Michael, the kind of look Michael usually reserved for painfully slow students.

"We're not going to the Korean restaurant for the same reason you didn't get on the Director's plane. We've reserved a plane to Nogliki."

"Why didn't we just stay on the GIP plane?"

"We couldn't take that into Nogliki. Only a few planes fly there."

Michael followed Nazer down the sidewalk away from the bus stop, wincing as the camera cases bumped against his damaged ribs.

"What kind of plane?"

"You'll see," Nazer replied with a faint grin.

—⦿⦿⦿—

Behind Michael and Nazer, the man in the leather trench coat pulled out his cell phone, dialed, and spoke in urgent, hushed tones into it.

Fifty-nine

—⁓—

"What the hell's that?"

Michael stared in disbelief at the ugly monstrosity perched in front of a maintenance hangar at the edge of the airfield, its twin propellers spinning lazily in the cold air.

"That's the quickest way to Nogliki," Nazer explained. "It's an Antonov An-24, a forty-four-seat twin turboprop manufactured in the 1960s in the former Soviet Union, designed for rough strips and remote locations. Those high wings protect the engine and blades from debris, which will be helpful where we're going."

"Does it still fly?"

A bemused smile flitted across Nazer's face.

"Unless Assistant Sa'id is being exceptionally cruel."

"Anyone else on the plane?"

"Just us and the pilot."

"At least we'll have room to stretch out."

—⁓—

The man in the trench coat peered around the corner of the maintenance hangar. Three men suddenly appeared at his elbow, dressed in black and carrying sub-machine guns. After a brief, hushed conversation, the four fanned out toward the tarmac. As Michael stepped toward the plane, the man pulled a snub-nosed sub-machine gun from inside his coat.

—⁓—

Michael had climbed half the steps to the open cabin door when the first shot rang out. In one fluid movement, Nazer dropped the two camera cases, drew his Sig Sauer P556 Swat semi-automatic pistol from the holster inside his jacket, and pivoted towards the firing. Over Nazer's head, Michael glimpsed four men running toward them with weapons drawn. As he tossed the two camera cases into the plane, the pilot revved the engines. The twin propellers kicked through the air, whipping Michael's parka in the wash.

While bullets pinged off the fuselage, Michael ducked behind Nazer and grabbed the cases the man had dropped.

"Who's shooting at us now?" Michael demanded.

"Who knows," Nazer said as he returned fire.

"Let's go!" Michael shouted.

Nazer nodded and began retreating up the stairs, shooting steadily. Two of the assailants had taken cover behind a dumpster and were firing from both sides. As Michael reached the doorway, he spotted a third creeping toward the plane's tail.

"On your right!" he shouted.

Before Nazer could react, a new barrage of gunfire cut the assailant in two.

"Who's shooting at them?" Michael demanded to no one in particular.

Longfellow peered over the luggage cart at the dead man. Melissa crouched next to him, gun trained on the dumpster's near edge.

"Nice shot," she called over her shoulder.

"Michael's on that plane," Longfellow said. "We've got to get on that plane."

"We have to get past those gunmen first."

Just then, the two gunmen behind the dumpster unleashed another volley, split this time between the plane and the luggage cart. Longfellow and Melissa ducked as the bullets chewed up the tarmac and the cart shuddered from the impact.

At the plane, Nazer had ducked inside. As he reached around the cabin door to return fire, Michael raced to the cockpit. There he found the pilot, frantically trying to raise help on his radio. Michael knocked the radio from his grasp and grabbed the man's long ponytail, snapping his head back.

"You call for help and we kill you," Michael barked in Russian.

The man gaped, revealing yellowed and missing teeth. Sunlight danced off his Yoko Ono glasses.

"Are you crazy?" the man replied in English.

"Get us off the ground now or you're dead."

Michael then turned and ran back toward Nazer.

———※———

Seeing the plane move, both assailants raced from the dumpster toward the stairs.

"Now!" Longfellow roared as he opened fire. Instantly, the leather-jacketed Russian's ear exploded, dropping him in his tracks. Melissa sighted on the man's partner, but before she could drop him, he squeezed off a triple-tap toward the open cabin door.

As the plane jerked forward, Nazer was thrown across the open door directly into the semi-automatic fire. Three holes stitched across Nazer's collarbone, splattering blood and bone. The force of the bullets spun the Saudi into Michael, who caught him as he fell.

"No, no!" Michael shouted, checking for a pulse.

It was no use. One glance at the blood pumping from the three wounds and the glassy look in the man's eyes revealed the awful truth.

Michael's head was just visible from the bottom steps as the Russian aimed and began to squeeze the trigger. Before his finger could complete its contraction, Melissa's pistol barked. A crimson stain erupted on his chest as her bullet severed his spine and ripped out the front.

Just as she turned to wave him forward, Longfellow pointed his gun at Melissa's head and fired.

The Deputy NSA Director didn't even have time to scream as the bullet whistled past her ear and thudded into the fourth assailant, crawling toward her under the plane's nose. Longfellow raced forward and caught Melissa just as her knees buckled.

"Sorry about that. There wasn't time to warn you."

Inside the cabin, Michael stumbled toward the door to close it, slipping in a pool of blood as the plane inched away from the stairs. Before he could close the door, a figure momentarily eclipsed the sun. He froze as the woman pointed a gun at him.

"I'm Melissa Stark, Deputy National Security Director."

It was as if she had spoken gibberish. But his confusion soon gave way to utter shock at the next figure to step through, pulling the door shut after him.

"Are you okay, Michael?" Longfellow asked.

Michael's mouth hung open.

"I'll get the pilot," Melissa said, hurrying toward the cockpit.

Longfellow stepped toward Michael and examined him, his gaze evaluating the cuts and bruises, the almost-shut eye, until he was satisfied that the blood was not Michael's.

"I've been worried sick about you."

Michael finally found his voice.

"Hal?"

Sixty

—◦◦◦—

Flying North Toward Nogliki

Michael perched on the edge of his seat, where Longfellow, the man Michael knew as Hal Jacobs, his mentor, fellow professor and department chair, had led him. Melissa joined them after covering Nazer's body with a blanket she had found in a first aid compartment. Michael felt like he was suffering from a case of vertigo, and not from the bucking and bouncing An-24.

"I don't understand. What are you doing here?" he asked as Hal knelt in front of him.

"I'll explain everything, but first, where's Julia?"

Michael closed his eyes, his pained expression saying everything.

"What happened?" Hal asked in a voice full of dread.

"She attacked them while we were at Abqaiq. One of our captors, Kasprzyk, shot and killed her."

Hal sagged into the chair next to Michael, ashen-faced, and stared at his hands.

"No," he whispered.

"I tried to stop it, but I couldn't." Michael spread his hands, looking from Hal to Melissa for absolution. "I stopped Kasprzyk from shooting her once, but . . . ." His voice trailed away as the names of all those he had failed to protect sounded inside his head, each one an accusation. *Dad. Mom. Janie. Milla and Katya. Julia.* He glanced sorrowfully at the blanket-clad corpse. *Nazer.* Who would be next?

Hal placed a rough hand on Michael's arm. "It's not your fault. It's never been your fault."

His mentor's hand looked older than he remembered. The knuckles were gnarled and purpled. Liver spots dotted the back. And it shook slightly, although that could have been the plane's vibration. It was the hand of an old friend. His only friend.

He asked again: "What are you doing here?"

Hal's sigh was almost as loud as the engine's throaty roar.

"It's a long story and we don't have a lot of time. I've been a field agent for the NSA since the late seventies, specializing first in Soviet and then in Russian affairs. Over the past ten years, I've spent most of my time on energy security issues."

Michael blinked slowly."I don't understand."

"You've been through a tremendous amount in the past few days and I wouldn't expect you to understand."

"You're not a spy. You're a scientist and a professor at Bowdoin College."

"I am a scientist and a professor. I was before the NSA recruited me and I still am."

Michael sat back and cast a long, searching look at the friend he thought he had known. As the plane bounced through an air pocket and the cold air leached through the metal skin, Michael began to work through the implications of what Hal had just told him, none of which he liked.

"Who knows about this?"

"No one outside the NSA, except you, now."

Hal laid a hand on Michael's knee.

"I'm so sorry I wasn't there when they came for you and your family, and Julia. The NSA sent me on a last minute mission, but I should have been there. I could have tried to stop them."

Hal's voice caught in his throat. He cleared it roughly and continued.

"The NSA is trying to locate Milla and Katya, but hasn't been able to find them. I, we," Hal shot a quick glance at Melissa, "believe firmly that they are still alive. Do you have any idea where they might be?"

Michael had winced at his wife's and daughter's names. Now he removed his knee from Hal's hand. "So let me make sure I understand this clearly. When you met me at the teen center, you were already working for the NSA?" Michael took Hal's silence as an admission and continued. "And when you got me into Bowdoin, the same? The same when you got me my job at Bowdoin and when you encouraged my research into the biodegradation of oil?" Hal had stopped nodding and sat, pale and still, like a witness on the stand who knew his darkest secrets were about to be exposed. "And when I received government funding for my research? When I scheduled my press conference?" Michael's anger burned in his chest. "And when The Global Group was plotting to kidnap my family, this entire time, you've been working for the NSA?"

Michael stood up and tottered across the shimmying fuselage away from Hal, leaving the friendship that had carried him from Janie to Milla and Katya discarded in the space between. He was shaking, from the turbulence, but more from the realization that the one person he had trusted the longest, the one person he thought would never lie to him, had. *Just like Mom and Dad. And David.* And the countless other people who had wormed in and out of his life.

"So this has all been a lie?" he called over the roar of the plane's engines. "You found me at the teen center because you thought I might be useful."

"That's not true," Hal said, standing up.

"And you trained me at Bowdoin so I could produce something the NSA could use," Michael said, backing toward the tail of the plane. Hal followed, hands up, pleading. Melissa, a step behind, watched the exchange through narrowed eyes.

"No."

"I'm an asset to you. That's all I've ever been."

"No, I . . ."

"You wound me up and sent me down this path, and now look what's happened. Where were you, where was the fucking NSA when they grabbed my wife and daughter?"

"That's enough. Time for crying's over," snapped Melissa, who had followed the two men to the tail of the plane. "My orders were to get Longfellow on a plane and get the hell out of here, but he convinced me to find you. Our government is after us for treason because of you. People have been killed because of you. We should all be heading to Washington right now to try to fix this, but here we are, trying to rescue your family."

Melissa stepped closer, green eyes sparking. For the first time, Michael noticed that she had a lisp that grew more pronounced the faster she spoke.

"You've got the United States of America in a hell of a position, Michael. The Deputy Director of the National Security Agency is on a plane to Nogliki to help you destroy Russian oil for no other reason than to save your wife and daughter. I've already killed at least one Russian back on the tarmac. Who knows how many crimes Longfellow's committed? The NSA, the Secret Service, the FSB and who knows who else are after us. As we speak, the President of the United States is meeting with the Russian and Saudi heads of state, in our last best chance to prevent the Middle East and North Africa from burning up and being lost to the Iranian mullahs or the ISIS fanatics forever. And because The Global Group kidnapped one mother and daughter from Brunswick, Maine, we may already have lost." She laughed ruefully. "I'm still trying to figure out how your family became more important than our national security, so don't cry to me about how abused you've been."

"Milla and Katya don't deserve to be sacrificed," Michael said. "They're innocent."

"No innocent person ever deserves to be sacrificed," Melissa responded, softer. "That's the definition of being innocent."

She rubbed her hands quickly over her face and blew out a long breath.

"Arguing doesn't get us anywhere. We're all in this mess to-gether. I'm hoping someone has a plan to destroy the Russian oil, save your family, and, I really hope, save the Middle East and North Africa for all of us. And, given how we blasted out of Yuzhno, I should point out that The Global Group or the FSB or whoever else was shooting at us, probably knows where this plane is headed. So how do we get off this plane in one piece?"

Michael glared angrily at Stark for a long moment, before nod-ding in détente, and returning to the front of the plane. He closed his eyes while his brain chewed on the problem of how to avoid the deadly reception undoubtedly waiting for them. Then he pulled the map of Sakhalin Island from Nazer's backpack and tracked their route. He turned to Melissa.

"I think I have an idea."

Sixty-one

⎯⎯⎯⎯

Molodaya Guardiya Industrial Storage Facility, Moscow

With an angry snarl, Akhmetalin kicked over the desk, scattering the files across the floor. His assistant, Leonid Stepanin, the only FSB operative Akhmetalin had brought into The Global Group, jumped out of the way of a hurtling laptop just before it smashed into the concrete block wall with a scream of electronic static then fell dark and silent. Akhmetalin stood in the middle of his office, on the third story of the industrial storage facility on Moscow's northern side, clutching his cell phone in his hand, trembling with rage.

"Why aren't they answering their phones?" he bellowed at Stepanin, who ducked again, afraid that Akhmetalin would find something else to hurl at him. "Where are my operatives in Yuzhno!"

The colonel stomped to the office window and peered east, as if he could see all the way to Yuzhno-Sakhalinsk. His operatives would have informed him if McKeon had not arrived. Something must have gone wrong, but what?

Akhmetalin pressed his burning forehead against the cool glass of the window. Behind him, Stepanin quietly righted the table and slid the destroyed laptop into his briefcase. He couldn't leave something so incriminating lying around. He straightened his shoulders and waited for the next outburst from his superior officer, praying hard that the cell phone would finally ring.

⎯⎯⎯⎯

FSB Headquarters, Lubyanka, Moscow

"What's he doing now?" First Deputy Yakovlev asked the agents conducting the surveillance of Akhmetalin's warehouse.

"He's standing with his head pressed against the window, sir," the agent with the binoculars reported through his throat microphone.

"He's complaining that his operatives in Yuzhno-Sakhalinsk haven't called," added the other agent wearing headphones.

In his office at FSB Headquarters, Yakovlev stroked his red beard and smiled a mean smile.

"Nor will they. Keep him under constant surveillance, but don't let him see you."

Yakovlev terminated the connection, picked up the phone on his desk, and dialed a number.

"This requires immediate attention," he barked as soon as the individual on the other end of the line answered. "There is a terrorist flying toward Nogliki on an An-24 out of Yuzhno-Sakhalinsk. His name is Michael McKeon. He is an American. He must be detained. You may hurt him, but do not kill him under any circumstances. I want him flown here, to me, immediately upon capture. Do you understand?"

Yakovlev hung up. He leaned back in his chair and stared at the ceiling. A high-pitched cackle spilled out of him, grating, like metal on metal. In the growing gloom, his goateed face made him appear like the devil his subordinates whispered about.

⤙∾∾⤚

Akhmetalin continued to stare out the window for several long, silent moments. Something was wrong. A warning light flashed on the edge of his consciousness. He had screwed up, but how? When?

Then, he knew. He turned from the window and strode toward Stepanin, who tensed, waiting for the blow. Akhmetalin gripped his junior officer by the shoulders and pulled him close in a bear hug. Stepanin, surprised and fearful, stood rigid. The FSB colonel placed his lips close to Stepanin's left ear and whispered. A moment later, he released the white-faced Stepanin. Akhmetalin nodded toward the exit, then walked across the room to the bathroom, turned on the light, and shut the door. A shell-shocked Stepanin turned robotically and walked toward the exit. His limbs moved mechanically, almost against his will, for, if he had had any choice, he would have shot himself right then.

—◦◦◦—

"One of them is leaving," whispered the FSB agent with the binoculars.

"Akhmetalin?" asked the agent with the headphones, for he hadn't heard any conversation in the warehouse office for several long minutes.

"The other one."

"Let him go. It's Akhmetalin that Yakovlev wants."

The two agents settled into their perch and waited for Akhmetalin to come out of the bathroom.

—◦◦◦—

Ritz Carlton, Moscow

In the center of Moscow, in his suite at the Ritz Carlton, NSA Director Stanley Billings opened his door to find two Secret Service agents posted outside. He stared impassively at them then shut the door. Things were spinning out of control. The one person he needed to reach was not answering his phone. Billings glared balefully at the door. This would not stand.

Nothing was lost yet. He could still regain control. He just had to get out of this hotel.

—◦◦◦—

Nogliki Airport, Nogliki, Sakhalin Island

Boris Ivanovich's head lolled side to side as he slept soundly in his chair in the blue and white air traffic control tower at the recently constructed Nogliki Airport. His snoring rattled off the metal walls, almost drowning out the sound of footsteps pounding up the stairs towards him. It wasn't unusual for Boris to catch a nap during his shift. Although air traffic had increased since Sakhalin Energy paved over the old dirt and stone runway and constructed the $40 million airport at Nogliki as the jumping-off point for the company's offshore drilling platforms, flights were still infrequent, leaving plenty of time for Boris to catch up on his rest. He needed it, because Boris lived with his wife, Voluntina, in a small house near the energy company's base camp that served as what passed for a bed and breakfast in Nogliki. Because no "guests" were allowed inside the base camp, the workers often met their "guests" at Boris's house. When their drunken carousing and carnal screaming didn't keep him awake, Boris' wife's snoring did. His wife snored like a Soviet helicopter: choppy and deafening.

As a result, Boris was too exhausted to hear the thudding of several pairs of boots racing to the top of the tower, just as he had been too exhausted to notice the plane that had disappeared from his radar several minutes before.

The first FSB agent through the door kicked the chair out from under Boris. The second grabbed the startled air traffic controller by the lapels on his jacket and yanked him off the floor. The third stuck his jowely, unshaven face into Boris' and demanded to know when a chartered An-24 out of Yuzhno-Sakhalinsk was landing.

"I don't have any record of a charter from Yuzhno," the flummoxed Boris stammered.

"There's a charter from Yuzhno," the third agent insisted. "And if you don't find it, you will go to Lubyanka."

Boris paled and hurriedly checked his records, but found no flight plan for a charter from Yuzhno-Sakhalinsk that evening.

"Sometimes they don't file flight plans," Boris explained. "They don't always follow the rules this far away from everywhere."

"Look!" the second agent exclaimed, pointing at the radar screen. "There's the plane."

Boris looked at the screen then shook his head.

"That plane is flying toward Yuzhno."

The third agent peered suspiciously at the screen.

"But from where? Did it take off from here?"

"No. There have been no flights this evening."

"It's flying on a direct line from here to Yuzhno," the third agent pointed out. "If it didn't take off here, perhaps it was flying here and then turned around." He glared at Boris. "Maybe because someone warned him away."

"What? I, I was asleep until you woke me up. How could I have warned him?"

The second agent pushed Boris toward the radio.

"Call him," the third agent ordered. "Tell him he must turn around and fly here."

With shaking fingers, Boris fumbled to turn his microphone on.

"Come in, charter. Come in, An-24. This is the air traffic control tower at Nogliki. Come in."

Silence.

Boris' voice climbed an octave.

"Come in, An-24! Please come in. This is Nogliki tower. This is an emergency. Answer!"

Sweat poured down Boris' back as he hunched over the radio under the agents' hostile glares.

"An-24 flying toward Yuzhno, come in now!"

"That's enough," the third agent snapped, grabbing Boris by the back of his collar.

"No, please!"

The other two agents grabbed Boris' flailing arms and legs and, together, the three agents dragged him down the stairs and out of the tower toward a waiting van.

"No!" Boris screamed. "My God, no!"

The third agent stepped back as the other two threw Boris into the van and climbed in after him. He slammed the door and walked toward the driver's seat. *They always scream for God at the end,* he mused as he scratched under his chin. *Time to alert the airport in Yuzhno to stop that plane on the tarmac.* He was disappointed that he had not apprehended the terrorist himself, but relieved that he could refer the problem to Yuzhno and get Moscow off his back. He shivered slightly as he thought of the struggling air traffic controller inside the van. Even the FSB agent was terrified of Lubyanka.

Sixty-two

Yuzhno-Sakhalinsk International Airport

The lead agent in Yuzhno shut off his cell phone and swore loudly. His fellow FSB agent glanced sharply at him from the other side of the maintenance hangar and raised an eyebrow. The lead agent beckoned him close.

"What is it?" the other agent asked.

"That plane that left here during the shooting apparently was headed to Nogliki."

"And?"

"And it turned around and is heading back here."

"Why?"

"Who knows." The lead agent shrugged.

The two agents stepped onto the tarmac and walked past a dead body surrounded by a FSB cleanup crew.

"The crew is not even finished clearing the scene and the plane is already on its way back?" the other agent asked incredulously. "Short trip."

"Very short," Nikolai said, pointing to the sky. "There it is. Hurry."

The two men raced down the tarmac toward the descending plane. By the time the An-24 taxied to a stop, they were waiting, red-faced and breathing hard. The lead agent checked the plane's markings. It was the same plane that had left less than two hours ago. The other agent rolled a set of stairs to the cabin door. Guns drawn, the two agents climbed the stairs and banged on the door. When no one answered, the lead agent nodded, and the other agent yanked open the door. Both stepped through, guns held chest high.

At the sound of a muffled groan from the cockpit, the agents sprang through the open door and nearly laughed at the sight. The pilot was stripped to his underwear and taped into the chair. His hands were taped to the controls. Another round of tape covered his mouth. The pilot struggled, wide-eyed, to speak through the tape. The agent leaned forward and ripped the tape off the pilot's mouth in one, painful jerk. The pilot gasped and licked the blood from his lips where the tape had pulled off skin.

"What happened? Where is the scientist?"

"They had guns. They made me land in a field outside Nogliki. Then they took my clothes and my cell phone and tied me up. They told me that if I didn't take off and fly back to Yuzhno, they'd kill me."

"Why didn't you call it in after you were in the air?" the lead agent demanded.

In answer, the pilot pointed to his ruined radio with a screwdriver sticking out. The lead agent cursed again and pulled out his cell phone.

—⟨⟨⟨⟨⟩⟩⟩⟩—

Across from the Molodaya Guardiya Industrial Storage Facility, Moscow

"Akhmetalin has been in that bathroom a long time," whispered the FSB agent with the binoculars.

"I haven't even heard a flush," the agent with the headphones replied. "We should call headquarters."

The other agent agreed. As he reached for his cell phone, a hand knocked it away. He spun in surprise just as a sharp clap filled his ears. Something red exploded behind his eyes. For a millisecond, he felt the piercing agony of his skull caving into his brain. Then he fell to the floor, lifeless. Leonid Stepanin quickly pivoted and shot the second agent in the mouth before he could even remove his headphones. Then he slipped the silenced Stechkin pistol back under his coat, turned and left the apartment, closing the door after him. *Now we're at war with the FSB, too*, Stepanin thought grimly. As he reached the cold, gray street, he turned up his collar, certain that he had just issued his own death sentence.

—⌒⌒⌒—

Nogliki

"Why did you take the pilot's clothes?" Melissa panted as she pushed her way through the thick undergrowth on the edge of Nogliki. After landing on a field south of the small town, she, Hal and Michael had skirted the airport, scrambling across the rocky fields and through the thick scrub toward town. Melissa was perspiring freely from the exertion and had unzipped her parka. Her hands were scratched and bleeding from when she had stumbled on sharp rocks. She looked in disgust at her soiled jeans. *When this is over, I'm going to burn them*, she thought.

"We didn't have time to check him thoroughly and I wanted to make sure he didn't have a cell phone stuck somewhere, or something sharp he could use to cut himself free," Michael replied over his shoulder as he climbed a small gulley, picking his way carefully over loose gravel. "Plus, his coveralls were a lot thicker and warmer than the linen pants they gave me in Saudi Arabia."

"If someone's following us, your misdirection with the airplane may have bought a small head start, but how do you intend to get to Molikpak?" Hal asked, referring to the offshore drilling platform. "Access is severely restricted. Even workers have to wait for weeks to fly by helicopter to the platform."

Michael paused before answering. He was still furious with Hal, but he didn't have the time or the energy to fight with him now. If they survived this, he'd deal with him then. He looked around at the workers' camp that had grown into a small town huddled on the stony plain a few hundred yards ahead. Nogliki consisted of the airport, a camp for workers waiting for transport to the offshore drilling rigs, and a few decrepit buildings and homes surrounding the camp. The camp, off to the right, with its tall metal fence topped by concertina wire and corrugated metal buildings resembled a prison instead of a way station. All in all, Nogliki was a depressing and foreboding site.

Michael's legs felt rubbery after the scramble toward town. With little to eat and even less sleep, adrenalin, tension and exhaustion had eaten away the last of Michael's reserves. He was empty, but there was no time to rest. He needed to move quickly and get off Sakhalin before all was lost.

"Al-Naimi prepared press credentials for Nazer and me," he replied. "We're supposed to be journalists reporting on the efforts to protect some birds. He also bought us tickets on today's helicopter ride to the platform. I'm sure he paid through the nose to move us to the front of the line. Unfortunately, the credentials have our photos on them. I can use mine, but neither of you look like Nazer."

"So how do we go with you?"

"You don't."

"Michael—!"

"While I'm on Molikpak, you can figure out how to get us out of here."

"You don't have an exit strategy?" Hal asked.

"I stole our exit strategy's clothes and sent him back to Yuzhno," Michael replied ruefully.

"Wonderful," Melissa muttered.

"According to Nazer, there's one home that rents out a couple rooms near the camp." Michael pointed to a wooden house with shuttered windows and a pronounced dip in its roof. "We can clean up there and use it as our base."

Hal nodded approvingly. Melissa closed her eyes and, for a moment, envisioned her big bed with its down comforter back in her townhouse in Georgetown. Then she opened her eyes and stared at the shack ahead.

"Lovely."

—◦◦◦—

FSB Headquarters, Lubyanka

"Why aren't they answering?" Yakovlev demanded. For twenty minutes, he had tried to raise the two agents conducting the surveillance of Akhmetalin with no luck. "Go over there and find out what is going on," he barked at the two agents standing shoulder to shoulder in front of his desk.

Sixty-three

⸺◦◦◦⸺

Nogliki

The boarding house run by a woman named Voluntina lay at the end of a deserted street of ramshackle wooden buildings, sagging in on themselves. A mangy dog with a stump for a tail eyed the three Americans hungrily from a rotting porch. Sea birds circled overhead and, underfoot, the musty smell of dark earth and mushrooms wafted from the ground. The Americans were so exhausted and desperate to catch a quick nap that they failed to check for a tail until it was too late.

As they neared the shack, the unmistakable sound of a bullet being chambered in back of them broke the silence, causing them all to freeze. Michael and Hal exchanged a chagrined glance. Neither could reach their weapons with their hands full of the cases of microbial solution. Melissa's hands were free, however, and she slowly reached for her Glock.

"Turn around," said a high voice from behind them with the barest hint of a Russian accent.

Gravel crunched under their feet as they turned. A woman had appeared with a gun. She was tall and slim in her mid- to late-thirties, dressed in hiking boots, jeans and a thick, dark waistcoat. Her blond hair and pale skin shimmered in the growing dusk. For a brief, heart-stopping moment, Michael thought it was Milla. She pointed the gun at him but her eyes darted between all three.

"You are Michael McKeon, but who are they?"

"Who are you?" Michael responded.

"The Director sent me to meet you."

"Do you mind pointing your gun somewhere else, then?"

The woman hesitated.

"Who are they?" she repeated.

Michael noticed Melissa's hand resting on her hip, near the Makarov hidden in the small of her back.

"They're my partners. They're helping me."

"The Director didn't say anything about partners. The Director is very upset that you missed the plane he sent and that you didn't meet your contact at the Korean restaurant."

Michael shrugged.

"Tell the Director to get over it. We have a job to finish."

The woman smiled and tucked the gun into her waistband.

"We need to get inside. Then we can discuss the next step. You are tired and hungry, yes?"

"Yes, very."

"Come this way, please."

An electric shock coursed through Michael as the woman brushed past him. She looked just like Milla: same height, same build. She even walked with the same determined gait. Melissa and Hal shook their heads in warning, but Michael ignored them. This felt right. He hurried after the woman, shifting the suitcases on his aching shoulders. Behind them, Melissa scowled suspiciously and slipped her Makarov into her jacket pocket, keeping her finger on the trigger.

The woman kept a fast pace as she led them down a narrow alley away from the boarding house.

"What's your name?" Michael asked.

She flashed a brief smile.

"I cannot tell you, for everyone's protection."

"Where are we going?" Hal asked suspiciously.

"Not far. The FSB, local police and Molikpak security are looking for you. I have to keep you hidden until it is time. There is a house nearby."

They followed as she turned left, then right, then left again through a series of tight, garbage-strewn pathways between the buildings clumped outside the oil installation's base camp. Michael hadn't seen or heard any sign of life since they left the boarding house behind. Darkness crept closer as the sun fell in the sky. A slight breeze reached them, carrying the sting of salt water with it. Michael shivered as the temperature began to drop rapidly. He bit back a groan from his injured ribs.

"So, after I'm finished, are you the one who'll take me to the Director?"

Without warning, the woman whirled toward him, gun-raised. Before Michael could react, Melissa's gun barked. The woman jerked as her throat erupted in a red spray. She collapsed onto the ground with a horrible gurgle, her eyes rolling back in her head. Melissa darted forward and shot her again. As the woman's feet stopped thrashing, Melissa snatched the gun and rifled through her pockets, coming up with a single piece of paper.

Michael stared, open-mouthed, at the dead woman who had looked so much like Milla, but whose features were now frozen in an angry death mask. Melissa stepped in front of him. She was talking to him, trying to show him something, but he couldn't hear her. He couldn't take his eyes off the dead woman. She held the paper in front of his face. A photo of himself stared back at him. Above the photo was an order from the Director: *Eliminate Michael McKeon before he reaches Molikpak.*

Melissa was already pushing him back down the alleyway.

"We need to get away from here before someone comes to investigate the shots."

Michael was in a haze as Melissa and Hal led him through the maze of buildings back towards the boarding house. They reached the boarding house without further incident and Hal quickly checked them in, stored the suitcases of inoculum in their room, and pulled him back outside. All the while, Michael's brain had been digesting the recent turn of events, reaching the only possible conclusion.

"Let's head into the forest," Hal suggested.

Michael followed silently, refusing to look at or respond to Hal or Melissa. He'd pulled into himself, as he always did when he couldn't face an awful truth.

As a robin's-egg blue truck lumbered past, carrying recent train arrivals to the base camp, the three Americans crossed a dirt road and climbed into the trees on a small mountain. Michael slipped once on some loose shale then stopped. The sea birds had disappeared. The trees deadened what little sounds of life emanated from the village. Melissa placed a hand on his shoulder and stared into his eyes.

"I know it's frightening to be shot at . . ."

Michael shook his head as Hal alternated between peering into the trees for assailants and glancing anxiously at Michael.

"It's not that," Michael said quietly.

"What's wrong, then?"

He couldn't ignore the truth any longer. And he was certain that it would kill him.

"The Director sent that woman to kill me before I reached Molikpak," he began. His voice caught in his throat.

"Yes."

"That means that he doesn't want me to destroy the Russian oil. He lied about that."

Melissa nodded slowly. Michael closed his eyes. Was she really going to make him say it?

"The only reason to keep Milla and Katya alive was to make me complete the mission. If Abqaiq was the only target, then the mission is completed. They don't need me anymore. And if they don't need me . . ."

He left the sentence unfinished.

"But if he didn't need you, then why bring you here?"

"What better place for a Russian to kill him than on Russian soil?" Hal said.

Melissa stared at Michael, horrified.

"Oh, Michael, I'm so sorry."

She reached out to him, but he pulled away.

Now that he had given voice to his fears, the reality of his loss overwhelmed him. Once again, he had failed to save someone he loved.

He was trembling. Blood rushed in his ears in a deafening torrent. He wanted to scream. Blinded by rage, he yanked out the Sig Sauer and began shooting, again and again and again, sending one bullet after another crashing into the nearest tree. Splinters flew at him, slicing his skin, but he felt nothing. Hot tears spilled down his cheeks. When he had emptied the magazine, he threw his gun to the ground. He didn't know what to do next.

Suddenly, Melissa's arms were around him, her face against his. He tried to push her away, but she wouldn't let go. They staggered together and fell to the ground, but she held on. He pushed and shoved, trying to get his feet under him, but she wouldn't let him up. She repeated his name over and over in his ear. Finally, like a fever, his fury broke. He closed his eyes as the trees spun dizzily around him. Then he collapsed. And cried. He cried for Katya. And Milla. He cried for Janie and his parents. He cried for himself, for the misery and loss that had gripped him and never let go.

When he could cry no more, Melissa relaxed her hold. She rolled off him and together they stared through the scrub trees at a comfortless gray sky. Hal knelt next to him as Michael wiped his eyes. Covered in dirt, moss and twigs, his limp body sank heavily into the soft, dark earth. A sharp breeze, raw with the promise of a cold rain, rustled the leaves. His fingers twitched once, then lay still. There was nothing left to type.

"What happens now?" Melissa finally asked.

But it wasn't Melissa whom Michael heard, for he was thousands of miles away, in his sister's bedroom, listening to his thirteen-year-old self ask the same question.

I wish I had a better answer for you, but the same question will always get the same response. We find the bastard who did this and kill him.

Sixty-four

Thirty minutes later, a hastily convened council of war occurred in the bedroom on the second floor of Voluntina's boarding house on the outskirts of Nogliki. While Michael pored over the maps and photographs from Nazer's backpack, strewn across the bed, Hal and Melissa kept watch from the window and door. Outside, a driving rain had begun to fall.

"Michael," Melissa tried again. "We need to get out of here. There's nothing more to do."

Michael ignored her, as he had for the last thirty minutes since announcing his intentions while lying on the ground in the woods.

"Going to Molikpaq now is a death sentence," Hal tried. "It won't accomplish anything."

"We're not going to Molikpaq," Michael muttered.

Hal and Melissa exchanged confused glances.

"Where are we going?"

Michael held up the map of Sakhalin II's facilities and jabbed a finger on the northeast coast about a third of the way down from the northern tip. "Here."

Hal peered at the location.

"The onshore processing facility?"

"I should have seen it before," Michael muttered, pacing around the small room. He shoved a straightback chair with two missing spindles out of the way. "I wondered why Molikpaq was the target. It didn't make any sense. In Abqaiq, they found the choke point where the microbes could spread throughout the system, but Molikpaq was just one rig. Knock it out and they still have two others. The Director didn't want to reveal Sakhalin's true vulnerability because he never had any intent of destroying the oil here."

"And the onshore processing facility is the vulnerable point?" Melissa asked.

"Absolutely." Michael held the map against the wall and traced paths with his finger. "All the oil in the entire Piltun Astokhskoye reservoir comes to the OPF before being pumped south. This is the choke point. Once inserted here, the inoculum will spread back through the offshore pipes into the entire reservoir and down through the onshore pipes into the storage facilities on Aniva Bay." He nodded to himself. "They'll be expecting me to head north to Molikpaq, but I'm going to head south to the OPF." Michael stared so fiercely at the small square indicating the OPF that Hal expected the map to burst into flames. "This is where I will kill the Director's oil." He glared at the others, daring them to try and stop him. "And then I'll kill the Director."

"Then we better go now," Hal said quietly from the window. "Because we've got company."

Sixty-five

By the time Michael, Hal and Melissa reached downstairs, two dark sedans had pulled to a stop in front of the boarding house, engines running, headlights knifing through the downpour. Hal and Melissa flicked off the lights in the living room and kitchen while Michael set the five cases of the microbes at the foot of the stairs. Outside, six figures slipped out of the vehicles, three from each, and moved silently in the shadows behind the headlights. The three Americans watched two split off and disappear around the corner of the boarding house, toward the back.

The unfortunate Voluntina picked this moment to ascend from the root cellar, muttering that her no-good husband was late coming home from work again. Hal met her with a hand slapped over her open mouth and a murmured order to return to the root cellar and stay there. The frightened woman dropped her basket and hurriedly retreated down the stairs, tripping over the spilled turnips and potatoes. Lightning blazed, momentarily illuminating the four men crouched by the vehicles. The boarding house's thin walls shook as the wind picked up, driving the rain sideways. Then all three dove to the floor as a new sound reached them: the rat-a-tat-tat of a thousand bullets slamming into the boarding house at once.

"Hail," Hal muttered sheepishly, picking himself up from the floor.

From outside a voice, amplified and distorted over a bullhorn, reached them over the drumming of the hail.

"Vuyhodeete!" Come out. *"FSB!"*

Michael, Hal and Melissa gathered in the middle of the small house, where the living room became the kitchen, hunched over in a tight circle. With a groan for his damaged ribs, Michael hoisted the strap with the five cases onto his shoulders.

"They won't wait long to storm this place," Michael said. "I don't want anyone else to get hurt because of me. You guys give yourselves up and tell them that I escaped into the woods. Tell them I'm heading for Molikpak. I'll try to slip away in the darkness."

"No," Hal replied as he slid over to the living room window and peered over the trim. "You and I will make a run for it. Melissa, you lock yourself in the room upstairs and tell them that we kidnapped you."

"Spare me the heroics," Melissa hissed from the kitchen window, where she was watching the two darker shapes move among the dark shadows. "We're all in this together."

At that moment, the men outside opened fire, sending glass shards and splinters exploding over the three Americans as they dove to the floor.

"Poslednee shance!" the voice called. *Last chance.*

"There's a small barn out back," Melissa whispered from the kitchen floor as she shook glass from her hair.

"I saw it earlier," Hal said. "There was a beaten path going to it, wide enough for a vehicle." He crawled to the root cellar door, opened it, and shouted down to Voluntina: *"Avtomobileh?"*

After Voluntina responded with a panicked stuttering of unintelligible sounds, he demanded again: *"Avtomobileh?"*

"V karaye," came the timid response. *In the barn.*

"Gdey kloochey?" Where are the keys?

"V zajheraniya," Voluntina whimpered. *In the ignition.*

Hal shut the door and belly-crawled back into the kitchen to Melissa and Michael. "Melissa and I will take out the two men in back while you take the microbes and run for the car."

Michael began to shake his head. "No."

"Don't stop. You need to be in the barn before the men from the front reach us." Hal stopped Michael's protest with a raised hand. "If we stay here, we'll all be caught. You're the only one who knows how to insert the microbes. There's only one road out of here, so, first chance you get, dump the car and find another one."

"No," Michael replied, his voice thickening. "We go together."

Hal glanced out the kitchen window as another bolt of lightning struck. The entire house shook in the wintry gale.

"They're moving into position," he muttered more to himself than to the others. He clasped a hand on Michael's shoulder. "Noble sentiment, son, but reality calls. We're not all getting out of here. It has to be you. They'll arrest us and Melissa will tell them who she is and it'll all get worked out."

Michael stared at Hal, knowing he was lying, then nodded once and slipped the strap back onto his shoulder and crawled to the kitchen door, ignoring his damaged ribs. He ducked into a sprinter's crouch, eyes blinking furiously, as Hal stood over him, one hand on the door, the other holding his Sig Sauer inches above Michael's head. Melissa waited at the window. There was so much Michael wanted to say to Hal, but he had run out of time.

"Now," Hal said, wrenching the door open, pistol spitting fire.

Michael lunged into the dark as Melissa opened fire from the window. The cases, swinging awkwardly, nearly pitched him over. Stumbling in ankle deep mud, Michael slid sideways then fell to one knee before righting himself. Panting, ribs screaming in pain, he lurched forward. Hal's and Melissa's rhythmic fire mixed with the staccato of the hail in a gruesome symphony. Then the Russians responded as another round of thunder shook the land. Slipping and sliding forward, with his arms tucked against his side, protecting his ribs from the banging cases, Michael hoped he was running in the right direction. The same hail and pitch-black night that hid him from the Russian gunmen also obscured the barn. He should have reached it by now, but it was difficult to measure distance in the darkness and with his struggling pace.

He sensed before he heard the lull as the Russians changed clips. A second, two, three passed, but no response came from the boarding house. His senses screamed at him to turn around and help Hal and Melissa, then he heard the bark of Hal's Sig Sauer followed by Melissa's Makarov, and redoubled his efforts.

When the lightning struck again, he was steps from the barn door, in full view of the Russian gunmen. From the shouts that erupted, he knew he had been spotted. Before the gunmen could fire, Hal and Melissa unleashed another volley, sending the Russians diving to the ground for cover. In the next instant, the front of the boarding house erupted in a hellstorm of automatic fire. The four gunmen in the front had joined the battle.

Michael grabbed the rusty handle and yanked the doors open, ducking through as a round of automatic fire turned one of the doors into kindling. Tucked in the barn, barely visible as the last illumination from the lightning strike bled away, was a battered, four-door, dirt-colored Lada sedan. Michael limped across the packed dirt floor and opened the driver's door, afraid that Voluntina had lied, but the keys were in the ignition. With a cry of relief, Michael dropped the cases of microbes into the back seat, climbed into the front seat, and cranked the key.

The Lada groaned softly, like an old man struggling to stand then settled back on its tires.

"Come on!" Michael demanded, turning the key again with no response. He paused and listened. He could hear the hail rattling on the barn's wood roof, but no shooting. No shooting was not good. No shooting meant that Hal and Melissa . . . no, he refused to finish the thought. The doors to the barn burst open and two men stepped into view, their flashlights blinding him just as he turned the key and the engine roared. Michael ducked as the men opened fire, jammed the car into gear and floored the gas pedal. With a horrible metallic screech, the car leapt forward as its windshield shattered under the barrage. One of the men jumped out of the way, but the other bounced off the hood then the roof.

Michael kept his head down as the Lada raced toward the house. The sedan bucked as automatic fire laced its rear quarter panel and trunk, but its tires remained intact. He desperately wanted to look for Hal and Melissa, but couldn't. If he made it past the house, he had a chance.

The dirt driveway ran in a straight line from the barn until it reached the house, then curved around the house to the road. The two FSB vehicles had been parked in the road, noses perpendicular to the house. If Hal and Melissa had drawn all the gunmen into the house, he should pass their vehicles before they could reach them. Then it would be a race. He didn't like the Lada's chances against the FSB vehicles, but he'd have a chance. That was all he could ask.

He kept the pedal pressed to the floor as he rounded the house and spotted one Russian racing across the front lawn. Both cars were still parked, lights on and empty. He'd made it! But, mere feet from the open road, something slammed into him with a horrible crunch. The steering wheel slipped from his grasp as the Lada spun in a tight circle toward the parked cars. In the moment before his head crashed against the window, Michael glimpsed a third car, identical to the first two, that had been lying in wait as a last line of defense. Then his car crunched into the first parked car and Michael's head exploded in pain. And he knew nothing more.

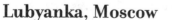

Lubyanka, Moscow

"We have McKeon," reported the voice on the phone. Yakovlev pumped his fist in the air. "We stopped him before he reached Molikpak."

"Good work," Yakovlev commended. "I want him on the fastest plane to Moscow."

"Yes sir."

The First Deputy hung up and gave a shout of jubilation. He had foiled Akhmetalin's plot. Now he needed to bring the colonel in. Just then, his phone rang again.

"Yes?"

It was the two agents he had sent to find his surveillance team.

"What is it?"

"They're dead, sir."

Yakovlev's sense of jubilation evaporated.

"Who is dead?"

"Both agents, sir. Shot in the head. Close range. Executed."

Yakovlev gripped the phone tightly, his fury mounting.

"And Akhmetalin?"

"Gone sir."

Yakovlev hurled his phone against the wall.

Sixty-six

Sheremetyevo-1, Moscow

The three FSB agents from Sakhalin were bleary-eyed and exhausted by the time their chartered flight arrived at Moscow's Sheremetyevo Airport at noon the following day. The captives had been sedated for the long flight across Russia, but the three agents remained awake and alert, knowing that any failure or mistake meant their death, if they were lucky. As a result, Gregoryi, the bald lead agent, was relieved when their wheels touched down and the plane rolled to a stop inside a secret hangar maintained by the FSB. As the hangar's doors scraped across the concrete with a loud screech, the plane settled on its wheels with a mechanical sigh.

Gregoryi peered out the window as two figures stepped out of the shadows and marched across the hangar towards them. Spotting their uniforms, he stiffened. He had not expected a full FSB colonel as a welcoming committee. He glanced at the unconscious McKeon, strapped into his seat, with a mixture of admiration and terror.

"Kto vam?" he whispered. *Who are you?*

Gregoryi beckoned to the two agents to follow him off the plane. He wanted to present his full team to the FSB colonel and his assistant. If he was honest with himself, he simply did not want to face the colonel alone.

Gregoryi and his two agents hurried down the stairs onto the concrete and stood at attention. The colonel was tall, dark-complexioned, with an arrogant nose and frighteningly black eyes. Gregoryi was glad he had brought his agents with him, but still wished he was back safely in Yuzhno instead of facing this dark devil in a secret hangar in Moscow.

"The prisoner is inside?" the colonel demanded with no introductions or niceties.

"Yes sir, sedated."

"You didn't kill him in the process of sedating him, did you?" The black eyes snapped. Gregoryi had to will himself not to step backwards.

"No, sir," the agent stammered. "We are trained in this."

"Very well. You three stay here. I will inspect him alone."

The three agents scrambled to get out of Colonel Akhmetalin's path as he stomped up the stairs. As he reached the top, he paused slightly and waited for the spits from Stepanin's silenced Stechkin. One. Two. Three. He turned to find the three agents slumped on the concrete inside widening circles of crimson.

"Put them behind the stack of tires with the two operatives Yakovlev sent to meet the plane then help me unload McKeon."

Akhmetalin stepped into the dimmed interior. The plane smelled musty, like damp, rotting wood. He had never been to Sakhalin, but assumed the entire island smelled like that. As his eyes alighted on McKeon's pale face, a sadistic grin spread across his dark features.

"I am going to enjoy this," he promised himself quietly.

Sixty-seven

Ritz Carlton, Moscow

As the brown-haired, mousy NSA analyst twisted uncomfortably in her chair, Chief of Staff Jack Rafferty did his best to appear sympathetic, or at least empathetic—he could never remember the difference.

"You've done the right thing," he told her, although any NSA analyst who so quickly gave up her boss didn't have much of a future in his or any other administration. "So, you overheard Director Billings order this 'Viktor' to assemble a team of operatives to capture Stark and Longfellow and to go in armed, is that correct?"

"Yes sir."

Rafferty held up a yellow slip of paper.

"And these are the three phone numbers that were dialed from the i-Phone Stark and Longfellow were using?"

"Yes sir. One is for Jigger, a computer analyst with the NSA. Another is an American cell phone that I wasn't able to trace."

Rafferty found it amusing that there could actually be cell phones that the NSA wasn't able to trace, but he kept a stern face. "And the third?"

"It's a Saudi cell phone, but it's not registered to anyone."

"And you didn't call any of them?"

She shook her head in the negative.

"And neither did Director Billings?"

Again, no.

"And he didn't keep a copy of these numbers?"

"Not that I saw, sir."

"Very good. Thank you. Please, do not discuss this with anyone except me."

Rafferty waited for the analyst to leave then peered curiously at the phone numbers, particularly the last one. He had almost decided to dial the number when a sharp rap on his door interrupted him.

"Come in."

It was Special Agent Frank Mayberry, looking even grimmer than usual.

"What is it Frank?"

"The two agents guarding Director Billings are unconscious. Judging from the hypodermic marks on their necks, they were both drugged."

Rafferty was out of his chair and across the room in the second it took his blood pressure to spike to dangerous levels. "And Billings?" he demanded, spraying spittle on the agent's chin.

"Gone."

Sixty-eight

GIP Headquarters, Riyadh

Sa'id al-Naimi stared at his computer screen in frustration. Before permitting McKeon to leave, he had insisted on inserting a GIP tracking device behind the American's left eye. In the past, the GIP inserted tracking chips under the skin, but the targets often dug them out. Al-Naimi had found few men willing to dig out their own eyeball.

When the scientist's GPS device indicated that he was flying west from Sakhalin, Al-Naimi had sent a team to Moscow, where McKeon's beacon had stopped. Shortly before they landed, McKeon's beacon simply disappeared. He opened a secure channel to the team's leader.

"Agent Mohammed."

"Yes, Assistant Sa'id."

"We are attempting to isolate the exact location of the beacon when it stopped transmitting."

"Yes, Assistant Sa'id. Do you think the American is trying to escape?"

Al-Naimi shook his head slowly.

"No, this is no escape. McKeon has been captured. I am certain of it. Prepare your team for an extraction once we have the location. I believe our target is being held in or near Moscow, most likely underground or some similar place that is preventing transmission of his tracking signal."

"Yes, Assistant Sa'id."

Al-Naimi closed the connection. Either that, he thought grimly, or someone just dug McKeon's eye out of his socket.

Nine minutes later, al-Naimi had McKeon's last known coordinates and ordered his team to head north to Moscow's suburbs. Thirty minutes later, the team leader's voice buzzed over the secure link.

"Assistant Sa'id?"

"Yes, Agent Mohammed."

"You may not believe this, but we're stuck in traffic. Putin has decided to head to his dacha and no vehicles can move. We're stranded in the middle of what has to be the most colossal traffic jam in the world with nowhere to go."

—*◦∕∕∕◦*—

FSB Headquarters, Moscow

First Deputy Yakovlev was not having much better luck. Akhmetalin had disappeared. His agents at Sheremetyevo had been killed and the scientist had been kidnapped, undoubtedly by Akhmetalin. Now, he was glowering impatiently while a cluster of sweaty computer analysts pored over business and government records, searching for any property Akhmetalin might be using as his hideout. He eyed the metal trash can against the wall and contemplated beating one of the analysts with it, but refrained. He recalled a conversation he had had with Akhmetalin just the other day.

"He has a dacha north of Moscow," Yakovlev announced. "Find it."

—*◦∕∕∕◦*—

Ritz Carlton, Moscow

Chief of Staff Jack Rafferty also looked like he wanted to beat someone to death with a trash can as he waited to tell the President about Billings' escape. While the President continued his private meeting with the Russian and Saudi heads of state, Rafferty pulled the yellow slip of paper out of his pocket and examined it again.

"Sir, did you hear that they're dropping barrel bombs again in Iraq?" his deputy asked breathlessly before Rafferty waved him away. His deputy was an annoying weasel of a man. Unfortunately, his father was one of the President's biggest fundraisers, but Rafferty promised himself he would find a way to fire him sooner rather than later.

Rafferty checked his watch. The President would be at least another twenty minutes. He looked at the third number and wondered again who Stark and Longfellow were calling in Saudi Arabia.

"What the hell," he muttered and dialed.

In the GIP's headquarters in Riyadh, a cell phone began to ring.

Sixty-nine

———

Razdori, Russia

Maria Demidova despised her neighbor. The seventy-eight-year-old grandmother had visited the small enclave of *cottedgi* outside Moscow since she was a girl. To her, the small wooden cottages smelling of wood fires and cooked onions would always be the soul of Russia. But as she gripped the hand of her six-year-old granddaughter and tottered up the unpaved driveway to her one-bedroom dacha, she knew wh she no longer had a village, a country or a soul to pass on. All three had been devoured by the government officials, *biznessmeny*, and *mafiya* who had invaded her country and her village. Demidova drew no distinction between the three. They were all equally corrupt and grasping. She had once respected Putin, but after being chased off the road twice daily by Putin's armored entourage, and after hearing of his decadent, fortress-like compound in nearby *Novo Ogaryovo*, the elderly woman knew that she had lived long enough to see the tsar return.

She no longer wished to live, especially since the corrupt government officials had given her beloved dacha to that black-eyed devil of a neighbor who had built a garish monstrosity with twelve bedrooms and a turret. *A turret, for Lenin's sake!* She clucked and shook her head. Her blue-eyed granddaughter stared at her questioningly, wondering if Demidova's disapproval was directed at her. The grandmother smiled sadly, patted her on the head, and urged her to hurry inside. She didn't like the idea of that bastard looking at her granddaughter out of one of his hundred windows.

He wasn't even Russian, well, not entirely at least. There was something of the East in him. Like Genghis Khan. Something foreign and feral. But the town officials had welcomed him with open arms, as they had all the others. When he needed to build a tunnel under her dacha to a helicopter landing pad through the birches, they had forced her to "sell." Not that she had seen a ruble. Nor would she. That was the saddest irony. Russia had sold its soul for something it would never even receive.

Demidova sighed heavily. Her arm hurt all the time now and her breath came in labored gasps. She would be dead soon. For that, she was thankful. With a last contemptuous glare toward the monster next door, she shuffled into her dacha to make sure her granddaughter had not tried to start a fire for tea.

As Demidova scolded her granddaughter for playing with matches, next door, in the basement of the monster, a woman was chained to a damp concrete floor. Her eyelids fluttered drowsily as her system struggled to purge the last of the sedative she had received in Nogliki. The dimly lit room swam before Melissa Stark's eyes. Her head pounded like a jackhammer and her mouth was painfully dry. She struggled to move, only to find that both ankles were chained to the floor. Thick iron clamps encircled both ankles and wrists, leaving her in a sitting position against the wall.

She had no idea where she was or how long she had been unconscious. The banging in her head made it difficult to think, but she tried to evaluate herself and her position. Nothing seemed broken, but the stiffness in her limbs indicated she hadn't moved for hours. Acid burned her empty stomach. She hadn't eaten in hours either. There were no windows, so she couldn't tell whether it was day or night. She was still in her clothes, thankfully, so the pigs who had captured her had not molested her while she was unconscious. Her parka was gone.

Where was Michael? She hoped he'd gotten away.

A man's groan interrupted her thoughts.

"Longfellow?"

The answer came back tired and raspy.

"Melissa?"

"Where are you?"

"I'm in the corner, farthest from the door."

Melissa spotted the faint outline of the door to her left and turned her head to the right. The effort cost her dearly, as needles of pain jabbed the back of her eyeballs. Finally, as her eyes adjusted to the dimness, she spotted the outline of Longfellow's body. He was handcuffed in a sitting position, like her.

"Where are we?"

"I don't know. I don't recall anything after they hit us with those syringes back at the boarding house."

"Do you think Michael got away?"

Longfellow waited a long time in the dank, dark basement to respond. When he did, his voice brought no comfort.

"Let's hope so."

Seventy

⸺◈⸺

They hit Michael three times before he woke up. The first time opened his upper lip. The second chipped a tooth. The third blasted the vestiges of the sedative from his system.

He opened his eyes. The room around him tilted and swayed. Michael choked down vomit and waited for his head to stop spinning.

"Open your eyes."

Slowly, painfully, Michael complied. The room had stopped spinning, but his head ached unmercifully. He tried to focus on the man standing in front of him. The man who had hit him was short, barely five feet tall, with square-tipped fingers and large knuckles that painfully reminded Michael of the walnut-knuckled Saudi he hoped never to meet again. He spoke English with a thick, Russian accent.

"Who are you?" Michael asked.

Michael never saw the punch coming. It exploded into the side of his jaw, snapping his head to the left. Michael spit out a bloody tooth and waited for the man to speak.

"Tell me exactly what happened at Abqaiq," the man commanded.

As Michael stared silently back, the interrogator cocked his elbow for another blow, then stopped at a knock on the door. While the man yanked open the door, Michael blinked blood out of his eyes. After a whispered conversation with a guard, the interrogator stepped into the hallway.

"Watch him."

The guard looked like someone who had once been thin, but had since gone to pot, with a full black beard, and a pianist's delicate, long-nailed fingers wrapped around a machine gun, which he silently pointed at Michael.

As soon as the door shut, the guard lunged. Michael tensed, waiting for another beating. Instead, he felt the man's hot breath on his cheek as his fingers scrabbled with Michael's handcuffs.

"My name is Grisha Medvedev. I'm a friend of Longfellow. They're going to torture you and kill you. We must get you out of here."

Seventy-one

—⟶⟶∼⟶⟶—

Moscow

Agent Mohammed of the GIP checked the clock on the helicopter's dash and frowned darkly.

"Another thirty minutes," he said over his microphone to the American operative in the back.

Nothing about this operation felt right. He was a Saudi spy operating inside Russia without consent of the government with an American operative in tow. And they were flying toward the dacha of a FSB Colonel to try to rescue an American who had attacked Saudi oil facilities. He didn't know the details of what the American scientist had done. All he knew was that this was the type of operation that landed spies in jail, if they were lucky.

"Go faster," the American operative urged. "We may already be too late."

The Saudi spy glowered at the controls as if by sheer force of will he could slow the clock or speed the helicopter, while the American operative placed a call to Chief of Staff Rafferty, who, at that moment, was hovering outside the door of a closed meeting between the American, Russian and Saudi heads of state. With no agreement and time running out, the three men had kicked their staffs out of the room for a principals'-only meeting.

As Rafferty ended the conversation, noticeably paler, he grabbed the arm of his counterpart on the Russian negotiating team, a senior member of the Russian Federation Council named Sergei

Bogdanovich, and pulled him into a nearby alcove for a quick, hushed conversation that none of the curious staffers could overhear except for one shouted word by Bogdanovich: "Microbes?"

To the surprise of the onlookers, the two men then strode across the hall and into the principals' meeting without even knocking. According to the U.S. Deputy Chief of Staff, who had sidled next to the door as it closed, Rafferty addressed each of the leaders in turn: "Excuse me, gentlemen, but we have an even bigger fucking problem than you can imagine."

No record exists of what was said in that conference room at the Ritz Carlton, but seven minutes later, when Rafferty and Bogdanovich barreled past the gawking staffers, the message they had been given was clear: FSB Colonel Vadim Akhmetalin's day was done.

Seventy-two

—⁓—

Razdori, Russia

Michael was in shock as the handcuffs fell to the concrete floor with a dull clink.

"Who are you?"

"My name is Grisha Medvedev," the man replied hurriedly as he lifted Michael off the chair and vigorously rubbed his arms and legs to restore their circulation. "I used to be in the FSB, but I work for myself now. I've known Longfellow a long time. I've been helping them try to find you and your family. We separated and I've been tracking an FSB colonel who's involved in the kidnapping of your family. This is his dacha."

Medvedev shoved a pistol into Michael's hands and pulled him toward the door.

"How did you get them to hire you?" Michael asked.

"The man who just left is named Leonid Stepanin. He works for the FSB, but," the giant patted his round stomach, "they don't recognize me any more. I wouldn't want to take my chances with the colonel, though. I used to work for him." Medvedev eased the door open and glanced down the hall. "We're wasting time. We have to get you out of here."

Michael grabbed his arm.

"Hal, I mean Longfellow, and Melissa Stark were with me in Nogliki. Have you heard anything about them?"

Medvedev's eyes lit up.

"I heard they brought two prisoners with you. That must be them."

Michael breathed a sigh of relief.

"Thank God. I was afraid they were dead."

"We all will be dead if we don't get out of here fast."

Both men froze at the sound of a key turning in the lock.

"Back in the chair," Medvedev hissed.

Michael raced to the chair and slumped into it, his head on his chest, and his arms in back. He still held the gun. Medvedev assumed his position near the door just as Stepanin strode into the room.

"Time to finish this," he said, stepping toward Michael. As he did, Medvedev hit him from behind with the butt of his machine gun. Michael was on the man as soon as he hit the floor. He grabbed his hair and jammed the gun into the man's ear.

"Where's the Director?"

"Pull the trigger. I won't tell you a thing. You're already a dead man."

"Medvedev?" Michael called. "These walls seem thick. Are they soundproof?"

"Almost."

"Good enough."

Michael shot the man in the knee. *Pop.* Stepanin groaned and grabbed for his wounded knee, but Michael kept him off balance.

"Tell me."

"Go to hell."

Pop. The other knee.

"Where is he?"

Pop. The rib cage.

Stepanin sagged, but Michael held him aloft. Thick, red blood leaked from his injured ribs and knees. The Russian had turned pale. Medvedev circled worriedly.

"The next one takes off your ear."

"Okay. Okay," the man panted. "He's out back, in the small dacha."

"Thank you."

Michael blew away the top of the man's spine and dropped him. Medvedev gazed at Michael in fear and awe.

"Are you sure you were never FSB?" Medvedev asked.

Michael raced past him to the door.

"Find Melissa and Hal. I'm going to find the Director."

Without waiting for an answer, Michael yanked open the door and ran out.

Next door, Maria Demidova glanced up from her grand-daughter and her tea to glare at the sound of a helicopter hovering overhead. That bastard next door was always hopping about in his helicopter. After a moment, she looked up at the ceiling again. She was no expert in helicopters, but this one sounded different.

Seventy-three

———

As Michael reached the first floor, he found himself in a hallway just off a mammoth kitchen filled with stainless steel appliances. The door to a giant, walk-in, sub-zero freezer was immediately to his left. Brass sconces illuminated a hallway of some type of black wood. A grand entrance hall stretched out in front of him. The lights from a chandelier sent shadows crawling towards him. To his right was a darkened library. The entire mansion felt like it had been recently constructed and was still waiting for its occupant to arrive.

A slight disturbance in the air current caused the hair on the back of his neck to stand up. He dove into the kitchen just as a hail of bullets chewed into the door frame. Michael slid across the tile floor as a figure leaped into the doorway. Bullets shattered tile and pinged off the metal appliances as Michael ducked behind a long, rectangular, stainless steel work table. He reached up and fired blindly over the table, but the gunman had opened the door to the sub-zero freezer and was hiding behind it.

Michael eyed the gas stove to his right and briefly contemplated severing the gas line, but Hal, Melissa and Medvedev were somewhere in the house, and he didn't want to blow them up. He sprawled onto the floor and peered under the work table. The freezer door was several inches off the ground. He could just make out the gunman's toes behind the door. He could hear the man's muffled voice, possibly alerting others to Michael's escape. Lying on his shoulder, he sighted on the left boot and fired. An anguished cry and a thud indicated he had hit his mark. Michael quickly rolled out from under the table and raced toward the door, slamming into it at full speed, driving it into the collapsed gunman with a satisfying crunch. Michael spun around the door and blew the top of the dazed gunman's head off.

Inches from Michael's head, the plaster exploded as another gunman opened fire. Michael stumbled over the dead gunman and fell behind the door. He jammed his pistol into his waistband and picked up the dead guard's machine gun as the gunfire kept up a steady metallic beat on the door.

Michael peeked around the door and spied the second guard crouched in front of the stove. He glanced around. The door to the hallway was too far. The guard would cut him down before he reached it. With a silent prayer that the others had escaped, he stuck the machine gun around the door, and emptied the clip at the stove.

The explosion nearly burst Michael's ear drums. The door wrenched on its hinges, but saved him from being instantly incinerated. He dove into the hallway just as a second explosion sent a ball of fire racing toward him. The force threw him against the wall. Gasping for air, he raced toward the back door and dove onto the grass as a plume of fire shot over him.

A painful crackling told Michael that his shirt was on fire. He quickly rolled until he snuffed it out then struggled to his feet, coughing as the superheated air seared his lungs. His eyes tearing, he spotted a small dacha of polished stone one hundred yards away, nestled into a grove of birches. Michael glanced around desperately. There was no cover. If there were any guards inside, they could pick him off at their leisure. He pulled the pistol from his waistband and ran. Behind him, the scream of igniting gas gave way to explosion after explosion. The windows blew out, sending a fusillade of glass shards. If Michael had waited an instant longer, he would have been cut to shreds. Instead, only a few splinters sliced into his back and legs as he raced toward the stone dacha.

Black dots danced before his vision as he reached the porch. He was surprised that no guards were posted at the dacha. Perhaps Stepanin had lied. Michael gritted his teeth and kicked in the door. He stumbled through, gasping for breath, then skidded to a halt. In the middle of the dacha's great room, in front of a large stone fireplace, tied to a chair, her head slumped to her chest, lifeless, with blood on her shirt, jeans and in pools on the floor, was Milla.

Seventy-four

With a strangled cry, Michael rushed to Milla's side. He dropped the pistol on the floor and quickly checked her pulse. As she murmured incoherently, he raced across the great room to the kitchenette on the back corner, grabbed a carving knife from the block on the counter, and ran back as fast as his depleted legs would carry him.

The carbon blade sliced through the rope like butter. As the coils fell to the floor, Milla slumped forward. Michael dropped the knife and caught her, pressing her to him, calling her name over and over again. He patted her once-beautiful blond hair, now matted with blood. After what seemed like forever, she stirred. Her eyelids fluttered open. Her ice blue eyes found his.

"Michael?" she whispered.

"It's okay," he croaked. His burned throat barely functioned. "I've got you. Where's Katya?"

The only warning Michael had was the slight shift in Milla's eyes to a spot just over his right shoulder. Then something heavy crashed into the side of his skull.

Seventy-five

M ichael instinctively rolled toward whoever had hit him. He
knew he had suffered extensive injuries. He couldn't hear
or see out of his right side. He couldn't even tell if his ear was still
attached to his skull, but he was acting without thinking. When he
felt himself slam into two feet, he grabbed one and twisted viciously.
He distantly heard a howl of pain then the world fell in on him.

Someone landed on him, pummeling and kicking him in a
ferocious flurry of hands and feet. Michael caught a flash of a dark-
skinned face, contorted in fury, and jabbed upwards. His fingers
found an eyeball and dug viciously. The assailant fell off, holding
his injured eye. Michael seized his opportunity and dove for the
knife he had used to free Milla. He grasped it and spun towards his
attacker just as the man was about to lunge. The man froze.

Michael shifted the knife to his left hand because his right was
trembling uncontrollably.

"Don't move," Michael ordered.

The attacker was a beast, tall and broad-shouldered with black
hair and a swarthy complexion. Michael took a small amount of so-
lace in seeing the man's right eye, reddened and screwed shut. The
other eye sparked malevolently. His chest heaved and his large hands
twitched for Michael's neck.

"So, we finally meet, Michael," the attacker snarled.

Michael recognized the voice. He gripped the knife tighter.
"You're the Director."

A nod. The Director never took his eyes off the knife in Michael's hand. Given Michael's battered condition he knew that the man wouldn't wait long to attack.

"Milla, get the gun. It's on the floor by the chair."

Silence.

"Milla? Get the gun, honey."

Sounds of movement. Finally a response.

"I've got it."

"Good. Bring it here."

"What are you going do to, Michael," the Director asked, a calculating sneer on his face, "shoot me?"

"Absolutely."

Out of the corner of his left eye, the only one working, Michael glimpsed Milla approach with the gun. Then his stomach fell as she circled around him and pointed the gun at the Director.

"Milla! Don't! I'll do it!"

He watched in horror as his wife stepped forward, narrowed her eyes, and sighted along the gun. Then, in one inexplicable movement, Milla flipped it around, and handed it to the Director.

Seventy-six

—◯◯◯—

Michael stood numbly, unable to understand what had just happened, as the Director placed a hand on Milla's shoulder and pointed with the gun.

"Please relieve your husband of the knife." He fixed Michael with a victorious glance. "Hand it over. I don't want to shoot you in front of your wife, yet."

Michael complied, letting Milla slip the knife from his fingers. She returned to stand, triumphantly, next to the Director.

"Perhaps you should explain, Milla," the Director suggested. "I think it would be more painful coming from your own lips."

Milla brushed the hair from her face and stepped towards Michael. A smug smile that Michael had never seen slithered across her face, turning her beautiful features ugly. She placed a hand on the Director's arm.

"This is my first husband, FSB Colonel Vadim Akhmetalin. He is also Katya's father."

Michael closed his eyes and began to sway. The rest was a surreal nightmare.

"Five years ago, Vadim learned of the work you were beginning on the destruction of hydrocarbons. He had been looking for a way to weaken Saudi Arabia and America, and your work promised to be the fatal blow he was searching for. What better way to destroy Russia's chief oil rival and frame its chief political rival than to have an American destroy Saudi Arabia's oil?"

Milla's eyes shone admiringly at Akhmetalin.

"He organized The Global Group to finance the operation, but he needed to distance himself from the operation, so he created the fiction of The Director. But he needed your technology."

"I considered offering to buy the technology from you, but I doubted that you would accept the offer," Akhmetalin interrupted. "And, if you rejected it, I risked exposing myself. I also contemplated simply kidnapping and torturing you for it, but, after researching your past, I guessed that you might be stubborn and tough enough to resist torture. I was right again. You have displayed a remarkable ability to survive. Yuri was supposed to kill you at Abqaiq."

"Is Kasprzyk 'Yuri'?" Michael asked.

"Yes. From your condition, I can see that the Saudi interrogation chambers are every bit as brutal as I have heard, but you survived them. If you had gotten on my plane from Riyadh, my operative would have dumped your body over the desert. Another operative would have killed you at the Korean restaurant in Yuzhno. Finally, you killed one of my best operatives in Nogliki. You are almost as tough and stubborn as me."

Michael ignored the compliment and continued staring at Milla. Was she brainwashed? Had Akhmetalin threatened Katya unless she said these things?

Milla picked up the thread.

"Since torturing it out of you didn't seem to be a useful option, we decided that you might respond to a threat against someone you loved, especially after losing your sister."

The words, delivered as mildly as if she had commented on the weather, were like an electric jolt through Michael's body. He stiffened then shivered.

"You made life easier for us by coming to that conference in Moscow." Milla ran a finger languidly across Akhmetalin's chest. "Vadim schooled me in the art of seduction and covert surveillance." She laughed. "You were easy to take to bed, but I needed you to love me, not just want me. You had to be ready to give up everything to save me. For that, Katya was invaluable. You loved her first, me second. I'm not sure you would have permitted yourself to love me if you hadn't already fallen in love with her."

Michael remembered how desperately he had resisted letting them into his life. It was Katya who had first touched his heart. Only then did he open himself to Milla.

Milla saw that her words rang true and smiled another ugly smile.

"Once you did, it was like a dam bursting. You never do anything half way. You hate or you love completely. Then, it was just a matter of waiting until you had perfected the technology. Once you were finished, we were ready to move."

Michael swallowed hard.

"Where's Katya?" he whispered.

Milla pointed to a door in the far wall.

"That door leads to a helicopter pad hidden in the birches on a nearby parcel. Katya is waiting for us in the helicopter."

He could barely get the words out.

"Does she know I've been trying to rescue her?"

"Of course not."

"Does she know that this was all a lie?"

"Don't be stupid," Milla replied testily. "She was too young to know Vadim."

"But what does she think is happening here?"

"She thinks we've been captured."

Michael started to sway slightly. He wasn't sure how much longer his legs would hold him. The fire behind him crackled and spit. A spark landed on his ankle. He let it burn. He was beyond pain.

Akhmetalin had stepped sideways, gun in one hand, knife in the other, with his head cocked to the side as an arrogant smile played across his face. He was enjoying this show.

"She must wonder what I'm doing, where I am," Michael said.

"She does, but soon she will learn that you're dead. Then she'll have a new father, her *true* father."

Michael flinched as Milla landed the shot with cruel precision. Katya's *true* father stepped next to Milla and flashed the knife through the flickering firelight to draw Michael's attention.

"I had hoped to restore Russia to its rightful place atop the world, but the current administration decided to work with your country and the Arabs." He grimaced in disgust. "A Middle East Marshall Plan just means greater American meddling where Russia should be acting unilaterally. With our natural resources, we are the dominant country in the world." He shrugged well-muscled shoulders. "But I had to take matters into my own hands. Now that I've destroyed Saudi Arabia's oil and framed America, those multilateral talks are dead and Russia is, once again, the preeminent power in the world."

Michael closed his eyes. The world had broken him one final time. But Akhmetalin and Milla were not quite done playing with their newfound toy.

"Vadim had planned to take his time torturing you, but when you escaped, we had to think quickly," Milla explained. "I cut myself and smeared blood to make it look like I had been beaten, then Vadim tied me to that chair."

Another explosion rocked the dacha.

"We'd better be going," Akhmetalin said. With a sadistic grin, he placed the gun in Milla's hands. "I think you should have the honor, my dear."

Milla's eyes narrowed into slits as she pointed the gun at Michael's chest. Michael raised his hands in self-defense.

"Don't do this."

"Good bye, my love," she whispered in the same throaty, vodka-tinged voice that had first caught Michael's attention.

Michael flinched at the sharp crack of a bullet. He waited for what seemed an eternity for the bullet to rip through his heart, shredding his life to bits, but nothing happened. A furious roar filled his ears then someone slammed into him, spinning him to the floor.

"Michael? Michael!"

A woman's voice. He could not place it. He must be dreaming, or dead.

"Michael!"

A hand shook his shoulder. Slapped him across the face. When he opened his eyes, he knew he was dead, because staring at him in consternation was Julia Donatelli.

"Come on, Michael! We don't have time. Akhmetalin's getting away with Katya!"

Seventy-seven

———

"You can't be here," Michael stammered. "You're dead."

Julia touched the bandage wrapping the left side of her head.

"Almost. Al-Naimi's goons found me and patched me up. Then he sent me along with one of his squads to rescue you."

"One of his squads?"

"Yes, but they got stuck behind Putin's motorcade, if you can believe that. The leader and I stole a helicopter and dropped it on Akhmetalin's front lawn. We were looking for you when the whole house blew up."

While talking, Julia had helped Michael to his feet. As the room came back into focus, he spotted something that made him sick. Milla lay dead on her back, the front of her blouse stained with an expanding circle of blood. Her ice blue eyes stared unseeing at the ceiling.

"I'm sorry, Michael," Julia whispered. "She was going to kill you."

Michael nodded numbly. He slowly turned away. He couldn't think about Milla, about her betrayal. There were only two things that mattered now, and both lay through the door in the far wall.

"He has a helicopter pad hidden through the birches a couple of parcels over," Michael explained. "Katya's in the helicopter. If I don't stop him, I'll lose her forever. Go get the Saudi agent and get your chopper in the air. I'll try to catch Akhmetalin before he reaches it."

Michael raced through the door and down a ramp into a tunnel. The underground passage was cool and smelled of dark, moist earth. Track lights fought against the shadows. Michael raced as fast as his aching body could carry him through the tunnel, trying to ignore the blood streaming down his face and the incessant hammering inside his head. To keep moving, he repeated one thing Milla had said: he hated and loved completely. He hated Akhmetalin and he was going to kill him. He loved Katya and he was going to save her.

The tunnel inclined upward. Without warning, Michael burst into the open. Akhmetalin had cleared a good-sized landing field amid the birches. A Mi-8 rested in the center of the clearing, its five-blade rotor already increasing in speed. Akhmetalin had reached the helicopter and was climbing up the ladder into its open door as Michael dropped to one knee and aimed. He would have only one shot. It was nearly an impossible shot in the moonlight with only one eye working, but he couldn't afford to miss. Michael steadied his tremulous right hand with his left, and fired. As the bullet ricocheted harmlessly off the fuselage, Michael aimed and squeezed the trigger again. The gun clicked on an empty chamber. With one last, vicious smile, Akhmetalin ducked into the helicopter. Seconds later, the ungainly bird lifted off the ground.

The Director had won. Katya was gone.

Seventy-eight

With an angry, desperate bellow, Michael threw the useless gun to the ground and stumbled into the clearing. The rotor wash whipped through the birches, tossing him like a rag doll to the ground as the Mi-8 rotated to its left and hovered directly over him, fifty feet in the air. A dark head poked out of the open door. It was just a black smudge against the night sky, but Michael knew it was Akhmetalin. The smudge grew larger. Akhmetalin was leaning out of the door. He pointed something down at Michael.

A machine gun.

Akhmetalin intended to kill Michael from the sky.

Michael didn't run. He spread his arms wide. He would welcome the bullet.

Suddenly, the smudge jerked and the machine gun fell from Akhmetalin's grasp, spinning and turning until it landed on the ground with a wet thud.

The smudge jerked again. Michael raised himself onto his elbows. Then, without warning, Akhmetalin pitched headfirst out of the helicopter. Michael scrambled to his feet as the colonel's blood-curdling screech rent the night air. The colonel's arms windmilled as he turned over onto his back, still screaming, legs pumping, trying to find purchase in the thin air. He turned over again then crashed into the ground, head first, with a sickening, bone-crunching, slap.

Michael remained frozen in place for a long moment before racing for the machine gun. He scooped it up and ran to Akhmetalin's body, but one look told him all he needed to know. The Russian's neck had snapped clean through as the impact shoved his head back into his shoulders. The permafrost had split Akhmetalin's face open.

The change in whine and intensifying winds told Michael that the helicopter had landed. He crouched against the wind and crab-walked toward the open door, anxious to discover who had thrown Akhmetalin to his death, and fearful what someone capable of that might have done to Katya.

As the Mi-8 settled on its skids, its rotors slowed their merciless beat. After a long moment, a tall, thin man with close-cropped gray hair stepped onto the ladder. He waved at Michael and beckoned him close.

"Hello!" he called over the rotor wash. "You must be Michael McKeon. I'm NSA Director Stanley Billings. I've been looking for you."

Seventy-nine

~~~

Michael inched forward cautiously as Billings stepped onto the grass. The NSA Director glanced at Akhmetalin's nearly decapitated corpse with disgust then smiled a thin smile, like a man who did not do so often.

"You must be anxious to see your daughter," he said.

Michael's heart leapt.

"Katya's inside? Is she okay?"

"She is. Go on. I'll give you two a moment, then we better lift off."

Michael flashed a grateful smile and hurried toward the waiting helicopter as fast as his injured body would move, skirting the craters and mounds left behind when Akhmetalin's workers cleared the trees for the helicopter pad. A few feet from the door, he stumbled over a left-behind root. As he fell, a shot sounded and his right shoulder exploded in agony. Crying out in pain, Michael rolled onto his left side, looking for the shooter.

Advancing slowly toward him, Billings sighted his Beretta on Michael's chest.

"What are you doing?" Michael panted as he pressed his palm against the wound, trying vainly to stop the blood pumping between his fingers. He dug his heels into the frozen earth, pushing himself toward the helicopter, but stopped as the NSA Director twitched the gun.

"You've shown a tremendous ability to survive," Billings said. "At Abqaiq, at the Korean restaurant in Yuzhno, with the assassin in Nogliki—you should be dead by now. The FSB managed to grab you before we could at the base camp, but Akhmetalin stole you back when you landed in Moscow. He was supposed to kill you, but he decided to have some fun with you, and now, it's up to me." The man sounded tired and annoyed. "Even now, you trip, and the bullet that should have gone through your heart, hits your shoulder instead. You're one tough bastard to kill."

"You're working with The Global Group?"

"I *am* The Global Group," Billings snapped. "Akhmetalin thought he was running this operation, but he was merely working for me. This was mine all along."

Michael pressed harder, but he couldn't stop the blood pumping out of him, warming the dark earth beneath him, releasing the dank smell of mushrooms.

"Why?"

The NSA Director straightened his shoulders and glared down at Michael.

"I am one of the few patriots left in our government. One of the few willing to do what it takes to protect this country from itself and from its sworn enemies."

"You're crazy," Michael groaned.

"Saudi Arabia uses its trillions in oil revenues to train and sponsor the very terrorists that attack us and Russia's even more of a threat than they were during the Cold War," Billings said as he signaled to the pilot to power up. "Back then, we had weapons that balanced each other. Neither side would use its nuclear weapons because it knew the other would respond."

Michael couldn't feel his arms and a terrible coldness was creeping up his torso. Billings stood over him, his suit coat and tie flapping as the Mi-8's blades chopped the air with increasing ferocity.

"But now the Russians have a weapon we don't: massive oil supplies. They produce almost as much oil as Saudi Arabia does. Even more importantly, Russia supplies most of Europe's gas and oil. That's the edge they've been searching for since the days of Lenin. With a flick of a switch, they can turn Europe cold. With that threat hanging over their heads, how long do you think our so-called European allies would stand by our side in a fight with Russia?" Billings asked.

He didn't wait for an answer, but jerked a thumb toward Akhmetalin's corpse.

"He tried to take over the operation. Killing Stark's assistant was dumb. It attracted unwanted attention from the President. And I knew he'd try to stop you at Sakhalin, but I hadn't counted on the FSB showing up."

He shrugged.

"So I didn't destroy Sakhalin. Thanks to you, I've destroyed the Saudi threat to American security and framed Russia for it. And in the process, this nonsense about a Middle East Marshall Plan is dead. It's still an American world and it always will be."

Michael had stopped listening. He arched his back, craning his neck toward the helicopter, trying to spot Katya one last time.

But it was useless. He couldn't see her.

"Fine. You won," Michael groaned, barely audible over the rotors' whine and the whipping winds. "Kill me, but leave Katya alone. Please. She doesn't know anything about my work, or The Global Group, or any of this. She can't tie you to anything."

Michael's voice broke as Billings' finger tightened on the trigger.

"You can leave her at the college with someone. Just give her a chance. Please!"

"No loose ends. Sorry."

As Billings squeezed the trigger, gunfire erupted from both sides of the clearing, tossing his body about in a macabre dance in the moonlight. While Michael struggled to remain conscious, Hal and Melissa stepped from the shadow of the birch trees, followed by a grim-faced Medvedev.

Hal and Medvedev raced to Michael, but Melissa stopped at Billings' body, staring in shock.

"I had no idea," she murmured.

"Get on board and make sure that pilot doesn't leave," Hal ordered Medvedev. "And find the first aid kit."

Hal winked in and out of Michael's dimming sight.

"Stay with me, Michael," he pleaded as he caught the first aid kit from Medvedev.

Michael grabbed Hal's shirt with a bloody hand.

"Katya," he croaked, "on the heli—"

"Grisha!" Hal shouted. "Is Katya in the helicopter?"

Michael fought to stay alive long enough to learn if Katya was there. He couldn't feel Hal cut away his shirt or wrap his shoulder in a bandage. He watched Hal's eyes, waiting, his fingers typing out Katya's name in a steadily slowing beat.

From what sounded like miles away, he finally heard Medvedev respond: "I found her, locked in a closet. She's fine."

Relief flooded through Michael as tears squeezed out of his eyes.

"Hal, take care of her."

The older man's eyes widened in alarm.

"Don't talk like that, Michael. You're going to take care of her. Melissa! Leave that bastard and help me get Michael on the helicopter."

"I had no one to take care of me," Michael persisted. "Promise you'll take care of her."

"I don't need to," Hal said as he slid around to Michael's head, motioning for Melissa to grab Michael's feet.

Hal's face was inches from Michael's. With his last remaining strength, Michael tilted his head back to meet his old friend's gaze.

"Please."

As Hal's eyes blackened in sorrow, Michael caught his own reflection. He was a ghost. He was, no longer, the one left behind, limping on with a depleted soul and punctured heart. He was, finally, going to die. It seemed absurd, but, despite everything he had endured, it had never occurred to him to give up, to die. He had loved briefly and fought mostly, but had always carried on. Now, he could, just, stop.

But he didn't want to. That was the funny thing, although funny wasn't the right word. He'd wanted to die for most of his life. But now, he wanted to live, whatever that meant. It's frustrating to get what you want when you don't want it any longer, Michael thought, as Hal finally answered his prayer.

"I promise."

Then the bright call of a birdsong reached him: "Daddy!"

As Hal and Melissa lifted and carried him toward the helicopter, Katya peered into his face, her long, blond hair pulled back in a ponytail and her green eyes wide with worry.

"You're hurt."

"You're going to be okay, sweetheart. I love you."

"I love you, too, Daddy."

With that, Michael's eyes slid shut; his fingers stilled.

Eighty

Botkin Hospital, Moscow

President Gavin Flanagan paused outside the doors to the emergency room that the Russian President had quickly commandeered and closed his eyes, listening to the heartbroken sobbing of Katya McKeon, whom they had just left clutched in Hal's embrace. Then he uttered a single word, an expletive that neither Chief of Staff Rafferty nor Deputy NSA Director Melissa Stark had ever heard pass his lips before.

"It was Billings, right in front of us the entire time," he said bitterly. Flanagan's face was drawn and gray, his telegenic good looks drained by the lack of progress in his talks with the Russian and Saudi leaders and the increasing violence throughout Northern Africa and the Middle East, compounded by Billings' betrayal, and the past thirty minutes the President of the United States had spent trying to console the inconsolable Katya. He closed his eyes and took a deep breath, summoning his last reserves of strength, and then placed a hand on Stark's shoulder.

"You're my new National Security Director, Melissa." As Stark's mouth opened in shock, he continued. "Billings and Akhmetalin set up you and your assistant with the bogus gmail account." He paused. Melissa looked stricken at the mention of her former assistant. "I'll call Dani's parents later today. I'd like you on the line with me."

Melissa nodded and discreetly wiped a tear away.

"It's my fault she's dead."

"Stop it," the President replied, a little harshly. "She worked for you, but you both worked for me, so if it's anyone's fault, it's mine. I should have discovered Billings' betrayal in time. I shouldn't have hired him in the first place." He wiped his hands over his face, which needed a shave. "We don't have the time to beat ourselves up. We have a lot of cleaning up to do and very little time. I need both of you with me at the talks." He paused again. "You sure that Julia Donatelli is healthy enough to make the flight back to Abqaiq with the fix?"

"No she's not," Melissa replied, "but she's our best option at the moment. Jack already ordered one of the doctors from the embassy to go with her."

"And our new friend at the GIP assures us that she will have any assistance she needs," Rafferty added.

The President glanced at the door again. They could hear Hal murmuring quietly to Katya.

"I have a granddaughter about her age," Flanagan said quietly. "Jack, I want some of the Marines from the Embassy here with them. They'll fly back with us on Air Force One."

"Yes sir."

"I want to talk with Longfellow and both of you about an idea I have."

"Yes sir."

Melissa cleared her throat.

"Sir? About the Russian who was with Longfellow and me," she began.

"You mean 'The Sword'?" President Flanagan asked with a raised eyebrow.

"Yes sir. He was a very big help, instrumental. We wouldn't have gotten out of there without him."

"That's high praise for someone who tried to kill you a few years ago."

"Shoot, not kill," Melissa corrected with a trace of a smile. "Anyway, he's made a lot of enemies in this country."

"He's made a lot of enemies in many places."

"He came here to help us and I'd hate to see him caught and punished as a result."

"If I knew where he was, I'd have to tell the Russian President." A twinkle appeared in his eyes. "So it's a good thing that I don't know that he's already slipped out of Russia and returned to his wife in London."

"Very good, sir."

The President watched Melissa peer once again through the emergency room doors at Katya and Hal.

"You look like hell, Melissa."

Melissa nodded slowly. She'd washed her face and pulled her hair back, but a nasty, purpled bruise covered her right cheek. Cuts and scrapes lined her face and hands. Her eyes were red-rimmed with emotion and exhaustion, and her clothes were ripped and filthy. She quickly looked away from the dark blood stains on her fleece and jeans, pushing away the images of frantically trying to stop Michael's bleeding as the helicopter raced to the hospital. She wanted to scream and cry and vomit all at the same time.

"I've been in hell, sir," she said quietly.

"We're not out yet," he replied. The President placed an arm around Melissa and another around his burly Chief of Staff. "Let's go see what we can do."

Conclusion

—⟊⟊⟊—

Brunswick, Maine

Over the next six weeks, the initial turmoil in Washington, DC, over the mysterious disappearance and death of NSA Director Stanley Billings quieted once it was discovered that he had fallen off a cliff while hiking in Colorado. Because of the severe trauma to the body, the casket was closed out of respect for the family.

In Saudi Arabia, the Kingdom renewed full oil production and attributed the slight reduction in output to poor technical readings and the vagaries of measuring the true capacity of aging oil reservoirs. One group of conspiracy theorists warned that Saudi Arabia was running out of oil. Another group warned that Saudi Arabia was simply playing games to manipulate global oil prices. No one noticed that Sa'id al-Naimi received special honors from the King. In a private ceremony in the King's palace, Khalid Nazer and Fouad al-Dossary were posthumously honored with Nazer's parents and al-Dossary's wife and son in attendance. In Moscow, President Putin honored Dmitry Fyodorov. Unfortunately, Fyodorov had no family to attend. In a special exception arranged at the highest levels of the American, Russian and Saudi governments, a gray-haired NSA agent stood quietly in the back of the rooms in Riyadh and Moscow, honoring his fallen friends.

President Gavin Flanagan's popularity soared as he announced the Middle East Marshall Plan with the Saudi and Russian heads of state at his side. Despite ominous rumblings from the mullahs in

Iran and the Prophet in the Levant, a vast array of nations signed on, pledging support in exchange for democratic reforms.

In Brunswick, Maine, Hal Jacobs and Julia Donatelli returned to Bowdoin and quickly disappeared into Bowdoin College President Ethan Halsey's office. A few days later, President Halsey announced a new, substantial grant that would pay for a major addition to the Hatch Science Center, with construction to begin immediately. Neither President Halsey nor Hal ever disclosed that Julia had been and remained an active NSA agent, and had originally been placed at Bowdoin to help protect Michael.

It was late May. Finals were finished, the students had left, summer had arrived several weeks early, and the campus custodial crews had left the windows and doors open in the empty dormitories, relying upon the summer breeze to chase away the lingering aromas of dirty laundry, greasy pizza, burnt coffee and stale beer. All was quiet as a group of four solemnly processed across campus.

Hal listened as a tall, thin man with a long, slightly morose face and white hair asked about the addition to the Hatch Science Center. It was striking how closely President Halsey resembled Ichabod Crane.

"It'll be finished by the end of the summer," Hal said.

"And the portions of the building that I'm not allowed to know about?" Halsey asked with a wry smile.

"Those will be done too."

Two women walked to Hal's left.

"You must be happy to get out of Washington," Julia Donatelli said to Melissa Stark.

"Always," the NSA Director replied. "How are you feeling?"

Julia touched the white scar on her temple.

"Much better. The doctors tell me that I'm very lucky. And that I have a hard head."

Evening had fallen and the few workers left on campus had gone home for the day. As the muted sounds of traffic sifted through the pines, the four continued their journey in silence until they reached their destination. Melissa Stark took the lead, rapping gently on the door. When there was no answer, she glanced at Hal, who nodded, and rapped again, louder. She was ready to knock a third time when the door flew open and Michael McKeon stood before them.

"I didn't think you were going to let us in," Hal said with a smile.

Michael shifted uncomfortably then stepped back and motioned for them to enter.

"I just put Katya to bed," he said, walking stiffly through the kitchen and into the living room. "I took her to Popham Beach today after church."

"When did you start going to church?" Hal asked, arching an eyebrow.

Michael glanced toward a picture of his sister, recently placed on the mantle. "I made a promise to someone a long time ago that I never kept. I was reminded of that promise recently. It's time I changed a few things and honored my promises."

Michael settled himself painfully into a chair by the window.

"Katya had a great time at the beach, but was exhausted. I think she's asleep already."

Melissa, once again, took the lead, claiming the chair facing Michael while the other three perched on the couch.

"How are you doing?" she asked.

"My broken nose and bullet wound are fine. The cracked ribs and chipped vertebra will take a while longer to heal, and the right orbital bone around my eye isn't progressing as well as the doctors had hoped."

"Are you still getting the headaches?" Hal asked.

Michael nodded then smiled wanly. "But I'm alive."

"You gave us a real scare," Hal said. "The surgeons at Botkin Hospital spent hours trying to repair the damage. They didn't give you much of a chance because you had lost so much blood. It was the happiest moment of my life when you opened your eyes and looked at Katya and me."

Hal's voice had turned rough. He cleared his throat and blinked rapidly.

"The warm weather helps, doesn't it?" Julia asked. Michael nodded as a strained silence suffused the room.

"You probably saw that we announced that a crime syndicate had kidnapped you and your family to extort money from Milla's Russian relatives," Melissa said. "Julia was caught in the middle. I personally briefed the Chief of the Brunswick Police and the Director of Campus Security and ensured that all agencies had closed their files. In fact, their files have now disappeared entirely."

Michael nodded again then looked to President Halsey.

"Thank you for giving me the semester off to recover and spend time with Katya."

"Of course," President Halsey replied in his reedy tenor. "I understand that you removed Katya from her school and have been teaching her yourself?"

"That's right. We need the time together."

"If you don't mind my asking, how is she doing?"

Michael took a long, slow breath as the others waited.

"Better, I think." He glanced at Melissa. "The counselor the NSA provided helped. She doesn't have as many nightmares and she doesn't panic if I leave the room." He pointed at a drawing on the coffee table: a brown dog stared excitedly out, pink tongue lolling, sitting on a field of green under a blue sky. "The counselor has her draw her feelings. Bright colors and happy pictures are much better than what she was drawing after we returned from Moscow. But it's still day to day."

"Do you think you made the right choice, not telling her what Milla did?" Melissa asked quietly, glancing at the picture of Milla, Michael and Katya on the mantle, not far from the one of Michael's sister.

Michael grimaced in pain as he shifted and looked out the window. Just feet away was the sidewalk where David and his men grabbed him. He closed his eyes and thought of the new bed and empty closet in his bedroom. He didn't dare remove Milla's pictures, not so long as he needed to pretend, for Katya's sake, to grieve his late wife. But at least she was gone from his bedroom.

"Yes. She needs to have good memories of her mother."

"It'll get better," Hal offered.

Michael silently weighed Hal's words for several minutes before responding: "For Katya, possibly. I hope so. She has good memories to hold onto. That may give her the base she needs to build on."

"What about you?" Julia asked.

Michael paused again, staring out the window.

"I don't know," he said quietly.

"Have you talked to the NSA's counselor?" Julia asked.

Michael made a face. "She talks about moving beyond hate to acceptance; forgiving, even if not forgetting." He shrugged ruefully, his gaze flicking across the others before returning to the window. "I'm not sure I'm built that way. Right now, I'm trying to forgive my parents for what they did to Janie." He flashed a smile. "It's only taken me twenty-five years. Maybe in another twenty-five, I'll be ready to forgive Milla. We'll see."

After another uneasy silence, Michael cleared his throat and turned to the others.

"Has there been any fallout from delaying the announcement of my work?" he asked.

"No," Hal replied. "We issued the press release that more testing was required. I went through your files and deleted any reference to the ability to capture and destroy the natural gases produced by the bio-degradation of oil."

"Good."

Michael gazed at the others while they exchanged covert glances. A warm breeze flowed through the open window, rustling Katya's drawing, and carrying with it the shouts of children playing. Finally, he decided to move things along.

"I doubt all four of you stopped by just to check up on me. You clearly have something you want to tell me. What is it?"

Hal cleared his throat and began.

"Since your adventures in Saudi Arabia and Russia, a lot has happened. As you know, Melissa has become the new NSA Director. Your adventures have opened everyone's eyes to the grave new threats to energy security. In response, President Flanagan has created a new agency called the Energy Security Agency, working with, but not under, the NSA. Its mission is to protect the United States' energy supplies from any and all threats."

Hal cleared his throat again.

"The newly independent ESA will be housed here at Bowdoin in a secret and secure level under the Hatch Center. Obviously, President Halsey has been kept informed."

The President nodded. Michael remained silent as Melissa picked up the thread.

"President Flanagan has asked Hal to head up the ESA and he's graciously agreed," she said.

"And I've asked Julia to be my deputy director," Hal continued.

"Well, I guess congratulations are in order all around," Michael said.

"And I'd like you to be my other deputy director," Hal said.

Michael narrowed his eyes.

"You want me to do what?"

"I want you to be my deputy. Help us get this organization off the ground."

"I'm no spy," Michael laughed, then turned serious. "What I did out there revived a part of me that I thought I had buried. Killing came too easy. I'm afraid of what would happen if I continued. I want to bury that and focus on better things, like Katya." He paused, then added, more to himself than to the others in the room, "I don't even know who I am anymore."

"You're wrong there," President Halsey replied. "You're a brilliant professor and if you want to remain solely in the classroom, then you will always have a place here at Bowdoin. However," he said as he leaned forward, his sharp elbows resting on bony knees, "sometimes we are called on to do the unexpected. I never intended to be president. I always assumed I would spend the rest of my life teaching the Classics, but here I am."

"With all due respect, President Halsey, it's not exactly the same. No one tried to kill you."

"That's true. Some of the deadliest people in the world tried to kill you, and here you are, alive, having saved your daughter and prevented a global catastrophe. It sounds to me like you are exactly what this agency, and this country, needs."

"And we will continue to research and teach here at Bowdoin," Julia added. "That's our cover."

"Michael, we need you," Hal implored. "The world is growing more dangerous. New energy and security threats crop up every day. We haven't been able to identify the other members of The Global Group, but they're out there. And now we have the threat that someone else will discover how to weaponize your microbes. Despite the best efforts of this country and of Saudi Arabia to keep that a secret, word will eventually leak out. It'll become a threat that other countries must acknowledge and counteract, like the nuclear bomb after Hiroshima and Nagasaki. We may very well be on the precipice of a new microbial arms race."

"You don't understand," Michael snapped. He pointed at the ceiling. "I have a little girl sleeping upstairs who lost her mother and has been through hell. She is entitled to a safe and secure childhood. My sister and I never had that, but she will. I can't give her that if I'm running around the world to fight bad guys."

"You're wrong," Hal replied solemnly. "That's the *only* way you can give her a safe and secure childhood."

Melissa stood up and smiled at Michael.

"We'll leave you alone, Michael. Please say hello to Katya from me?"

"I will."

Michael walked the four visitors to the door. As Julia stepped past him, she suddenly turned and hugged him tightly. Michael winced from his sore ribs. She still smelled of vanilla and almonds.

"This is your home now," she whispered fiercely. "Katya's too. Everyone here cares about you. We'll be your family if you let us."

Then she let him go and stepped out into the fading light. The four paused on the front walk after Michael had closed the door.

"What do you think he will do?" Julia asked.

"He'll do the right thing," Hal replied quietly.

After the four had left, Michael sat in his chair by the window, his fingers typing his thoughts in a brisk staccato before settling into a somber, heavy *adagio*. Finally, his fingers stilled as the sun slipped below the pines and shadows claimed the room. Then he sat some more, listening to the crickets and frogs call and respond, until, finally, with a soft sigh, he climbed the stairs to check on Katya.

THE END

Notes

The science behind microbes that consume oil, including turning oil in hard-to-reach areas like Canada's Tar Sands into natural gas, has been documented, but no microbes have been developed to pose the threat discussed in this book.

Yet.

The places and facilities referred to are all real places. I did take a few liberties with the facilities at Abqaiq. If you're looking for the deoxygenation tower where Michael McKeon inserts the microbes, you won't find it, but the facility is otherwise largely as I have described it. Similarly the facilities on Sakhalin Island are largely as I have described them, although readers looking for Voluntina's bullet-ridden shack will be disappointed. While Chekhov did describe Sakhalin as "Hell," and I think Michael McKeon, Longfellow, and Deputy NSA Director Melissa Stark would agree, Sakhalin has been discovered, to a certain extent, by tourists enjoying its extremely rugged climate.

Unfortunately, the violence and unrest continue in the Middle East and the Middle East Marshall Plan is my creation. Any novel set against the backdrop of the Middle East and Russia runs the risk of being passed by events almost instantly. Undoubtedly, things on the ground will have changed many times by the time this book is published. Let's hope for the better.

Despite the presence of Longfellow, Julia Donatelli, and Michael McKeon, I don't mean to suggest that every professor at Bowdoin College is a spy. As to the precise location of the Energy Security Agency, well, I will never tell. Maybe in the next book . . .